“Le[...] to be a thing of the past [...] The book takes us on a [...] nnecting us to a deep m[...]

[...]krishnan Pillai,
Author of Chanakya's 100 Best Sutras

“Shared struggles, diverse choices, triumphs—a profound exploration of resilience”

- *Saksham Garg,*
Author of National Bestseller, SAMSARA

“A compelling emotional saga of a complex mother-daughter relationship. Gripping.”

- *Neil D Silva,*
Author of Maya's New Husband

“As a schizophrenic who dealt with quadragenerian parents, and saw how people in rehab are handled, this was a restorative read.”

- *Kunal Roy,*
Psychologist (MA in clinical psychology)

“Letters to my mother is a meticulous take on parent-child dynamics. As a psychologist, I saw several of my patients in it. Riveting read.”

- *Vijaya T Rai,*
Senior psychologist, Founder/CEO,
Silverline Counselling and Learning Centre

In this captivating epistolary novel, the author masterfully weaves a narrative across three generations and 70 years, immersing readers against the historical events.

- *Harshil Shah, Books Barista*

Letters to My Mother

Vikkas Arun Pareek

VISHWAKARMA PUBLICATIONS
VP

Letters to My Mother

1st Edition published in India by Vishwakarma Publications in August 2023
Reprint - January 2024

ISBN - 978-93-93757-03-6

Disclaimer

This is a work of fiction. Names, characters, places and incidents are either the product of the author's imagination or are used fictitiously and any resemblance to any actual person, living or dead, events or locales is entirely coincidental.

Published by:
Vishwakarma Publications
34A/1, Suyog Center, 7th Floor, Gultekadi Marketyard Road,
Giridhar Bhavan Chowk, Pune: 411037, Maharashtra, India.
Mob. : 9168682200
Email: info@vpindia.co.in
Website: www. vishwakarmapublications.com

Cover: **The Book Bakers**
Typeset and Layout: **Vishwakarma Publications**
Printed at: **Square Digital, Pune**

₹ 350/-

To my mother
Alka Pareek

Meera
(2001 & 2015)

Chapter 1

Meera (2001)

MEERA WATCHED AS the second plane crashed into the Twin Towers on her television screen. It was repeat footage. She had turned the television on after Sujit messaged her.

URGENTLY switch on your TV NEWS—the message read.

Damn you! How about a simple I Love You message? Idiot— she thought.

She reached out for the remote that was still on her belly. She had probably slept with it, thinking about him and not really watching what was on TV earlier in the afternoon when he left after lunch. She could still taste the wonderful fish he had cooked for her. Her roommate was out then, and she wanted to make the best use of the time.

They had had their first kiss. It was not what she had imagined it would be, but she could see that Sujit was more nervous than she was.

Meera knew the channels on which news was shown; those were her favourite channels anyway. After all, she was studying mass communication and was an aspiring journalist.

Now, she stared blankly at the screen for a minute or two to realise the depth of what was playing out before her eyes. It didn't look like news; it looked like some scene from an action movie. She rechecked the channel.

In big, bold letters, flashing on the screen, the message was clear.

US UNDER ATTACK

FIRST PLANE CRASHES INTO NORTH TOWER: 8:46 AM EDT

SECOND PLANE CRASHES INTO SOUTH TOWER: 9:03 AM EDT

Breathing hard now, she understood the gravity of the situation. The world would change. No one had ever dared to attack the US, let alone wage an attack of this magnitude.

"OH, MY GOD!" she shouted into the phone.

"I know!" Sujit replied.

"OH, MY GOD!" she repeated.

"I know!" Sujit repeated.

But Meera kept a stoic face. "I think they deserve it!"

"What are you saying?!"

"Why not! Boss around the whole world, and this is what is bound to happen."

"Come on! How can you say that? They are saying, hundreds of people have lost their lives, not to mention the lives of the passengers on the planes."

"I know I am being awful, but I just don't like those who boss over others."

"If you want to be a successful journalist, you have to keep your stupid views and emotions to yourself."

"Yeah, yeah, how was your practice? You have a big match coming up!"

Sujit was to play in a football tournament next month. The gossip in the club was that the selectors for the national team would be there. He was trying all he could to avoid distractions so that he would be selected for the national team. And the first thing he was trying to keep away from was Meera.

"You are the biggest distraction."

"Oh!"

"Oh… what?"

Meera took a couple of minutes to reply. "No, no, it's okay. It's probably nothing."

"No, tell me… is anything wrong?" Sujit asked.

"No… it's fine."

"If you don't tell me, then forget about our date tomorrow."

"Ahh, you are very difficult sometimes! No... sorry, most of the times, you are so irritating!" Meera said quickly. "It's just that my mother is in New York now. I am wondering if..." She broke off.

"Wow! This is the first time you have said anything about your mother in the last one year," Sujit rejoined in a gleeful tone.

"There's nothing to say. As I said, it's probably nothing!"

It was one year since they had met, and they had their first kiss only today. He would need to teach her a thing or two—Sujit thought after disconnecting the phone.

Will she find out? Will it be too soon? We just had our first call two months ago, after years of no contact. I don't want my mother to think that I am looking forward to this newfound connection we now have—Meera thought after disconnecting the phone.

"No, let it be! I hate that woman anyway. Let her die," she said to herself.

"Why? I will come after my term finishes in March anyway. Why do you want me to come now?"

Meera broke into a cry as she said that. She had planned to go to Mysore with her friends during the winter break, but her father now insisted that she come to Delhi.

"I would not have called you if it was not important," Adarsh said in a stern voice.

"Please! I have to study for my exams."

"There is a lot of time for the exams. What is it really, Meera?"

"I have planned a trip to Mysore with my friends. I didn't want to tell you as you would not have allowed me to go."

"And now you think I'll allow you, and you'll go?"

"Yes, because you are very sweet. I didn't want to tell you as you worry too much."

"When are you going? Dates?"

"Day after tomorrow and will come back after Christmas."

"So... you can still come here on the 27th."

"It takes two days to reach there."

"I will send you the flight tickets. You can be here and then return before your classes start in January."

"Wow! Why are you spending so much?"

"Don't worry; it's nothing. I only ask you to travel by train as you are still a student and you need to learn the value of money."

"Stop with your *gyan*, Papa. Is everything okay?"

"Yes, we are all well. I just want to spend some time with you. It's been so long."

"No, it has not been that long. I just visited a month ago at Diwali."

"Meera!" Adarsh said in an I-will-not-listen-any-further tone.

"Okay, send me the tickets. I never get to spend the New Year with my friends!" she made a final complaint and disconnected the call.

Meera had promised herself that she would celebrate Sujit's selection and treat him with some more compassion on New Year's Eve. That seemed unlikely now.

"What is this?" Meera looked around the house for any clues as to why her father had called her back all of a sudden.

She was expecting the worst… maybe her Kavita Maa or even some distant relative… but then she was relieved to see that the house was in the same order. Maybe it was even a bit cleaner than it was during her Diwali visit.

Her gaze turned to a midsized box on the dining table. It was unusual for something like this to be on the table, for her father was quite particular about keeping his stuff in its proper place. The box was not heavy either. She picked it up to see what it was.

"Leave it there and come and sit with me," he said.

It's unusual for him to behave in this manner; he is certainly trying to avoid answering me—she thought.

"I know you haven't sent for me to ask about my trip or studies. Please tell me what this is about. I am getting worried. We have been sitting here for an hour now, and you have asked me about all the things in the world, but the one question I asked—about that box, you haven't answered. Besides, you keep looking at that box as if it will come and bite you," said Meera.

Her father took a deep breath and began pacing across the room. Then, in slow, halting words, he said, "Did you hear about 9/11?"

"Everyone has heard about that." But even as she said that she felt a sense of discomfiture.

"Your mother was in the building, and she died during…"

Meera looked at her feet, she looked at her father, and she looked around, but she did not look at the box. She now knew what it contained.

"Okay."

"Okay?" Adarsh asked with surprise.

"What do you want me to say, Papa? That I am not sad; I am not crying, and I am not even bothered? You could have easily told me that on the phone. It doesn't change our lives one bit."

Adarsh turned towards his daughter in shock. His voice grew louder now. "Don't be so cruel," he said. "I have not brought you up to disrespect the dead."

Meera fell back into silence. She looked again at her feet. Images of her mother flashed before her eyes. They seemed quite distant now. Her heart was full of emotions. She knew she didn't care, but still, her breathing was much heavier than usual.

"She left you her money and this box, it came with her will," Adarsh continued.

Meera laughed.

"I have directed our lawyers to transfer the funds and put them in a trust in your name."

"I don't want her money."

"Then burn the money," Adarsh said angrily.

"Why are you shouting at me?" Meera yelled back.

His daughter's words did not make Adarsh bow down. Instead, he became agitated. "Because your mother is dead now! I know you did not love her and did not care about her. Neither did I, but Meera, I am disappointed with you. The principles I have taught you do not mean disrespecting the dead. Whatever problems I had with her, were ages ago; I am over them now."

"So? I am not over them," cried Meera.

"And now you probably never will be."

That last sentence hung in the air for some time, leading to an uncomfortable silence.

"What is in the box?" Meera asked finally.

"I don't know. I have not opened it. It is meant for you."

"I don't want anything to do with it."

"That's fine! I will throw it then."

With those words, Adarsh picked up the box and threw it in the backyard along with the other rubbish.

Meera kept looking at her father, and without looking towards the backyard, stormed towards her room.

"Where are you going? We are not done yet" her father asked in a calmer voice, wanting to reconcile.

"I think we are," Meera replied as she lowered her head and walked out.

For the next three days, Meera continually looked at the box lying there in the open, in the cold and dusty weather.

Then, on the third night, Meera saw her mother. "Take it, Meera. It will bring us closer!" the lady told her vacantly with a hollow look in her eyes. Meera woke up with a start doubtful whether what she had seen was a dream. Or was she just remembering the one time her mother had forced her to take cocaine?

She looked outside the window. The box was still there. *Why had they not collected it along with the other rubbish?*

She went down and stood next to the box, staring at it for a long time. How much time? She herself did not know. Staring at it thus, she completely lost track of time.

"You can take it with you. If you still don't want to open it, you can throw it somewhere over there," her father said suddenly from behind her, making her jump. Then, after a while, he said, "She can't do you any more harm."

"She can."

Meera (2015)

"PUSH! PUSH HARDER!" the doctor instructed her.

Meera was exhausted. It was two days since she had been trying to push, but her baby was refusing to come out into the world.

"Push, baby… push harder!" Sujit said, half-panting.

"You, mother fucker… You push hard if you want to…" Meera shouted back.

Sujit's mouth fell open at the cuss word. He looked at the doctor and said quickly, "She is not usually like this. But this is really taking a lot of time…"

"I know. I've seen worse; don't worry," the doctor said to an embarrassed Sujit. Then he added, "You go out and get these medicines."

Sujit quickly jumped at the opportunity and, waving to Meera, rushed out of the room. The pungent smell of phenyl in the hospital corridor was more welcoming in comparison to the atmosphere inside.

"It's coming!" the doctor said in excitement. "One last push, I promise," he assured Meera.

Meera thought that with this final push, her life, not the child would definitely be out of her,

"Sujit, stop laughing!" an embarrassed Meera said for the fourth time.

"Okay, okay, I will try…" he said, and they both laughed.

Meera was holding her daughter, and Sujit was narrating the incident of her birth, despite Meara's reminder that she was the first one to hear the baby's cries. He was not even there!

"For a few seconds, the doctors thought that you had passed away. But within minutes, you began to snore. By the time I reached, they had cleaned our little princess and were ready to wake you up for the first feed."

He laughed some more.

"She is so pretty… just like me," Meera said.

"That she is!" Sujit agreed. His laughter had subsided now, and there was a proud glow in his eyes, the kind new parents are blessed with.

"What will we call her?"

"Jia."

Meera's mind flashed to the tunnel of her past, and through that tunnel, unrestricted, she could see the box and her mother. The thought of the box scared Meera. She had not thought about it for almost a decade now, or maybe more—yes, definitely more.

She tried to remember the colour of the box. *Was it blue? Was it brown?*

Unbidden, a struggle grew within her now. She wondered why she was thinking of the box after so many years. What had suddenly brought that thought to her?

She looked at Jia. The baby was sleeping on her stomach, moving her little fingers. Was she having a bad dream? Meera pushed her chair back so that it began to rock. The baby evidently liked it, for a calmness soon settled on her face. She probably felt secure. And that made Meera feel secure.

Later, during the night, Meera mentioned the box to her husband.

Sujit's response was to raise his brows and crease his forehead in a frown. "Why are you thinking about it now?"

It was fourteen years now that Meera had had the box. Forget opening it; she had not even discussed opening it. Every time they moved houses; the couple had altercations about the box. Sujit had lost count of the times he had asked her to get rid of it, but Meera wouldn't listen.

"If you are not going to open it, why do you keep lugging this burden?" he asked, knowing that there would be no definitive answer again.

"I don't know." Meera avoided his gaze. Instead, she focused her attention on Jia's little game with her father's bracelet.

Sujit seized the opportunity to change the topic. "She has turned quite naughty already," he said. "Can't believe she is already nine months old!"

"I am scared, Sujit. What if I turn like *her*? What if I harm Jia?" she said with tears running down her cheeks.

Sujit understood what she was thinking. With a deep breath, he said, "You are not like your mother, or at least like what you have told me of her. You will never harm our daughter."

More tears rolled down Meera's cheeks.

Sujit mustered all the strength he could and said, "Meera, why don't you open the box? Why don't you find out what your mother has left you? Maybe you will learn something new, something nice about her. Maybe she has left you a letter?"

Meera got up shaking and pulled the box out of the cupboard.

"When did you get it here? I thought it was in the attic."

She smiled. It was a wan smile, designed to hide her true emotions.

"You should not have gone up to the attic," Sujit said. "The stairs are rickety—not safe. You know that."

"I love you."

"You can't get away by skipping the issue. You know that, right? Anyway, open it now and see what my mother-in-law has to say," Sujit said.

Meera looked at him. Her feeble smile had told him all about her fears and insecurities. Truly, she could not gather the courage to open the box.

Sujit came forward. "Let me help you."

"No, I have to do this. I just hope that it doesn't break me further, so much that I end up harming Jia."

"You will not. Now open it."

After a last doubtful look at her husband, Meera finally opened the box. The first thing that hit her was the smell of old paper. She put her hand inside the box and took its contents out.

She found a carefully folded letter, a jewellery box, a necklace, an antique-looking ring, a hand-painted picture, and another set of brown envelopes that looked like they had some papers in them.

She opened the letter. It read:

Dear Meera,

25 Nov 2001

I am Simon, your mother's friend. To be honest with you, we were more than friends. Now that we will soon know each other well, it's best to start with honesty. We met a couple of years ago and had planned to get married the next year.

You must have heard of what happened when I called your father a week later.

I am really very sorry. You must be feeling terrible at this moment. I know how difficult your relationship with your mother was, but trust me when I say this—she really cared about you. In fact, you were the only person she really cared about in her entire difficult life.

I loved her. I hope that after hearing from her, you will be able to forgive her and probably love her too. You will find letters that she wrote to her mother telling her all about you. I have read some of those letters. In the bundle are some old letters that she didn't let me read, but she always said that they held a great value for her and that you would learn a lot about her after reading them.

We have her funeral services on 24th Jan. We don't have the body, but we will perform her memorial services and want to celebrate her life. Inside this envelope, you will find tickets to New York. If you decide to come, your mother in heaven will be very happy. We will wait for you.

Meera, I know this will be sudden for you, but I am sure you will honour her last wishes.

Also, your grandmother, Shakuntala, is living in the Manav Sansthan Central Home. After your grandfather's death, she decided to move there. I have spoken to her, and she will be really happy if you pay her a visit too.

Manav Sansthan
Building 6
Ramnagar Lane, Delhi.

Hope to see you soon! There are so many things I would like to tell you about your mother and just talk to you about her.

With love,
Simon Jones

Meera read the letter twice and then handed it over to Sujit. Sujit read the letter with a blank expression. He looked back at her.

"They waited for you back in 2001," he said after reading the letter twice.

Meera opened a smaller envelope. It had her tickets to New York, a hotel reservation, and address to her mother's apartment in New York.

"Sujit, my grandmother lives… or lived… thirty minutes from where I have been living for the last five years," she said with guilt in her voice.

"How could you have known this?"

"I don't know." That was all she could say, gasping. It was difficult for her to absorb these sudden revelations.

"The letter says, *'I hope that after hearing from her, you will be able to forgive her and probably love her too.'* How will you hear from her?" Sujit asked Meera as she looked at the other envelopes.

"Maybe these letters…" Meera picked up the set of larger envelopes, her hands shaking, and showed them to Sujit.

Concerned, Sujit took the bundle from her and held her hand as they nervously looked at the old letters in front of them.

Shakuntala

(1946 - 1955)

Chapter 2

THE NEXT DAY, when Sujit returned from football practice, Meera was still sitting in the same position he had left her. Without saying anything, he kept looking at her. He wanted to give her as much time as she needed to take the first step.

"I have not read them yet. Just arranged them chronologically," Meera said after what seemed like hours.

"Are you finding them a bit intriguing now?"

Meera didn't reply.

"I am sorry, I didn't mean it that way. I know you are treating this as a test of your sanity. Do you want me to read them along with you?"

"Yes, of course. Why are you even asking?"

"Not sure… it has something to do with your family."

"My family is with the living, definitely not with these dead."

Sujit sat down beside her. "Give me the first letter."

"No, you go and change. I will read it first."

Meera opened the letter. It read:

Dear Maa,

12 Nov 1947

How are you? I miss you and Papaji a lot. I wish I were with you in my home.

Everyone here is quite nice. They take good care of me. I sleep with Maaji. She takes good care of me, too. She scolds me sometimes, but she loves me a lot.

I don't like Shekhar. You know, Maa… one day when I called him, he was with his friends. Maaji had asked me to call him for dinner. He came to me angrily and asked me why I had addressed him by his name. He also complained to Maaji. She scolded me and asked me never to take his name as he is my husband. But Maa, he is not nice to me, and I don't want him to be my husband.

Masterji comes once a week and teaches us math. I don't like math; I like science, social studies and history. Shekhar likes all subjects. He gives all the answers quickly, too. And then he teases me for being slow.

Maa, Pitaji took us to the Independence Parade on the 15th. It was very beautiful, and I really liked it. I want to tell you all about it. We did so many things after the celebrations were over.

We reached early that day though we had reserved seats, quite close to where Panditji was. There were so many people standing—I counted until a hundred and twenty and then started again from one as I am still learning to count.

We had reached at 7:30 in the morning. It was very crowded. Our carriage could not go all the way, so we had to walk a bit. I tried holding Shekhar's hand as I was scared, but he pushed me, and I fell. My new dress was spoiled. He laughed at that. I don't like him, Maa. Please take me away from here. Panditji hoisted the flag (after three hours). There was a lot of noise among the crowd, and someone told Pitaji that the police had had to lathi-charge the people to control them.

Everyone shouted, cheered, and waved as the Indian flag came up. We shouted too. I saw Shekhar so closely for the first time. He was also shouting and laughing. I like his smile, but I don't like him. Please, Maa, take me back.

I saw it first, the rainbow in the sky. I showed it to Shekhar, but Shekhar told Maaji that he had seen it first. It was really very beautiful. I really liked it, Maa.

I wanted to go home, but Shekhar wanted to see the monkey and snake shows. So, Pitaji had to take us away from the seating area and into the crowd. But when I reached there, I really liked it. There were three snakes, and all of them were dancing to the tune of the snake-charmer's instrument, and then we saw the monkey who was also dancing. Pitaji gave me one anna and Shekhar one anna too. Shekhar gave his anna to the monkey man, and when I was trying to give my anna to the snake-charmer, he snatched my anna and gave it himself instead. The snake-charmer even played another tune for him. But that was my anna. I hate him! Please take me away from here.

I miss you and Papaji a lot. Everyone is nice here, and everyone takes care of me. You don't need to worry about me. When will you call me, Maa? I want to come home. Give my love to Papaji.

Your beti,
Shakuntala.

"You know… on reading your grandmother's letter, I watched a couple of videos on our Independence, and now I am all patriotic," Sujit said. "The British divided our country. It was their plan from the beginning." Then his tone became the one of frustration, "And the politicians were all part of this game."

"Keep your conspiracy theories to yourself!" Meera said, and she picked out the next letter to read.

Dear Maa,

16 Jul 1948

Maa, I am very angry with you and Papaji. Neither of you spent time with me during the wedding, and I was given so much work to do. I was not able to even talk to you.

I can't wait to come home. Three months! It has been so long since I have seen you. Pitaji has agreed to leave me with you for six months. I want to come as soon as possible—right now, if possible. The only thing I will miss here is my studies, I really like them. Masterji even said last week that I am doing really well. You know, Maa, I saw a smile on Pitaji's face. He was really happy to hear me being appreciated. Shekhar does not get much appreciation now. He does not want to study.

Maaji told me that now that I am thirteen, I will be a woman soon. I must try to keep Shekhar happy and get his attention. I was quite embarrassed when she asked me to smile whenever he saw me or our eyes met; and she told me to clean his room at least twice a day so that it would give me a chance to be with him. But do you know what he did? While I was cleaning his room, he came from behind and shouted at me for touching his things. He even pushed me! When I cried and went to Maaji, she scolded me instead and said that I was not doing enough to keep Shekhar happy.

Maa, now Shyam is also married, and his wife has come to live with us. Maaji loves her more as she is very fair and more beautiful than I am. She also wears better saris than I do.

Shyam is not like Shekhar. He always tries to find a reason to be with Rukmani, and is very polite to her. Maybe, because everyone thinks she is very beautiful. I don't like her, though, as she always stares at me with her big eyes.

Maa, you know what I did that day? I put extra chilli in the curry that she had prepared. No one ate her curry, and Maaji scolded her too. But she is so cunning! She put salt in the lassi I had prepared the next day and then laughed at me when I got scolded.

Maa, it was better earlier when Shyam used to play with me. Now he does not even talk to me and only revolves around Rukmani.

Maa, you tell me what I should do so that Shekhar also revolves around me as Shyam does around Rukmani. One day, I saw Shekhar hiding something in his shirt. When I asked him what it was, he shouted at me. But I could see it was something red. I am not sure if it was blood as he did not show any sign of pain, and because he was shouting at me, I ran away from his room.

Maa, when you meet Shekhar, you scold him. He does not treat me like Shyam treats Rukmani.

Give my love to Papaji. I can't wait to come and stay with you.

Your beti,

Shakuntala.

"Read this 1950's *Kyonki Saas Bhi Kabhi Bahu Thi*?" Meera joked and handed over the letter to Sujit.

"Yeah, really! So, it happened back then as well," Sujit remarked when he had finished the letter.

"Why not? I think this happens in all generations, across centuries," Meera said. They both laughed.

Dear Maa,

17 Feb 1950

Maa, you won't believe what I experienced. We went to a theatre to watch a movie called Har Har Mahadev last month. It was really exciting to watch it on such a big screen. I sat next to Shekhar, and during the movie, our hands touched twice. I looked at him, but he looked away.

I really liked the song "Shiv Shankar bhole bhaale bhakton ke rakhwalle", and I sing this song a lot. Maaji asked me to sing it for our Aarti as well. Since then, I have been singing it for the Aarti daily. Rukmani and I sing the Aarti. I really like her; she is my best friend.

Maa, I have done something really, really wrong, I have never lied to Pitaji here, but when Shekhar asked me to do so, I couldn't say no.

Last week, Maaji asked me to take lunch for Shekhar and Pitaji to the kacheri. When I reached there, I saw Shekhar in a fight with a couple of boys and they were all hitting one another. When I shouted, Shekhar looked at me and asked me to go away from there and also not tell anyone about it.

I ran to the office and left the food there. When Pitaji asked me if I had seen Shekhar on the way, I lied to him and said "No". I ran home and cried, waiting for Shekhar to reach home safely. In the evening, Pitaji came and took all of us to the hospital; Shekhar was unconscious. Maaji was crying really badly, and Pitaji again asked me if I had seen anything, and I again lied.

I thought Shekhar would be very angry with me. But when he woke up, I took tea for him; he smiled at me. He took my hand and said that he was very happy that I hadn't said anything to Pitaji.

I know that Shekhar is not well and it will take him about three months to heal, but that was the best day of my life.

Now, whenever I see him, I find that he is already looking at me. Sometimes, he looks away, and sometimes, I look away.

I wish that my friendship with Shekhar becomes like that of Shyam and Rukmani's.

I miss you, Maa and Papaji, too. I don't know when we will meet again.

Your beti,

Shakuntala.

"Let me look up this song *Shiv Shankar Bhole Bhale* something…," Sujit said as he opened the YouTube app on his phone.

They listened to the first video that came up. It was 2 minutes and 50 seconds long.

"It sort of grows on you, doesn't it?" Meera said, pleased that they had found it.

"No way! I am not going to listen to this. Just because your grandmother sang this in her daily Aarti some seventy years back, it doesn't mean that we should also be listening to these oldies," Sujit said, making a face.

"I am not saying that," Meera said, and looked away, slightly hurt.

"Okay, let me play this again, just to make you happy," Sujit tweaked her ear.

"Turn down the volume a bit. Jia will wake up," Meera said, giving him a kiss on his cheek as she got up to make some coffee.

"Do you want some coffee?"

"Yes."

Dear Maa,

17 Nov 1952

How is your health now? How is Papaji? Did you get the backyard wall repaired after it was broken by those goons? Papaji is almost forty now; he cannot act like someone of twenty and pick a fight with people like them.

Please take care of yourself. Shekhar has sorted out all the issues with those people now. They will not trouble you anymore. Here, Pitaji and Maaji are quite tense these days. They are worried about Shekhar. Pitaji beat him up really badly for coming home drunk yesterday. His hands began to bleed as he tried to shield himself from the blows. Even Maaji did not say anything; she simply kept standing next to Shyam. She has always loved Shyam more. Shekhar is her elder son. He has his bad habits, but still... I don't understand Maa—if I had a brother or sister would you have loved them more than me?

I have always supported Shekhar and will continue doing so... I knew before anyone else when he had had his first drink as he had told me about it. Also, when he took his first puff of a cigarette, I knew about it. But I did not tell anyone, not even Rukmani, with whom I share everything that happens in this house.

Pitaji was saying that he might send Shekhar away from Delhi for a few months or even years. I cannot live without him. Seeing him daily is the best thing for me; I love him, Maa.

I know that he also loves me... He has not said it to me, but I know he loves me. We also don't speak to each other at night. He just comes, closes the door, looks at me once, and then turns off the lamp.

Whenever you are in Delhi next, I will take you to Hotel India's Chinese room. They have recently opened it, and Shekhar took me there for dinner. To be honest, I didn't like the food there, to start with; it was all very weird to see, long worm-like things that they call noodles. But when I tasted them, they were the best thing I had ever had. They served them really well too and took good care of us. Shekhar told me he knew someone there, but I can't remember the name. I like going there with Shekhar, and especially to Connaught Place. There are so many places to eat and shop! He always gets me something expensive each time we go there.

But I am worried. What if Pitaji sends him somewhere? What will I do?

Please take care of your health and that of Papaji's. I am well and happy here.

Your beti,

Shakuntala

"I have heard about this. This is at Nirula's, isn't it?" Meera asked, coming out of reading the letter.

"Yes, I think. Let me find out," Sujit said. He proceeded to confirm it with the restaurant, and then he said, "They had closed the Chinese room back in 2006."

"Ah, we could have gone there and experienced the moment, too," he continued.

"Yeah, I was thinking on the same lines," Meera replied.

Dear Maa,

12 Aug 1954

How are you and Papaji? I am well. Please don't worry about me. Maaji, Rukmani, Shyam, and Pitaji are taking good care of me.

It has been a month now since Shekhar went for his army training. I received a letter from him three days ago. He had written it within the first week of reaching there.

He is also doing well, but I miss him here as I am all alone. Besides, they make him work really hard. He said that one day Commander Baldev made him do five hundred sit-ups. His arms and legs ached terribly after that, but I know he is strong and tough. He will not back off easily. He has made a friend too from Punjab, whose family had come to live in India after the Partition.

I can't sleep at night without him. I have developed this bad habit of placing my head on his shoulder and sleeping. He always stayed motionless so that I didn't wake up. No one does that for me now.

Rukmani suggested I go and live with him wherever he is posted once the training gets over. I can't live without him.

I see him everywhere. I see him in the morning, I see him in the afternoon, and I see him in the evening. But when night falls, I realise he will not come to me, and I am all alone.

This morning, I fought with Maaji and Pitaji because they have sent him there. Now they don't even talk to me nicely. I have said "sorry" so many times, but they don't listen. I don't want to stay in this house; I want to go where Shekhar is, to be with him.

Shekhar said that they might send him to the Pakistan border, where he would kill a hundred men alone… I don't want him to go to the border as I don't want him to get into danger.

Maa, what should I do?

I will not be able to come in November, as we might go to Vaishno Devi during the Diwali break.

I am missing you, Maa.

Your beti,

Shakuntala

"Wow! Was your grandfather in the Army at that time? He must have taken part in the Indo-China War of' 62 and the Indo-Pak War of' 65," Sujit said.

Meera looked out of the window and kept quiet.

"What is the matter?" asked Sujit.

"I don't know anything about their lives. I don't know if he took part in it or not, or if he died fighting for our country, and all, because of that woman…"

"Your mother?"

"Yes"

"Well, not entirely."

Meera looked at Sujit. She knew he was right.

"It's like… these letters are a part of someone else's family and not mine. I am entering into their lives somehow and am not being allowed to do so. It feels very odd."

"I am sure you are. Otherwise, your mother would not have sent them to you."

"I want to sleep now—I will read them tomorrow," Meera put the letters into the box and stood up, yawning.

"Don't start without me," Sujit told her before going to the kitchen to get a bottle of water.

Shakuntala
(1956 - 1964)

Chapter 3

"WHY DIDN'T YOU tell me about Simon?" Meera complained to her father in the morning. She also told him about the tickets to New York and that Simon had mentioned his call to her father in the letter.

"So… you have opened your mother's antique carton, finally?" Adarsh asked.

"You knew what was in it. Did you also open it back, then?" Meera asked in surprise.

"No, I did not open it. Simon told me that he would send tickets, so I guessed it might have a letter or some sort of communication from him along with your mother's things in the box."

"You are right. There is a letter. But why didn't you tell me about the call?"

"I wanted it to be your choice rather than a circumstantial decision. You would have been emotionally pressed to go to New York, which would not have done any good either," Adarsh said. "If you would have opened the box then, given it a thought, and then decided to go, it would have been your choice. I would not have stopped you from going—at least not after her death. Now say something…"

"I would not have gone," Meera concluded.

"I thought so, too. So, what's in the infamous Pandora's box?" Her father chuckled, trying to make the discussion easier.

"Nothing much… my New York tickets and a bunch of letters."

"Ah, those letters that she wrote to her mother and her mother to hers."

"You knew about it?"

"Yes, I was married to her, however, briefly. I know a thing or two about her. You won't believe it probably, but there was a time when I really loved her."

"Okay, I have to go now."

Meera did not hide the fact that she was disinterested in her father's story. She disconnected the phone and looked at the pile of letters that were now lying on the dining table.

She looked at a letter from 1995. Wondering why it was unopened, not delivered and read back then—what part of the story of her mother's life it contained, she slowly opened it.

Dear Maa,

26 Apr 1956

How are you and how is Papaji? We both are doing well here. I have moved to Rewa in Vindhya Pradesh. It's very far from Delhi—I have never been so far from Delhi ever in all my life!

I had thought that without Maaji and Pitaji, Rukmani, Shyam and Kishore, I would be lost here, but now, I am with Shekhar after almost two years.

Maa, when I came here two months ago, Shekhar hugged me in front of all his servants. They all laughed, but I was very embarrassed. Shekhar took two days' leave, but we didn't go anywhere. We were most of the time in our bed, in the room. He made love to me during the day. He has never done it in the daylight before this; we always used to make love to each other during the night.

Earlier, he used to drink all the time. But now, he has changed. He used to fight with everyone, once he hit me with the bottle on my back, but later he made love to me all night, so I did not mind. But now, he takes one glass and drinks slowly. Sometimes, he takes almost an hour to finish one glass. He is also very gentle now.

I am so happy, Maa, that I am finally with him. He cares about me, too, and I want him to be with me all day and night. I get bored when he goes for his duties during the day and wait for him to return.

Our servants told me that Shekhar is the favourite of his several seniors as he works really hard. He has also made many friends. Every now and then, we are invited to someone's house within the same army compound. He also invites his friends for dinner at our home.

He asks me to cook something special every time, but I don't do that. I ask the servants to do that. Why are they here, anyway? I don't want to work and get tired, now that my husband is so respected here and is at such a good post. There is no need for me to work.

Maa, you had asked me to come and stay with you for some time, but I can't come now. I have just come here, and I don't want to leave Shekhar again for long. We have so much to do here—so many people to meet, and Shekhar expects me to be with him whenever we go anywhere. I will write to you if I make a plan to come.

Please take care of your health and also of Papaji's.

Your beti,
Shakuntala

"You know… I just love the Army life—It is so dignified and classy," Sujit said.

"Yeah, but there is danger, too, isn't it? I went to cover a skirmish about six years ago and saw how brutal it was. The army life is not all about classy parties—it's more about the sacrifice for the country that the soldiers make," Meera replied sternly.

Sujit, at once, knew he had hit an emotional cord. "Sorry… I know your cameraman lost his life. But it looks like your grandmother was all into the classy parties and heavenly sex. Your grandfather was a stud too. Even I can't fuck for two successive days and nights," Sujit said, with naughtiness in his tone, trying to bring Meera out of a difficult memory.

"I can take it for two days and nights, and I am sure you can give it to me. Let me motivate you a bit," Meera winked, moving closer to Sujit.

Dear Maa,

19 Nov 1956

How are you? How is Papaji? You didn't reply to my previous letter. I hope everything is well with you both.

Maa, a lot has changed over the last couple of months. Even our state Vindhya Pradesh is no longer in existence—They have named it Madhya Pradesh. I met so many people who are unhappy with the merger, but I think there are more who are in favour. Anyway, we don't have a say in it.

Shekhar is doing well. His love for me grows by the day. He takes care of me like no one has ever done, but he has to go on assignments for days and sometimes, for weeks. He says that they are running short of men, and he needs to cover other areas as well. In some places, there is some unrest due to the merger. I feel very lonely...

Maa, I have done something terrible, and I don't know what to do now. Please burn this letter after reading and do not show it to anyone. Shekhar was out for two weeks, and he had asked one of his jawans to stay at home, just in case I needed something.

One night, it was dark, and I did not know he was standing there; I went to get something to eat and stumbled upon him. I think he was intentionally standing there. We fell to the ground, and I fell over him. He was bare-chested. We looked at each other for a while, and then I stood up and went to my room. Maa, I will not lie, but I had to resist the feeling of grabbing his body and making love to him.

I don't know what I was thinking. I will go to hell for thinking about a man other than Shekhar. If Shekhar finds out about him, he will leave me or kill me. He will be hurt and feel terrible. He loves me so much, and I love him, too. Then why, Maa, did I feel this way when I touched another man's bare body? I ran to my room and closed the door behind me. I did not lock it. I wanted him to follow me—I wanted him to come to me. My hands and legs were trembling. I could not stand and I fell to the ground near the door.

The only sound I could hear was of my racing heart beating very fast, faster than I had ever felt. I don't know what I was thinking at that time. Could my strong desire have led him to my room? He opened the door and stood there for a very long time. I could see only the outline of his body as it was very dark.

Maa, God will punish me for this. I don't know what I was thinking. I gathered my courage and senses and stood up. He came closer—our bodies touched each other. I had a choice to make. If I had gone for it, I might have regretted my decision for the rest of my life, or it could give me the pleasure that I so desperately wanted then, and no one would know.

I closed the door.

I will now always have to live in fear. What will happen if Shekhar comes to know? I love him, I really love him, but these thoughts are killing me from within.

I don't know what to do. Please help me. Please, could you and Papaji come here for a few months?

Your beti,

Shakuntala

"OH, MY GOD!" shouted Sujit, jumping off the chair.

"Hey, Jia is sleeping in the next room."

"Oh, my God!" Sujit whispered, sitting back on the chair.

Meera didn't know what to answer or how to react.

"Did they do it?" he asked.

"I don't know. I was not there."

"This could mean that your entire lineage is… different."

"Shit!"

"Shit!"

Dear Maa,

1 Sep 1957

How are you? How is Papaji? We are doing well here. Sorry, I was not able to write to you sooner. You know… I have a daughter now whom we have named Janki.

Maa, it was horrible—more than you had explained to me. I had the pain for almost three days before Janki decided to come out. Maa, when the doctors told me that it was a girl, I couldn't control my tears. I was shocked, disappointed, and angry. You know how much I have longed for a boy. After Kishore, I wanted a boy more than ever.

Everyone will now love only Kishore, and no one will love Janki. They won't love me either. I cried when I first saw her; Shekhar cried too, but he was smiling—he was happy. I thought he would not love me anymore as I have given him a daughter, but he is happy. Every week, he invites people to show the baby off. Maa, she is beautiful, but not what I wanted. I wanted a boy for myself; I never wanted a girl.

Shekhar says now that we don't need another child. We have Janki, but I want a boy. Why did God have to punish me in this way?

I, sometimes, can't even bear to look at her. I leave her crying, I leave her in the sun, and I leave her hungry, too.

I have faced so much trouble for this child and now... When the doctor gave her to me for the first time, I cried a lot; I didn't even want to hold her.

I am worried about my family now—I am worried about Shekhar's family, his name and his legacy. Who will take care of us in our old age? Janki will not do that. She will go to her family and will not worry about us like a son would have done.

I hate her, Maa. She has come in between Shekhar and I. Shekhar loves her a lot. He would have loved a boy more; he just doesn't know. He even slapped me when I told him of my feelings towards Janki.

You tell me, Maa, if I am wrong. However hard I may try, I can be in your life in only a limited way. I couldn't have taken care of you and Papaji like a son and his family would have done.

Maaji is very lucky. She has Shekhar, Shyam, and Rukmani and I to take care of her and Pitaji and now Kishore, too, who is the apple of her eye.

What will be my position in the family now that I have given birth to a daughter?

Shekhar's friend has a Kodak Pony II camera which works on colour slides. I am attaching a photo of Janki.

I am not feeling well these days. I have asked Shekhar, and he has written to Papaji. If he agrees, I will come there and stay with you for a couple of months.

I don't know what to do, Maa. I have always wanted a boy. I can't love her now; I can't love her ever.

Hope to see you soon.

Your beti,
Shakuntala

A single tear rolled down Meera's cheeks. Sujit hugged her.

Dear Maa,

23 Jun 1959

How are you and Papaji? Sorry I was not able to write sooner. You have also moved from Delhi. How is Baroda?

Shekhar has been posted to Kashmir, and I am in Delhi. There are times now when I am not even able to recall his face. I live with his pictures now. Maa, am I a bad person in saying that I don't care about our country? I just want him to be near me.

Janki is two now. She looks like her father and whenever Shekhar is in Delhi, they don't leave each other. I was wrong—Shekhar loves Janki. Sometimes, I think he loves her more than he loves me, or maybe he loves her even more because he knows that I can never love her as he does.

She is the centre of attention in the entire house. Maaji and Pitaji are so happy when they are with her! Rukmani once told me that she was getting jealous, as all the love is now divided between the two children, and Janki is getting the larger portion.

Rukmani has turned quite nasty. Even if I just sit for a moment, she has a problem with it. Now, it is not my fault that I have servants, and she is still working as a housemaid does. I have refused to work with her so many times. I have also asked Pitaji and Maaji to hire servants, but Rukmani thinks that it is a waste of money. Is it my fault that we have more money than her?

I even bought one dress for Kishore, when I bought a couple of them for Janki. Do I have to buy an equal number of dresses for both? I did that only because Rukmani said that Janki could also wear her brother's clothes. But how can a girl wear a boy's clothes? Even Maaji agrees with her, though.

I think I was happier with Shekhar, away from Delhi.

They can keep their precious granddaughter and make her wear whatever they want to, and anyway, we may finally go and live with Shekhar in about three months.

Maa, there is no one to take care of you and Papaji. Please take care of yourselves. If you need any money, don't hesitate to ask me.

Your beti,
Shakuntala

"Money and power change people very quickly," Sujit said.

"You can't judge a person by what he or she did years ago," Meera replied.

"Yeah, but true nature never fades away, and it comes back in some form or the other."

"People change," countered Meera.

"Not sure about that, really. Maybe the situation around them makes them shift gears. But an inherent nature never or, let's say, rarely changes," Sujit philosophised.

"Maybe." Meera put the letter down.

"And, you know what? Your grandmother was a real stuck-up woman… Sorry," was Sujit's immediate apology in case Meera's newfound love for her maternal family would cause any trouble.

But Meera only smiled. "I think so, too," she said.

Dear Maa,

23 Aug 1962

I hear that there will be a war between India and China. I have heard Pakistan will also attack at the same time.

Shekhar has sent a letter from Pangong Tso near the McMohan Line. He says not to worry for now as there will be no war. Panditji will find a solution.

I am very worried for him, Maa. I don't know what to do. I have been sending him a letter every week and have to wait for a month to receive any reply from him.

For the first four or five days, it's fine as I read and re-read the letter and knew that he is safe, but after that, every second has been like a hammer.

I am very proud, Maa, of the fact that he is serving the country. I fully support him. He is very passionate about our country. The only other thing he is passionate about is Janki. I don't let my worry spill into words lest it may trouble Shekhar.

But I miss him a lot, and whenever I cry, Janki comes and wipes my tears. Her smile strengthens me; she is the only one I have here. I can't even go to Delhi now, and you know why.

I am worried about Shekhar. Will he be fine? I have been hearing of so many soldiers losing their lives. These are not just their lives; they are of ours as well.

Please pray for me. Pray for Shekhar, too. I promise I will be a better wife and mother and love him more than I have ever done.

Please pray for us.

Your beti,
Shakuntala

"Did he survive the war?" Sujit asked.

"How would I know? Even I have just found out that someone from my family took part in any war for the country. See… I have goosebumps!"

"I hope he did. Howsoever self-centred your grandmother is or was, she really loved her husband."

"Can you say that for sure, knowing what she did?" asked Meera.

"Or did not do," Sujit finished her sentence.

"That will be an unresolved mystery unless we find the answer in these letters. Will you open it?" Sujit asked Meera.

But Meera was stunned. "I don't know…" she mumbled.

"You have arranged them chronologically. Next is your mother's letter."

Janki

(1965 - 1970)

Chapter 4

Dear Maa,

29 Dec 1965

The darkness terrifies me. I hear voices when I sleep at night. Someone comes to my room every night, and someone also comes to the window. I want to sleep with you in your room so that no one can come near me.

I don't like it when you scold me. Rajan's mother never scolds him, he had told me. His mother buys lots of gifts and toys for him, too. You also buy a lot of toys for me, but you don't play with me. A few days ago, I learned a new game at school. Will you play it with me? I promise that I will be a good girl.

I miss Papa. He is still fighting with the bad people. He used to play with me and bring toys and dolls, when he was with me. My favourite is Nancy which he had brought last year when he had come to stay with us for two weeks. I want to stay with him.

Only Rajan plays with me in the evening.

I like pink. My room, my bed, my chest of drawers—are all pink. None of my classmates have pink in their rooms, but you had got that done when I asked you for my birthday. Still, only Rajan and I play in my room. You never come inside.

When I had got up last night, I got hurt by the corner of the bed. I cried outside your room for a long time, but you didn't open the door. It was hurting, Maa, and I couldn't sleep for a long time. I went to the fridge and took some ice. It was cold, and I couldn't hold it in my hands. You scolded me in the morning saying that I had peed in the bed. I promise I didn't do that; it was the ice that had turned into water.

You always ask me to go to my room when you drink and cry. I know you miss Papa, too, but Papa is brave. He will defeat all the bad guys and come home. Don't worry. I am always with you.

I know you write letters to Nani. You told me once that you write a letter to her every month. I will write you a letter every month too, and to Papa as well. I will also write letters to Dadi, Dadaji and Nani. Will you send my letters to them?

I don't like the brinjals and ladyfingers that you force me to eat.

And, yes, I want the new pink dress we had seen in the shop the other day, for my next birthday.

Your dear daughter,
Janki

Meera read the letter twice, just to consume the information. To start with, it was very hard for her to open the letter. She looked and relooked at the folded letter for an entire day before she could gather enough courage to open and read it. Sujit, meanwhile, had waited patiently.

This was the first time that she was reading and getting to know something about her mother apart from the unpleasant interactions she had had with her. She could never see beyond the mountain of hate she had carried for her.

Imagining her mother at the age of eight, seeking her own mother's love and attention, made it seem as if her younger self and her mother were in the same boat.

She did not pity her; no, she did not. She told Sujit that, but there was still a gap that emerged in Meera's mind. She wanted to fill that gap with her preconceived notions of her mother, but not with this new image of her—a child similar to herself. Truth be told, Meera had wanted her mother to be a bad child, a spoilt brat, so that she could justify her becoming what she was at a later age.

"Can the parents be blamed for what becomes of a child?" Sujit asked.

"Not entirely. People make their own choices, and the mistakes they make are their own," Meera said, still submerged in her thoughts.

Sujit did not want to let go so easily. He stressed further, "But, don't they get coloured by what they see of the world, or what they understand about it? Don't they try to fill the gap they see in the world?"

"It's still about the choices one makes. No one forces you after a certain age. Not even your parents force you about the things you do or say. Your character builds that for you," Meera replied, not agreeing with Sujit's philosophy.

"But aren't parents responsible for making or shaping that character?" Sujit asked as he handed Meera a cup of coffee.

Meera smiled to convey her thanks. "Yeah, but no one is perfect. Even parents are human, and it's not as if there is a course for how to do things right!"

Sujit smiled. He had made his point.

"Don't compare my situation and generalise. It's not fair," Meera grumbled.

"And what you are doing is painting a little girl on the basis of what she becomes later on, and judging her. Is it fair, then?" Sujit said, shifting over to his left shoulder.

"I am not doing that," Meera ran a hand over her daughter's head.

"Yes, you are."

"It's difficult."

"You are a hypocrite, then. All I am saying is to give her a chance. If she did not have a good childhood or did not get the love she deserved, this was bound to happen," Sujit explained patiently.

"Not necessarily," Meera snapped and walked away.

Sujit knew he could not win for at least now, but he was happy that, at least, this gap or vacuum that Meera had faced all her life, was now up for discussion.

Dear Maa,

25 May 1967

I hate you. I will leave you and will never come back. I hate Papa too; he also wants me gone. I will not write any more letters. I hate you—I hate you—I hate you.

Please, don't send me to Nani's home! Please! I will not trouble you and Papa. I don't want to go; I want to live with you and Papa.

You told me that I would have a little brother, but then you said that God has taken him away. Then again, you said God had sent my little brother back, and that he would return in two months. But again, Papa told me that God called him back. You are lying! Both of you are lying! Why would God call him? You must have sent him away somewhere like you are sending me now. No one will come to you. I don't want to come to you, nor does my little brother.

I will drink milk and eat all vegetables also. I will study, I will study a lot, and get good marks—better than Rajan, I promise! But please, don't send me to Nani's place.

You like Rajan more. Whenever he comes home, you talk to him even if you are not well. But when I come to you, you don't talk to me. You don't even look at me; instead, you shout whenever I come near you. Nani loves me a lot; I will be happy with her.

Papa leaves us, goes on his duty and does not come back for months. Who will take care of you when you are alone? I don't want you to be alone. I will take care of you. I know you are not well, and I will look after you like I do for Nancy.

Nancy also likes to be here with you and Papa. How will Teddy and she live without you? How will they sleep? Who will feed them? Who will take care of them when I am at school? All my friends are here. Who will talk to me there? Rajan is here too. How will I play with him there?

I don't want to leave Rajan. He is my best friend. He cares about me and gives me chocolates. I really like to play with him. I become the groom, and he is my bride when we play. Who will play with me there? Please, don't send me.

Please, Maa. Please.

Your dear daughter,
Janki

"This is really sad. Why would a parent do that to his child?" Meera said. She seemed exhausted with the letter's contents.

Sujit tried to work it out in his mind. "Well, I think, in this case, your grandmother was a psycho. She only thought of herself, her money and her ego—that's all!"

"Perhaps she had a strong desire for a boy? How can a parent discriminate between a girl and a boy, though? I would never do that to Jia!" Meera said.

Meera picked little Jia up and hugged her. Sujit embraced the two of them and said quietly. "The world was different in those times."

Meera mumbled through Jia's hair, "I will never ever send Jia away from me, not even to the hostel."

"Sometimes hostels are good. They instil discipline," said Sujit.

"But at what cost? The children miss being with their parents."

"She used to write a letter every month. Here, we have only two of them. Now that really sums up her childhood, doesn't it? I wish she had a better one!" Meera said. She looked down at the two letters that were now lying open in front of her.

"You are not using any swear words," teased her husband.

"I don't need to, and I don't want to, either. It's not that I can't. I can, and I have used those words before to address her. It's just that a lousy childhood does not mean that your monstrous actions will be justified once you grow up."

"I can't defend that," said Sujit.

"You don't have to," said Meera.

Dear Maa,

5 Mar 1968

How are you? How is Papa? I am fine now. Nani was really worried about me when I had chickenpox last month. I had high fever and boils all over my body which were very itchy. Now I am fine... You know, Maa, I spread chickenpox to five other girls in my class!

Nana loves me a lot. He was very sad when I was sick. Nani was sad, too. Both of them made me sleep in their room, on a different bed. Nani told me that she and Nana also had chickenpox when they were of my age, so they would not get it again. Nana told me that you used to cry a lot when you had it.

But I didn't cry at all, only once I did when the itching was very bad. But, otherwise, I have been a brave girl.

Now, let me tell you the best thing that has ever happened. I am in love, and every girl in my school is in love with them! I got a chance to see and meet them. Nana took us to Rishikesh, where I got a chance to see and meet Paul. Actually, I love all of them. I love John, George, and Ringo as well. I love The Beatles, Maa. But I want to marry Paul.

He was in a red shirt, and he was looking so good. We saw him from a distance. Nana took us into the Ashram, but we were not allowed to go near him. I wanted to stay longer, but as I said, no one was even allowed to go near them so we had to leave. I will have their memory with me till I die. I will tell my kids that I saw The Beatles up close, and I will also add some bits like I shook their hands and Paul gave me a hug.

Take care of yourself and we will meet when you are here. The last time, only Papa had come. Is your health okay now? I can come and take care of you if you and Papa wish me to do it. I miss you a lot.

I love you.

Your dear daughter,
Janki

"Hey, do you want me to read your mother's letters? Next, she'll probably write about her menstruation cycles and teenage kiss," Sujit said, giving Meera a flying kiss.

"So, what's new for you? You have experienced both, haven't you?" teased Meera.

Sujit rolled his eyes. "Not the menstruation cycles, but yeah, a lot of teenage action."

"Really, you never told me about it!" Meera pulled his hair.

"What should I tell you? All of it was with you!" he said. Then, he came closer to her and gave her a kiss on the lips.

Dear Maa,

15 Jun 1970

I don't want to leave this place. I really like it here. I don't want to go to Delhi to Dadi's house. I have so many friends here now. As it is, I go for two months to Dadi's house during summer. Why do I have to go and live there? I will have to change my school again, and make new friends. I am not good at making new friends. It had taken me so long to make friends here. Why do I have to do that all over again?

You don't care about me—you only care about what others say. If Dadi wanted me there, you could have said that Janki likes being at Nani's house and wants to stay there until she returns to me.

You don't want me to come and live with you. You don't want me to live happily, either, now that I am happy here. I hate you. I can't leave my friends and go there. What about my piano and painting class? I had fought with Nani for the piano classes. She wanted me to go to cookery classes. But she listens to what I have to say and puts her opinion before me, unlike you, who just tells me to go and live in a new place, leaving everything behind.

Why didn't you ask Papa to tell Dadi that I can't come now? I have studies also. In two years, I have my tenth standard Board Exams. Our tuition teacher has told us that we need to start preparing from next summer onwards to get good marks and take up Science. I want to be a doctor. I have always wanted to be a doctor. Why don't you understand my situation?

I don't want to go, and that's final. You have never loved me; you have never cared about me.

I hate you.

Your daughter,
Janki

"What is her problem? Why can't she be happy with whatever she's got?" Meera grumbled.

"What do you mean?" asked Sujit.

"I meant if she goes to a new place, she will make new friends and see new things. Then, why is she complaining?" Meera pushed the letter aside.

"Why did you complain when we moved from Mumbai to here?" countered her husband.

"That was different. I had work there—I had contacts there. Here, I had to make contacts all over again."

"So how is it different from a thirteen-year-old who does not want to leave her friends, and does not realise that there are new friends and a new life waiting for her in Delhi?" Sujit asked.

"Okay, I get your point."

"Sujit 1 Meera 0," smirked Sujit, putting Janki's letter in front of Meera again.

"Sujit 1 Meera 10,000!" Meera put her head on Sujit's shoulder.

Shakuntala

(1965 - 1970)

Chapter 5

Dear Maa,

8 Nov 1965

I have to be strong for him. My Major is fighting a war for our country, and I cannot be weak in front of him and others. We all assemble and listen to whatever is happening on the radio. Even the senior officers do not say much. I would have been happy if he had gone to fight against Pakistan, but I am still happy that he is protecting our nation at the China border.

I do get very scared sometimes, but I have to be brave — I have to be brave for Janki. She really misses her father.

She asks too many questions. I am trying to make her independent by making her sleep in her room. Sometimes, she cries a lot at night and comes and knocks on my door, but most of the time, she is very brave. She has her father's courage.

She does not have any qualities of mine. Maybe, my son will have my qualities. Pray for me, Maa, that I do not lose him this time. The doctor says that everything is going fine with my pregnancy. I just can't wait for this war to get over so that my dear husband and son arrive at the same time, and we can live like a happy family, and it's not very long now.

I am feeling a lot better now, and the doctor says that I am doing very well despite having all complications last time. Maa, I don't want to think about the past; I must stay focused on the present.

I am also careful; I do not allow Janki to cling to me often. In fact, I stay away from her, but she does not understand. I have to be careful, right? This time, I don't want anything to go wrong.

Shekhar said he would come by 10th Dec, before the birth, if the war is over. I am just praying that it does get over soon.

I want my son to be just like Major Ram's son, Rajan. He is a very sweet kid, and I try and plan things in such a way that he spends a lot of time at our house so that I can see him, and my son forms to become just like him. You know, Maa, he wants to be a pilot! I want my son to be a pilot, too. Janki does not want to be a pilot though; she wants to be a doctor. She is really inspired by our resident doctor here, Doctor Fatima.

How are you and Papaji? Please take care of your health. Sorry that I don't write letters that often now. You know what I have been through. All that time, Shekhar wasn't with me, either. I understand his passion, and I love my country too, but there are times when I need him.

I am alone, Maa. Please, you and Papaji, come and stay with me for some time.

Your beti,
Shakuntala

"She lost two kids," Sujit said, and his shock was evident in his voice.

"Yeah, it's really sad. But, perhaps, after getting what she wanted, she might have paid some attention to my mother?" Meera said.

"Or, worse, neglected her completely?"

"Yeah, whatever happens, happens for the good," agreed Meera and picked up the next letter.

Dear Maa,

9 Aug 1966

I am not fine. How can I be fine? How can I be fine ever? I have lost two sons—the sons whom I had always wanted since I got married.

Everything was fine, Maa, everything had been fine! They said that the baby was fine, and I would deliver it in about two weeks. It was earlier than we had thought, but they said there was nothing to worry about. When he was born, he did not cry. He did not cry, Maa! I could see his little arms and legs. He wanted to come to me, hug me so that I could love him. But they took him away.

Shekhar did nothing to stop them, Maa! He did nothing to stop them!

I don't want to live anymore. I don't love anyone anymore. This was all because of Janki. She was not well and fainted, and I had to hold her until Shekhar came running. The pressure might have caused this. She is responsible for this. She wanted it to happen.

No, Maa, I am wrong. Janki loved her little brother. She used to come and talk to him along with me. We used to sing songs for him. We used to make him laugh and feel him move inside me.

But I can't love Janki now. I have tried very hard to look at her and love her, but I can't. I can't look at her eyes longing for the love that I can't give her now. She understands that I am upset with her. I try to give her love but am unable to do so.

Shekhar has also started staying away from me. I just cannot understand him any longer. What if he leaves me? He has never told me that he wants a boy. He always tells me that he is happy with Janki, but I know that it is a lie. He wants a son as badly as I do. What if I am all alone, and there is no one to take care of me? Janki will go to her family and never look back. And, why would she? I have not been a very good daughter either. I don't take care of you and Papaji as I should. Janki will do the same to me, too. And, when Shekhar and Janki are not with me any longer, what will I do? Where will I go?

I am not able to sleep now, and it has been months like this. I tell Shekhar that I need my drinks and pills to sleep. But he does not listen to me. The hate that I generate towards Janki while thinking all night, makes him really upset. I don't want that. I want to be happy again. I want to be as I had been before.

She will never have a brother now. I need to save my family, but I can't think of doing so without my drinks or pills.

You didn't make me strong, mentally or physically, which is why this has happened to me. Maybe, Rukmani did not want me to have a son and she had cursed me. Who knows what is going on in that devious mind of hers?

I am going mad, Maa. I don't want to leave my family. I know Shekhar and Janki still love me, and I want to love them back, but I can't, especially to Janki.

Help me, Maa, help me!

Your beti,
Shakuntala

"She has gone through all the phases of depression," Meera said.

"I can see that," Sujit replied.

"She is angry with herself and the people around her. She feels guilty for not loving her family..."

"And also fears losing them," Sujit said.

"And also, grief, which is too much for her to bear. But why does she want a son so badly that she is ruining her entire family?" Meera rubbed her head in frustration.

Dear Maa,

28 Dec 1968

Maa, you will be happy to know that Shekhar has been promoted to Lieutenant Colonel last week. We had a ceremony and a party, but I didn't care.

I don't even want to know that Janki is doing well in studies. She had also taken part in some debate competition, but please don't write about her.

How are you and Papaji? He is still too young to have heart surgery, but it's good that you are taking care of him. If you need any money, I can ask Shekhar to send some. You have also not taken any money for taking care of Janki.

I have made new friends. Their husbands are below the rank of Shekhar, but I like them. They listen to me and don't judge me like the wives of the senior officers here. I hate those seniors' wives; they are so bitchy about me. Now they are saying that I sleep around with everyone I meet. According to them, I have even slept with the chef of the restaurant. If I like the food and I praise the man, that's it... it is enough to get them started.

They do not know what I have been through, that I am lonely and angry—angry with everyone, and the only thing that keeps me going is my drinks. What if I fell on the road, isn't Shekhar supposed to pick me up? Are husbands not supposed to help their wives when they are in trouble, or are we only playthings and child-bearing machines?

Shekhar has also changed. He fights with me and tries to control me. He has even asked the canteen manager not to give me any alcohol, but he does not know that I have friends all over the place.

He pulled me out of the party that night and kept me locked inside the room for the entire time. I was only trying to be friendly with the colonel. He would become a Colonel in two or three years; why is he so scared of his seniors now? You know, Maa, he had to call off the party when I kept on screaming in the locked room. I thought he was going to hit me when he entered the room, but he held me tightly and slept. He cried. I don't see him crying that often, but what is the point now?

He has said that he will take me to a doctor. Am I mad, Maa? Will he put me in a mental asylum?

He doesn't care about me. Ever since Janki left, he does not talk to me like he used to before. He blames me for letting her go as if I would do something to her. I am not mad. I know that she is my daughter.

Will you take me if Shekhar puts me into a mental asylum? Please ask Papaji to do that. No, don't tell him. He is not well now.

I love you, Maa. I can't even cry before Shekhar now. He thinks that I am making that up, but I am really sad and lonely. I want my old Shekhar back. I want my son back.

Your beti,
Shakuntala.

Later, Meera went to the clinic with Sujit for Jia's birth vaccinations. Seeing her child in pain, she said, "She's constantly crying. I can't see her like this."

"We have to get it done, though," Sujit tried to comfort her. "Our little princess has to be brave. It's terrible to see her in pain, but we must do what is right for her, isn't it?"

"Yeah, it just saddens me to see someone you love, in pain. I have told you about Marshall, our German Shepherd. We had to put him down because he had contracted this disease. I just felt terrible, and it took me ages before I could convince myself that it was for his good."

"Aren't you overdoing it? This is our daughter, and she is getting regular birth vaccinations," Sujit teased her. "There's nothing to feel bad about it."

Meera looked at Sujit speechlessly.

"Don't worry! We have to take hard decisions, and I am sure we will take many of those in our lives ahead, but we will take them together."

Dear Maa,

13 Apr 1970

I am well now. I returned from the hospital last week. Whatever happens, happens for the best, and now, I understand that. I could have killed myself as I could not live with myself. I could not live with anyone around me. I was in very bad shape. Yes, I think it was good that Shekhar admitted me to the hospital for three months.

No, I am not ashamed of the fact that I had to go there as I was not able to handle myself. I have learned a lot. I have learned a lot about myself; I have learned about Shekhar, too. I have always loved him, but now I love him more than ever. I respect him a lot for bearing with me all these years.

I have let you down, Maa; I was not there when you needed me; when Papa needed me, I wasn't there, either. He went through surgery, probably because of me, but I was not there to support you—to be with you. My little angel is there; I am sure she is very strong and must have stood beside you. I am sorry that I had not been a good daughter. But I promise you that I will try to be a better one now.

I cannot make up for the lost time, but I will try to be a good mother to Janki. She needs me, and I need her even more. I had always thought that I would be loved and respected by my in-laws, and that Shekhar would only love me if I gave him a son —someone who could carry the family name forward; I always thought that I would have a son. That and only that, trust me, was why I wanted a son rather than a daughter. Even after my first miscarriage, when the doctors said that I should not try for another child, I forced Shekhar. I forced him and myself, and all that time, I did not realise that the one whom I wanted the most, was all along by my side. Janki was waiting for me—waiting for my love.

I had been a bad mother but I am not so anymore. I know you had written that you can no longer keep Janki, but Maa, Shekhar wants her to go to her Dadi's house. He is still worried about my health and has warned me that I may return to what I was before... I am scared, too. But I am strong now, and I am feeling good too. Still, I am not sure if I will break down again; the next time I don't want my daughter to see me in this state.

I should have called her; she would have been my strength, but I am also worried that she will bring back my weakness and that I might not be able to control myself.

I have promised myself that once I feel stronger, I will bring her to us and never leave her again. Even Shekhar does not like being away from her.

Lastly, Maa, I don't know what to say to Shekhar. He has suffered a lot because of me—more than I have. He has stood by my side throughout our marriage, but I have always wronged him. I am very lucky to have him as my husband, and I have promised myself that I will take care of him throughout my life and not give him a chance to be upset.

I will also come to meet you and Papaji once I feel better. Pray for me, pray for my family. Now everything will be good. I will make everything like it was before, even better.

Your beti,
Shakuntala

Meera called her father early the next morning.

"Papa, how are you?" she asked.

"I am well. Why are you calling so early? Is everything okay?" Adarsh asked with a yawn.

"Yes, everything is fine…"

"Are Jia and Sujit fine?" Adarsh interrupted.

"Yes, yes, they are both fine. I just called to say that I love you a lot."

"Ahem, ahem, what happened suddenly? Do you want anything?" teased Adarsh.

"Come on, Papa! I am getting emotional, and you are making fun of me!" Meera said with a pout.

"Okay, okay… I love you too, beta. But, why suddenly? What happened?"

"Nothing has happened. I just realised that life is too short, and I just wanted you to know," replied Meera.

"You are making me anxious now."

"Okay, bye! No one can talk to you properly early morning. Bye!"

"Bye… take care!"

Janki
(1971 - 1976)

Chapter 6

Dear Maa,

15 Dec 1971

I am praying for Papa every day. You don't worry. Colonel Shekhar Saxena is a very brave man; he will fight and win the war for India. You have started drinking again. Why don't you listen to Papa? Why do you have to trouble everyone like this?

Dadi has not said anything, but she is also worried about you. Only if you call and ask for forgiveness will she forgive you, and you can then come and stay here, too. I don't care personally, but Dadi is upset for Papa also for he might be worried about you being there.

I know you don't care, but I am telling you that two months ago, I had won the 1st prize in the interschool painting competition, and last month, I won the 1st prize in a piano competition. Dadaji has kept both the trophies on the top shelf in the drawing room, and whoever comes home, he tells him all about it. He also calls me and introduces me to them. At first, it used to be embarrassing, but now I am used to it. Both Dadi and Dadaji, as well as Shyam Chacha, are forcing me to take up more advanced classes, but these days I am not able to concentrate on anything.

Dadi sits in the puja room for at least five to six hours daily and prays for Papa's safety. When the war is over and he comes here, I will ask Papa to talk to Dadi so that you can also come here.

I am liking it here. Earlier, I was angry with you when I came here from Nani's house, but I am happy now. Everyone loves me a lot. Rukmani Chachi makes dishes for me, whatever and whenever I ask for.

The only person who troubles me is Kishore. Do you know what I did? I saw him smoking, and I told Dadaji. He got a beating from Dadaji and Chacha, and a scolding from Dadi and Chachi, and they all told him that if he took his anger out on me, he would get more beatings. But I also help him. He really likes a girl who is a year senior to me and two years junior to him. Her name is Radhika. She is very beautiful, and they both look good together. At first, he did not have the courage to go and speak to her and asked me to help him. So, we are even now. He cares about me, but when I talk to him about boys, he gets angry and starts yelling. Once, he even punched Rajesh when he gave me a rose.

If you wish, I could have come to live with you and taken care of you, but I know you don't want me to be there. Even Kishore has told me that you have never loved me. He also says that I am not your daughter. Is that true?

Please reply.

Your daughter,
Janki.

"Do you think your great-grandmother would have forgiven your grandmother so that she could go back to the family in times like war?" asked Sujit.

"We don't know how bad the real picture was," replied Meera.

"Still, I had thought events like wars bring families together."

"There has to be an attempt from both sides, at least."

"Stubbornness runs deep in your family," Sujit philosophised.

"You bet."

"But at least, it looks like your mother is finally happy—first with her Nani, and now with her Dadi's family," he said.

"Yeah, that's true."

"You know when I was young, my Dadi had not let me feel the void my mother left in my life. Obviously, the extended family helped me a lot," Meera told him.

"Looks like history repeated itself. You and your mother had a similar childhood."

"But I didn't turn into a person like her—drug addict, kidnapper—you name what!"

"Because you had me from a very early age," Sujit said and came closer to Meera.

"Still, I have a few things to learn, and I am afraid I might go astray," Meera said with a wink.

Dear Maa,

26 Jul 1972

The only difference between now and all these past years has been I can see you now, every day, whenever you try to ignore me. You ignored my letters, but I continued writing them. Now, I try to talk to you, but you ignore me. Why did you call me here to make me lonely again?

But now, there will be more differences. I will not give you these letters. But I will still keep writing them as this is the only way I can vent my frustration towards you. I cannot say anything or fight with you; as Papa says, you are still very fragile, but I know the monster deep down is very much around.

Why did you call my school and ask the teacher how I was doing? She mocked me in front of the entire class, and all my classmates laughed at me. They think I am weird as I don't speak to anyone. They also think that I don't know how to make friends. They don't know that I have had lovely friends and I had to leave them, not once, but twice—first, when I moved out of Nani's place, and then when I moved out of Dadi's place. Why did you do this to me?

I had still thought that after all these years, you would be happy to see me but you are worse now. Why do you drink all the time? What satisfaction does that give you? Even the servants were laughing when Papa picked you up from the garden and took you into the room. Are you not ashamed of yourself?

You fight with Papa. You scream in the night, and still Papa cares for you. Rukmani Chachi loves me more than you do. I was so happy at Dadi's house. She and Dadaji, Kishore and Shyam

Chacha loved me. They had taken care of me while Papa was fighting for our country, and you were drinking to death.

Why don't you just die? I hate you.

Your daughter,
Janki.

"At least you have one thing in common with your mother," Sujit said.

"What is that?" Meera knew the answer, but she didn't want to spell 'that' out loud. That would make it real; it would also mean that now, she was feeling bad for her mother.

"Hatred towards your mother," Sujit said.

Dear Maa,

8 Mar 1973

Welcome back! I hope you have had a good time at the mental asylum. Okay, I know it was not a mental asylum, but you should have gone there. Only they can treat you.

But, thank you! All my life I had blamed myself as I felt that there was something wrong with me, which is why you didn't love me. But once you told me the real reason, I knew that it was not me; it was you. It was your selfish greed of wanting a boy instead of a girl, and you didn't flinch even once while telling this to me.

I don't care if you don't love me because I am a girl. Papa, Dadaji, Dadi, Kishore, and everyone else, who matters to me, loves me. I have always longed for your love. I had waited for you outside your room. Even when I was miles away, I had waited in the hope that one day, you would come and pick me up, hug me and say that you love me. I had been a fool all this time. All you wanted was a boy, and you had never wanted me. How could you have come to pick me up?

Why did you want a boy, anyway? What can a boy do that I can't? Maybe, they can smoke, drink and roam around, which I don't do now, but now that you had wanted a boy, let me do all that a boy can do and punish you.

Because of you, the feeling which I will carry with me for my whole life is now a bad memory of my first kiss. I said I didn't care when you told me about your feelings for me, but I cried the whole night and at the school during the recess. I met Rajan. Yes, we have still been meeting even after you told my teacher and asked me to stay away from him. I was crying in the far corner, and he came as usual. He was concerned about me. I think he loves me. I just jumped onto him and kissed him. Tears were rolling down my cheeks, some going into our mouths, while I kissed him, but I didn't care. I kissed him. It felt salty with the smell of curry and a cigarette, but I liked the sensation and touch of his lips on mine.

I wanted to show you that I am no longer the little girl you never wanted. I can take decisions, and I can make things work for me as a boy would do. Why should I cry and sulk in the corner like the girl you have never wanted?

I have never liked smoking. When Kishore smoked in front of me, I used to throw his cigarettes away. But I smoked my first cigarette with Rajan. I coughed throughout my last session of the school, but I still smoked, and I could still smell the cigarette in my mouth. My head is still heavy with the kiss and the cigarette, but I hope that you are happy now.

I will always remember my first kiss along with the pain that you had given me and the reason I chose to go for the kiss. I will probably never be able to love again in my life.

Thanks a lot, Maa, thanks a lot!

Your daughter,
Janki.

"So, what was your first kiss like?" Sujit asked.

Meera avoided the question. Instead, she said, "You know it's a weird thing? The first guy I kissed was also named Rajan."

"Oh! I didn't know that you are into older guys," teased Sujit.

Meera gave a sarcastic laugh. "Very funny! It was a different guy."

"So, how was it? You didn't answer my question."

"It was okay. Nothing so great to be remembered." It was an obvious lie, though. Meera's first kiss had been magical. She has, perhaps never felt that way again, not even with Sujit.

"That's a lie! Come on; you can tell me. I have told you about the girls I have been with."

"I have told you—it was nothing."

Dear Maa,

17 Aug 1974

You are a monster. The more I try to stay away from you, the more you come and hover around me. What is your problem? Why did you have to tell everyone that I know how to play the piano? I have quit playing it long back. It's so embarrassing, and moreover, you don't care about me. So, why the sudden affection and love towards me?

You don't even know how much I hate you. You are so stupid; you don't even know that I went to see a film, Ankur, with my friends about three months ago, and since then, I have been going almost every night. There were not many girls or women in the theatre, but I was in good hands. No one can touch me now that Pratap is with me. We went to his friend's house; he stays alone. Pratap asked him to go out and he made love to me all night, and by the time you and Papa had got up, I was already in bed. It bleeds, you know? I am sure you know. I cried too, but Pratap was very gentle.

I know you were watching me from the gap in the door when Suresh came to return the books. That was just an excuse. He had been trying to get into my pants for a long time. I would have never encouraged him, but because you were peeping, I went near him and kissed him. He will cherish that for all his life now. He then slid my hand into his jeans. It was so difficult to get rid of him afterwards. But I don't mind the attention, you know? It's because of you that I have this strong desire to seek attention.

Do you know what they call me now? Shama told me that they call me "military slut". I hope you are happy now. I relate more to Rajamma from the movie Ankur, but my friends call me Laxmi.

You have spoiled my life. Now, not even my friends ask your permission to meet me. They feel the same about you as I do. We have so many names for you that we call you behind your back. Even as you were leaving just now, I said… "Mad woman!"

You will never hear the words I call you, as you have now gone completely mad. Papa also does not like you. Why don't you just die?

I can never forgive you for what you have done to me—to my innocence. You pushed me into smoking and having this uncontrollable desire to get love and attention.

You know, I tried ganja? I didn't want to do drugs, but Vivek and his friend—I do not even remember his name—gave it to me. They insisted that I take it and promised me that they would protect me if anything happened. I don't remember much, but I am sure both of them fucked me. I told Vivek that he didn't need to drug me to fuck me. I even told him that he and his friend could fuck me together if they wanted.

I have become like this because of you, to punish you, and the best part is that I am not even ashamed of myself. Initially, I used to worry about what Papa would think. But I know that he will never get to know, and I will ensure that. I love him and I will never make him sad.

Why didn't you kill me in your womb itself? It would have saved so much trouble. All the sleepless nights that both of us have spent crying would have been avoided.

I hate you because of what you have made of me, and you never attempted to correct your mistakes, either. The only thing you know is how to judge my friends and me. At least, they are vocal about what they want from me, and, in return, give me what I want.

Your daughter,
Janki.

"Was that a rape?" Sujit asked, refusing to believe what he had just read.

"Didn't look like it, and anyway, I do not expect anything better from her."

"Well, she was lonely and acted out of revenge."

"There is a certain point up to which you can harm yourself in the name of revenge. After that, it becomes a choice and then a part of your nature. I think by this time, it had become more of a sort of morbid satisfaction in doing what she was doing, rather than a childhood trauma," Meera said with narrowed eyes.

"Forgiveness is not easy."

Dear Maa,

14 Jul 1975

One of the goals of my life has been achieved. It was for a short period, but still, I did spend time in jail! Even though it was only for two nights, I have achieved it.

You should be proud of my actions instead of complaining about them. I went to save the country like Papa does on the border. You were not there to see what we had seen. We were in front of Parliament, and there were thousands of students and supporters and activists guided by JP Sir and other leaders. We were very close to them. They will eliminate the corruption in the Government and remove the corrupt Prime Minister Indira Gandhi.

Now, I can't do much as you have held me a prisoner in my own house. But trust me, the Emergency will dissolve, and when it does, I will go again to fight corruption! You know Papa told me that he was proud of me, and a day will come when history will be written in favour of those who have stood against the mammoth evil that our society faces today.

But you will not understand that. You are only worried about who will marry me, who will look after me if I continue on the same path. I am fed up with hearing your whining every day. I just want to leave this place and go away to either Dadi's or Nani's house, but you won't let me do that either.

If I want more love, is that my fault? When you had seen me with those two boys, you told Papa instead of keeping it to yourself. He didn't say anything, but I understood. It would have been difficult for him to imagine his precious little daughter in a threesome, but why did you tell him in the first place? You don't want him happy, either. I saw the look on his face, the disappointment in his breathing. He has not been keeping well for the past two weeks now, and I can't even go near him.

You can think or say whatever you feel like to me; I don't care! But now you have embarrassed that one person who has stood by me all my life. How do I face him?

You are so selfish and self-centred that you cannot see anyone's happiness except yours.

Your daughter,
Janki

"I thought slipping hands into someone's underwear in front of your mother was hitting rock bottom, but I was wrong. It was having this threesome," Sujit said.

"It's exciting in a sad way," Meera said and regretted it immediately.

"Whoa, wait a minute! Have you ever had a threesome? Please say 'no'!" Sujit could not control his anxiety now.

"No, relax! I have not." Meera pulled his hair.

Sujit smoothed his hair. "So, what are you saying?"

"I just said that it would be… just different!" Meera burst out laughing.

"I never knew you were sort of a… kinky kind of girl," said Sujit, frowning.

"Threesome is not kinky," Meera argued.

"Okay, Madam Kamasutra, what is it, then?"

"I don't know! Wouldn't it feel good if more than two hands were feeling you?"

"It would, I guess," Sujit teased back, and then switched on the television.

"Imagine… I and one more girl begging your attention!"

"I can imagine that," said Sujit. "Now imagine this… I and one more boy begging your attention!"

Meera jumped out of her chair. "I don't want to imagine that!"

"Why not? Why do I have to do anything to a girl, then?"

"Fair enough! I have never thought of it. Should we try it?"

"No, this is up for discussion only, no action," Sujit warned.

Sujit had already gone far enough with the idea.

"Anyway, where do you find such people?"

"Google."

❍

Shakuntala

(1971 - 1976)

Chapter 7

"WE HAVE A problem…" Sujit called Meera from work.

"What is it? Did you not find anyone for our threesome?" Meera teased.

"I am not joking. It's about Amit and Nisha. They are fighting like India and Pakistan," Sujit said.

"What happened? What did your best friend do this time?"

"Nisha called. She said that he is cheating on her."

"Is he?"

"How would I know?"

"He is your best friend," said Meera.

"Doesn't mean that he will tell me who he sleeps with," countered Sujit.

"We are visiting them in the evening. What are you going to do?"

"Reading how Grandma reacted when my mother had a threesome."

"Damn, I can't read it today! We will be spending our entire evening consoling them," Sujit grumbled.

Dear Maa,

23 Oct 1972

I can see her every day. I want to run to her, hold her in my arms and never let her go. But I don't know what happens and I stop. I am not able to find the courage to overcome my guilt. I have had always wanted a boy, hoping he would be with me in my old age and take care of me. Janki will go away and will never be with me as I would like her to be. I can't live with that loss of having no one in my life.

But now, things are different; I want to know more about my daughter. One day, she was preparing a sandwich for herself and her father. I went into the kitchen and was scared to see her holding the knife incorrectly. It could have hurt her. I wanted to go near her and teach her, protect her, and help her, but I couldn't. I just couldn't go near her. I went out of the kitchen. I heard Janki's and Shekhar's laughter after couple of minutes and was assured that she was fine, and that she hadn't cut her hand or anything.

I can't overcome the guilt of what I have done to my innocent child.

Shekhar has also changed. He flushed my Old Monk in the toilet right before me. That was the only thing that gave me some oxygen to live on a daily basis. I don't care about the past. They have to understand what I am going through. Janki came in when I was throwing the empty bottle at Shekhar. What would have she thought about me? I had to shout at both of them to leave me alone, and then I couldn't sleep the whole night. When Janki was asleep, I went to her room and slept in the chair next to her. I love her, but she will never know this.

Last week, Shekhar had said that he would send me to the hospital again if I didn't behave well. I can see the helplessness in his eyes, but why does not he understand that I am beyond recovery? The best option for me is death.

I know both of them—Shekhar and Janki need my love, and I am trying a lot to pull myself together for the sake of my family. I don't want others to feel satisfied and believe that my family will not stay together for long.

Please suggest what I should do to come out of this miserable life and make Janki and Shekhar happy? How do I redeem myself?

Every night, before sleeping, I make a promise to myself that tomorrow will be different—tomorrow will be a new day. But, in the morning, the uncontrollable urge and mammoth guilt ruin my entire day.

I don't want to go to the hospital. I just need a little help from Shekhar to come out. I promise I can come out and be a

better mother and better wife. But how can I forget my sons, my two little sons who were taken away from me? Why am I being punished like this, Maa?

Your beti,
Shakuntala

"What did he do this time?" Meera was trying to calm Nisha and get some information out of her between her tears.

"I saw Amit naked from the waist up," Nisha cried, "and his secretary was leaning on his chest." She started crying out loud. "He can't control his desires. I should never have married him."

In another room, Sujit asked, "How was she, bro?"

"Super hot!" Amit replied and winked.

"Did you fuck her?"

"No, man! I know you think I am a dog, but this time I didn't do anything. She was insisting that I show my 6-pack abs to her, and when I took off my shirt…"

"You took off your shirt in the office?" Sujit said.

"She is really hot, man!"

"Okay, okay!" Sujit waved at him to continue with the story.

"So, when I took off my shirt, she leaned on me and said that she wanted to kiss my abs. How could I say no to that? And then this…" He pointed at his groin. "…sprung into action, and at that time, Nisha opened my office door. I don't know how many people would have seen that…" Amit trailed off.

"If you didn't do anything wrong, then be strong and don't budge."

"I really love Nisha. I don't want to lose her."

"Then be careful with these sluts," cautioned Sujit.

On their way home, Meera asked Sujit, "What did Amit tell you?"

"He really loves his wife," said Sujit.

"So, what do you think will happen now?"

"He didn't do anything."

"You don't have to justify that to me. Even Nisha knows he didn't do anything," said Meera.

"Then why is she troubling him like this?"

"So that your stupid friend is a little more careful the next time."

"How will he redeem himself now and regain her trust?" Sujit whistled.

"It's really difficult, but they will get back on track. I wish my Grandma had been able to redeem herself as well."

"What does that mean?"

"Read it yourself!"

Dear Maa,

7 Apr 1973

I have not taken a drop of alcohol in the last three months. It was really difficult in the beginning, but Dr Shyamlata made sure that I did not suffer alone. She used to sit with me even after her duty hours. I have learnt a lot and have faced my fears. The biggest loss in my life is not my sons; it is not giving Janki the love that she deserves.

The only way I thought I could redeem myself was to come clean in front of her—tell her about my fears, and I hoped, I prayed, I wished, and I thought that she would understand me and help me build this family up to what it should be.

It took me days and weeks to build up my courage, I have been told this several times in the therapy sessions and Shekhar also, when he had come to visit me. He has been understanding and supported me. He even laughs now and tries to cheer me up, but I can sense the detachment we have in our relationship. I had thought all that would change, but I was wrong. Telling the truth to Janki has thrown us further apart.

She had a childlike innocence earlier, which I do not see in her now. When I told her, she looked at me as if some weight had been lifted off her shoulders. But some has been added to mine. She said she doesn't care anymore, but I know she does. I heard her cry all that night but was not able to go into the room to talk to her. What could have I said? I can't do any more damage than I have already done to her.

She is different now—she wants to prove me wrong and take revenge. I don't know what it is and how she intends to do this, but I hope she does not harm herself while teaching me a lesson.

Dr Shyamlata had warned me of this reaction. This was the worst! If I don't handle her well now, she will never forgive me and hate me her entire life. Dr Shyamlata told me to stand next to her and try to speak to her. When she would speak, she was indifferent at first, but showed signs of anger later on, which is good, she said. This means all that anger she has had stored inside her, will come out, and probably we will make a new start.

I am ready to take in any kind of anger from her. She can even throw things at me or hit me. But when I go near her, she is indifferent and remains so throughout. I try to provoke her; I try to question her about how she is feeling, but she just looks back at me with a blank expression. I asked Dr Shyamlata about this and she is also concerned.

So far, all my efforts have been in vain, but I have not lost heart, nor have I gone back to my old ways of coping. I will make every attempt to redeem myself and save my family. I am making her favourite dishes. I keep a dress ready for her when she comes in. I have even bought her a radio. I had to literally snatch money from Shekhar. He thought I would go and buy Old Monk. I had kept it a secret. But when I gave it to her, I could see a sudden expression of surprise and happiness, but it was momentary. Seconds later, she flung the radio onto the bed and stormed out of the room.

She spends a lot of time outside now. I don't like Rajan. He has grown up to become a bully and a misbehaved boy, not the sweet little boy he was earlier. I am afraid when she spends time with Rajan, it is not good for her. I hope she has made new friends here.

Shekhar seems lost in his own world, but at least I can communicate with him. He is more secretive now, but I have to give him time as well, now that I am fine. I can't expect everyone to just fall in line—It will take time. Things may not be as good as they had been before, but at least we will be in a better state. I have spoiled this home, but I will rebuild it; no one can deter me again, not even myself.

I will also try and speak to Rukmani and Maaji and seek their forgiveness as I have hurt them as well.

You must be really ashamed of me. But the promise, that I have made to myself, will yield results. You will, once again, be proud of me.

Your beti,
Shakuntala.

Meera threw the letter in frustration. "Parents do so much damage to their children without knowing it."

"But she wanted to come clean and hoped that they would make a new start," Sujit said.

"There is no new start after this. I could never reconnect with my mother, even if she had been alive today," Meera said.

"Parents are human too, and they have equal rights to make mistakes. I am going to sleep."

Meera looked at Sujit for a minute and said:

"I will continue reading…"

Dear Maa,

14 Nov 1974

Maa, my hands are trembling as I write this. The situation has gone from worse to hell. I saw Janki putting her hands into a boy's underwear, and she knew that I was looking at her. What has she become? Why is she doing this? Calling me names behind my back, disrespecting me in front of her friends… these things are common now. I do get hurt, but I can't do anything about it. But, this… this behaviour at the age of seventeen is beyond imagination. How can she even think of doing something like this? If she can do this in front of me, God only knows what she must be doing behind our backs.

I feel my strictness is justified now. I do not let her go out of the house after seven in the evening. We had a big fight, and Shekhar supported her. He said she has grown into a responsible girl who can take care of herself now. He does not know half the truth, and I don't want him to know it, either. It's my fault, and I will rectify this.

She smells funny too. I suspect she has been drinking. But when I confronted her, she said she could never be like me. At least, due to her anger, she will never drink.

I am fighting this battle at two ends now. I know Shekhar is having an affair. What I don't know is when it had started. That is my fault too, and I am sure it must have started when I was in a miserable condition. I do not blame him or the woman; I blame only myself, and I will gradually win him back. I know he loves me a lot and that he has always loved me. If he did not, he would have left me for this woman. I am sure I can win my husband back, but I don't know how to win my child back. She has gone far away from me.

She didn't even wash her hands after that and came directly to the dinner table with that look and a smirk on her face! I had to shout twice, and I made her wash her hands before she put anything in her mouth.

Maa, I have failed. I have failed to become a good mother, a good wife, or a good daughter. But you have been my anchor in all this. If it were not for your support and guidance at each step, I would not have survived. I would not have had this courage to fight every day to try and save Janki if at all she could have been saved.

I know you and Papaji are not keeping well these days. If you wish, I will not bother you with my troubles as I don't know when and how they will end. At times, it looks as if they will end with my life, and I don't want them to end like this. I don't want to leave Janki with only negative thoughts about me.

Why don't you and Papaji come here and stay with us for a couple of months? Even Shekhar feels this would be good. He rightly believes that Janki will be happy if you are here at home with us.

Please write with your consent on the plan, and we will arrange the tickets for you and Papaji.

Pray that I succeed and manage to create some order out of this chaos.

Your beti,
Shakuntala

"How would you react if your parents see you kissing or having sex with someone?" Meera asked Sujit. They were at the breakfast table. Unable to resist, Meera had read the letter with Sujit.

"Embarrassed, I guess," Sujit looked down. Meera knew something was not right.

"Did it happen to you?"

"No, not sex, but once I was watching porn. This happened when I started watching porn."

Meera was intrigued. "When was that?"

"When I was eight," Sujit answered, handing over a slice of bread to Meera.

"Wow, so young!" exclaimed Meera.

"My dad came in. I was so embarrassed at the dinner table that day, but he was cool. He even joked and told my mother that they should get me married. You should have seen me then."

"I am seeing you now. You are as red as a tomato with just the memory of it. I can imagine what your state would have been then!" Meera teased him as she picked up his plate.

"Okay, I am off to work. Don't read without me!" Sujit blew her a kiss and left for work.

Dear Maa,

28 Nov 1975

The water has finally risen over the bridge. She can have and do whatever she wants, but not in my house. After so many years, Shekhar and I are finally close. Bringing two guys in our house in the name of studies and having sex with them in my house—I can't stand this!

I know that Janki's behaviour and rebellious nature is partly, or even if I say largely, my fault. Yet, I have never done anything that should make her do this. At this age, these are her own decisions. They are born out of revenge against my behaviour towards her years ago. It's not that I have not tried to make amends and compensate for that time. She can't punish me like this. NO! I can't tolerate this. I had to tell Shekhar, but I did not tell him the whole truth. I did not tell him that there were two boys. I did not even tell him that they were having sex. I just told him that her loving daughter was kissing a boy while pretending to study.

He did not confront, scold her or even say anything to her, which has had a powerful impact on her.

She is not even slightly ashamed of what she has done, but is upset and blames me because her father has stopped talking to her. It serves my purpose to control her, so I don't care what she thinks.

I am really sorry for Shekhar. He loves Janki a lot, and this half-truth made him very upset. He is avoiding her completely and not telling me anything about how he feels. He blames himself for this, which is completely incorrect as this is not his doing; this is not even my doing. This is entirely Janki's fault; this is her decision—this is her choice of life, and whatever pain she has been carrying from her childhood, does not justify this action.

Am I incorrect in saying this, Maa? You did not teach me not to love a girl-child—you did not teach me to drink and fall sick all the time or misbehave with elders. Those were my choices and my regrets. I have to carry that burden, and God knows that I have tried—I have tried hard to redeem myself, and my efforts have paid off with Shekhar.

I will not help her reconcile with her father now; I am not the punching bag that she has been used to, anymore. I can see the surprise in her, but enough is enough; I may have been the worst mother in the world, but even then, I do not deserve this from my daughter, if, at all, I would want to call her my daughter now.

She has crossed all limits, and her staying at home all day and pretending to study, will not make up for her atrocious behaviour.

I am ashamed that she is my daughter.

She thinks she is very brave for going to jail for a social cause and experimenting with her life like this. But, you tell me, Maa, is my anger justified, or do I still bow down before her and let her do whatever she wishes to?

Eagerly waiting for your reply, I cannot think straight now—I need your help now more than ever.

Your beti,
Shakuntala

"So… do you still think swinging is a good idea?" Meera said as she was sorting out the next letter to read.

"No one is policing us here, and I have found someone," Sujit gave her a big wink.

"What? Really?" Meera's eyes fell wide open.

"It's a couple," Sujit said.

Meera glared at him. "Are you fucking mad? I am not doing it!"

"Don't… I will!"

"Yeah… go ahead if you want! But I will never do it with three people at the same time."

"Really? Can I go?"

"Don't even dare… without me," Meera said with a wink.

Janki

(1977 - 1982)

Chapter 8

Dear Maa,

4 Jan 1977

You have won, and I have lost. Your evil has no limits. It's been more than a year, and still, Papa and I do not make eye contact, and nor have we had a proper chat. I have accepted that as a new normal, but what you have done now, is beyond my imagination.

HE IS MY FATHER. Why don't you understand that? Not letting me see him, will only make me hate you more. But that's what you have wanted from the start, anyway.

Life has become a joke for me. I don't have anything to look forward to in life now; I don't have any meaning left in my life. It's been one year, and I don't get urges to have drugs, sex, or even light up a cigarette. I just want my father to look at me, talk to me and hug me.

If anything happens to him, I will never forgive you for not letting me see him. You didn't even tell me that he had had an accident. I came to know only two days later from someone else. I want to see him as I don't have anyone other than him. If anything happens to him, I will also die.

I did as you had asked. Even though at that time I wanted to run away from rehab, I stayed as I thought Papa will... But I was wrong. You never stopped feeding him lies about me, and he may now never know how much I have left behind for him.

There were days, in fact weeks, when I would shiver in fever. Even the doctor said that I should call someone from home. Still

I faced all that alone, just in the hope that Papa would smile at me—his daughter—with love in his eyes.

How can you blame me for what I did at the hospital today? I had travelled for eight hours, and every second of those hours, I had prayed a thousand times for Papa, for him to get better and to live. And, YOU DIDNT EVEN LET ME SEE HIM! I hope that you will remember the punch on the nose now, and you must bleed—I wish you bleed to a painful death.

I WILL SEE HIM, AND I WILL TAKE CARE OF HIM. And, you cannot stop me. He is my father. Even if he does not love me, I will win his love and respect back.

I will not go to rehab now, even if you kill me for that. Even if Papa does not want to see me for another ten years, I will stay here and look after him.

You have won, and I have lost.

Your daughter,

Janki.

"Could that have really happened?" Sujit looked amazed.

"Anything could have happened. My dear Grandma could have done anything. I see now that she was actually the villain," Meera said all of this expressionlessly, without moving one muscle on her face.

"Still… not letting a daughter see her father in that critical period—what if something had happened to him? She might never have got to see her father again."

"Why are you getting so worked up?" Meera asked.

"Promise me, promise me, whatever happens between Jia and I, even if we are not on talking terms, and I am on my deathbed, you will let her see me and that you will not stop her. I know I would want only one thing at that time—to see my daughter. I am sure Colonel Grandpa must have wanted the same," Sujit's voice was choked with frustration.

"Jia is not Janki, and I am not Shakuntala," Meera said with a smile. "That is not who we are. Maybe a part of me, but that part I have never seen. You and I would never do something like this."

Dear Maa,

8 Mar 1978

Maa and Papa looked at me for the first time in two years, and it felt like an eternity. He smiled at me. I know he will never forgive me, but, at least, now he has acknowledged me as his daughter again. There is one corner of my heart that wants to thank you, too. At least, you love him. You have helped him a lot, and it's only because of you that he is now walking again. I still get shivers when I recall the incident.

I will be so proud when, in four months, Papa will be Brigadier.

But I can sense the tension between you both. I hope it's not because of me or my marriage. I can see how you both shy away from each other at certain times. I sincerely hope that you are not becoming the bitch you used to be, and troubling Papa, once again. Or, maybe he is fed up with you like I am, and he has decided to leave us, now that you spend a lot of time with your NGO. Don't worry; I will pray to God that your sins are not forgiven.

But today, I don't want to talk about you—I want to talk about the new family that I will be going to. I don't know where to start from. They have more than 15 people living under the same roof; this is actually four times more than we live together.

Adarsh's brothers, sisters, so many cousins, and Dadaji, Dadiji—Adarsh introduced me to his maternal side as well. Adesh Bhaiya is bit serious, or maybe he just pretends being so. But I really like to hang out with Atul and Arti; they are just adorable. I don't like his first cousin Mala. She is a snob, and I see myself in her. She seems happy, but I know that is not a happy place to be.

Do you know that I actually lied that I am going to Agra with Shilpa? I am sure you don't mind that. This will not harm anyone. I had actually gone with Adarsh and his gang and one more addition—Amol, Arti's boyfriend. This will be the first love marriage in their family, and I wish you could have heard the plans they had made. Every two seconds, they were planning another escape route. One second, they wanted to run away; in the next instant, they wanted to marry in a temple.

One thing that I am writing now—and which I had never thought that I will, at least to you—is 'Thank You'. Adarsh is the only right thing which you have done for me. That sunset where he held my hand quietly, and we saw the sun fade away behind the Taj is the scene that I will cherish all my life. He didn't say a word—He didn't have to. The red twilight said everything he had wanted to say.

But I lied to him. He looked at me with those sweet eyes of his and asked me if I had been with anyone before. He asked me to trust him and tell him honestly, but I lied to him just to be with him and did not tell him anything. Now that I am his, I don't need anyone else, anyway. Did I do right, Maa?

I can't wait to get married.

Your daughter,
Janki

"You are not getting your dinner today," Meera looked up from the letter and said with anger in her voice. Sujit recognised it at once.

"You don't start that again! I have told you that I will take you to the Taj, but we have matches lined up."

"Don't you dare start with your matches. Ten years has been a long enough time, and I have asked only for one thing—a romantic evening at the Taj."

Sujit knew this would not go easy. He had to eat out tonight. He looked into Meera's eyes and said, "Fine, I will eat outside." There was still hope in him that she would stop him.

"Fine," said Meera, pulling up another letter from the stack.

Dear Maa,

18 Nov 1978

I am scared. Amma and Baba want their son and daughter-in-law to go to Beijing for their honeymoon. It seems everyone is going there. But I don't want to go to China. Papa had fought against them in '62. Do you remember how difficult that time was for us?

There is another reason why I don't want to go abroad. You remember my friend Suresh whom you saw me with? He died earlier this year. He left for Dubai to meet his parents from Santacruz Airport in Bombay. His plane crashed into the sea soon after take off. I am scared. I don't want to die now that I have Adarsh in my life.

In any case, I will convince Amma against it, either today or tomorrow. She is not like you. She is sensible. Well, that is a relative term. You know that she has OCD. She washes her hands every other minute, and keeps checking if the doors are locked. I must say that Adarsh and all her children take good care of her, and they don't let her feel that she has got this disorder. She is very lucky. I hope my daughter will also take care of me like they do for Amma. Don't be surprised. I want a daughter, and unlike you, I will give her all the love in this world.

I had been very angry with you last week, but Amma told me to give it a week to contact you if I was still angry. Now, after a week, I don't feel the need to contact you, anymore—the past is not relevant to me.

She told me that you have told her everything about how you had wanted a boy and you could never give me the love that I deserved. I was very angry with you, but now, I think you were brave to tell her all that. She told me not to expect a mother's love from her; she would try to be my best friend and take care of me like an elder sister, and that no one could take your place. I don't know how everything will unfold—I don't know how my relationship with her would be, but one thing she said correctly is that no one can take your place. Your place is so much below the ground that no one can reach there.

Take care of Papa. I will come to see him in couple of months. There is one more bit of news that I wanted to write now, but I will only let you know when it is confirmed, or else it might get jinxed.

Your daughter,
Janki

"Your Dadi had OCD. You had told me that, but was it this bad? Did she have to check things every couple of minutes?" Sujit asked. He knew that Meera would be upset at reading about her Dadi who had been like a mother to her.

"It got really bad at the end. I am glad that she passed away. It was hard to see her in constant pain."

Sujit hugged her, and they sat quietly for a while. No words could have calmed down Meera now.

"Do you want to give it a break?" he said, finally.

Meera nodded a 'yes' as a tear rolled down her cheek.

Dear Maa,

27 Feb 1979

You won't believe what I saw, in fact, whom I saw. Her Majesty Queen Elizabeth II! Surprised? I had been, too when Adarsh told me a couple of weeks ago that she would be coming to inaugurate the Dubai International Trade Centre, and fortunately, I was there to witness it. I did convince everyone against China, and now, here I am—at the Chicago Beach Hotel in Dubai for my honeymoon. Well, not really, he had some work at TISCO as well, but we did get a lot of time. And anyway, we hardly go out. Most of my time is spent in staring at the ceiling walls in a pendulum motion or looking at the sheets or the pillow when he is behind me. He does not leave me for a minute. I get tired, but he is up again for another round. I may tell you in detail when we return in a couple of months.

To be honest, the building that she inaugurated, I don't like it that much. It stands 39 storeys high and is so big against everything near it. For miles around the building, it is mostly a desert. Adarsh tells me that Dubai will become the centre of the world in the coming years, but I don't see that. All I see is sand—lots and lots of sand. It's the same as our hotel—which looks like a big box, surrounded by pools on the beach, and at the rear, there's a vast scrubby desert stretching into the distance.

Yeah, coming back to the Queen—she looked radiant in the blue dress. I managed to see her from very close, which gave me a sense of purpose. She was a woman in the land where women do not have high ranks, posts, or even a say in things, for that matter.

Yet, she was there, walking side by side with Shaikh Rashid. I will never be the Queen, but I will live my life being Adarsh's queen.

You must have received the card. Suman, Mohan Mama's daughter, is getting married to Santosh, who also works for TISCO. I can smell something is not right, which I will check with my best friend now—the family reporter, Mala.

Also, why did you name your orphanage Manav Sansthan? We don't have anyone called Manav in our family. Don't get me wrong. I am not saying that you should have used my name for it. But you could have put Dadi's or Dadaji's name; Papa would have been happier then.

Take care.

Your daughter,

Janki.

"Hey, you were born in 1980, right?" Sujit asked mischievously.

"Yeah," Meera knew where this was going to.

"Are you a Dubai baby? Also, your mother had seen the Queen at that time. Maybe, that's why you are so beautiful!"

"Very funny!" Meera made a face.

Dear Maa,

4 Jan 1980

Adarsh's Nanaji is not well. Ram Mamaji has taken him to Bombay. We are also planning to go there. I am feeling really bad for Amma as she had just started to feel a bit better, and now she is all stressed again. Adarsh had spoken to Mohan Mamaji and he said that Nanaji is on borrowed time. I hope he goes to a better place. You may be wondering how I can say that, but there is no point in him living in this state. I pray to God that my death is sudden and not painful. Mohan Mamaji mentioned that they would delay Sarita's marriage, but Nanaji wants it to happen in his presence—not sure how they will manage that. They are thinking of doing it low-key, unlike Suman's lavish wedding. But Sarita insists on having a grand wedding. I think that she is behaving like a bitch. Can't she understand that her Dadaji wants to see her married? Adarsh is very close to Nanaji; he had an argument with her last week, and they are not talking to each other now. I tried to patch things up, but the two of us ended up fighting, instead.

You know Suman is expecting, and the good thing is that she is also in Delhi—not near our home, but not far, either. Santosh Jijaji drops her at our place every morning. And we both go for a walk for almost two hours. Mala is really jealous of my new friend. But she is so adorable; I will make it up with her. She wants all of me only to herself. She even comes and talks to my daughter when I am sleeping. Two days ago, Adarsh and I were sleeping, and she just came into the room and started talking to my daughter in my tummy. I woke up with a start, and she got a good scolding from Adarsh. I had to sleep in her room to pacify her.

You know, Maa, I have been writing letters to you all these years, but this is the first letter that I am actually sending to you. I think these letters have helped me vent out my frustration against you all these years, and it's good that they have remained safe with me. But I can write to you now that you will also become a Nani, and I actually thank you again for finding Adarsh for me.

Tell me… how do you feel about becoming a Nani and having a granddaughter? I know you must be thinking about how I could be so sure. But I can be! I can already hear her calling me Maa, placing her little hands on my cheeks and kissing me. I know that she will be a girl, and I will give her all the love in the world. She will be proud of me.

I know you will be probably disappointed again as you may want a son for me, too, but I am glad that I am with Adarsh during my pregnancy, and Amma is taking good care of me.

I could have found out the baby's gender when we had gone for sonography two weeks ago, but Adarsh said he didn't want to know it. It's an amazing feeling, Maa! How could you not love your child? It will not matter to me, even if it is a boy. I will still love him though I desperately want a daughter. It's an amazing feeling to see his small heartbeat on that small black and white monitor. Adarsh saw it first, and I started crying when even after several minutes, I couldn't see it. Adarsh had to pay for an extra one-hour session as we had crossed our time. After that, I was able to see it quickly within 5 minutes. He was cross with me for the next 20 minutes. But I had to see my princess's heart. When I talk to her, I know she is listening to me. I know she cares for me a lot and that she will always be with me.

I don't mind the puking and the sleepless nights. I just can't wait to see her in my arms. You know... Suman wants a boy. But I don't think she is as adamant as you were, and even if she will have a girl, she will be happy, but I do think that she will be happier if she has a boy.

Maa, I may not be able to participate in Kishore's wedding as much as I want to, as it will be my eighth month. Dadi, Dadaji, Chachi, and Kishore—all understand my situation. Chachi comes every other week to see me, and I was the one who orchestrated their match. Radhika owes me a lot, and one day, she will pay her debt.

I will write to you next when I have my little princess in my hands.

Your daughter,
Janki

Dear Maa,

27 May 1980

I held her, Maa! I held her in my arms. The doctor gave her to me, and she opened her little eyes to see me. I know everyone says that the babies can't see right away, but she saw me! No one believes me, but I know she looked at me and smiled. She was happy to see me, finally, and I was over the moon to feel her in my arms.

You must have been the Devil to not like a child like this, Maa. How could you not forget your desire to have a son when you had seen me for the first time? How could you not love me, then? But today is not about you and me. Today is about Janvi—she is my Jaan. I want to give her a name that is very close to my heart—she is so precious.

Adarsh cried when he first saw Janvi, and he became the butt of everyone's jokes, most of which came from Govind and Atul.

I am so happy, Maa, I am so happy! It's like I want to dance in the rain, holding Janvi in my arms! Both of us are smiling. I am telling you, Maa, that she will be very successful in her life, and that she will love me a lot.

I can go on and on about Janvi, but now, I am too tired and have to sleep, as she will wake up in another thirty minutes. I have to take that power nap, or else I will go crazy.

Before I go, congratulations and best of luck for your elections! Hope you win next month.

Your dear daughter,
Janki

"Aww, you are born, Janvi!" Sujit teased Meera.

"I didn't know that she wanted to keep my name Janvi. Yuck! What an old-fashioned name! Thank God that she didn't have her way."

"I like Janvi better than Meera. I will call you Janvi," Sujit said and burst out laughing.

"Sure, why not?" Meera said with a wide smile, shutting him up.

Dear Maa,

14 Aug 1981

First of all, congratulations! I think you are doing well with your NGO, social activities, and now, politics. This is a well-deserved win; Papa must be really happy.

Maa, it happened again—this time while I was sleeping. I felt like someone was choking me to death, and I vomited on the bed all over Meera and myself. Adarsh took Meera and cleaned her, while Mala helped me. There was, again, a lot of blood. Adarsh is not telling me what the doctor said. He just asked me to wait for the reports and assured me that nothing would be wrong with me. But I know that something is wrong. Maybe, these are the sins of my past life—my life before my marriage. I don't want to die.

Amol has done specialisation in neurology, and he said it could be cancer. I didn't tell this to Adarsh as he would have gone and fought with Amol. I don't want to die—I can't leave Meera without me. I want to see her all the time and live on to see her getting to school, finishing college, getting married, and so on.

But if I do go, please tell Meera that I love her more than anything else in my life—more than myself.

I have started to gather gifts for her that I would want her to have on her birthdays. I am putting together gifts from year two to year eighteen, and I will leave them with Mala so that she can give them to her.

I have bought a lovely keychain which has a fairy with wings spread high as if she is ready to fly. I will give her this keyring when she passes out of college. She can keep it with her for her entire life. And, there is this blue frock which says 'I love my Dad'; she will look so beautiful when she turns six or seven and wears this dress.

I have also bought this box in which she can keep her important things.

I will go out tomorrow to buy a few more things when Adarsh will not be at home. If he is there, he will not allow me to go outside.

There seems to be so much bad luck since Nanaji has left us! Atul's marriage is on hold. There is some argument Papaji had with Kavita's uncle, and now, he doesn't want Atul to get married to her. After two years of courtship, I don't think this would be possible. Papaji was a bit angry with me also when I favoured the marriage, but he didn't say anything as I am not well.

I hope the reports come fine. I don't want to leave Meera in a world where she does not know her mother. When I look at this fairy keyring, I can imagine how happy she will be when she gets it. I don't want to miss that smile!

Pray for me, Maa.

Your dear daughter,
Janki.

Tears rolled down Meera's cheeks as she put the letter back. Sujit saw the tears; he knew what was going on in her mind. The tears had been an integral part of Meera's life.

Meera opened the cupboard and pulled out a keyring that had a fairy with a broken leg. Her heart filled up on seeing it after all these years. She still remembered how much she had cried when Madhav, her cousin, had broken her beloved fairy's leg. She took the fairy keyring in her hands, recalling when Mala Bua had gifted it to her. In fact, the box, about which she read in the letter, was still with her with all her important documents. Mala Bua had gifted her that, too. She suddenly remembered her Bua's voice whenever she used to give those gifts, saying that they were from a fairy, and she should keep them safe all her life. Now, she understood why Mala Bua had stopped giving her gifts after she turned sixteen. Did it mean that all her lucky charms were from her mother—all those things with which she was still so attached, and had preserved some of them for thirty years?

She picked up her phone and dialled a number.

"Mala Bua…"

"Ah… Meera, my beautiful daughter! How are you? Why haven't you called me all these days? I had told you to call me every week… How are Sujit and my granddaughter, Jia?"

"Why do you always hesitate to take my name, Bua? I had not paid attention earlier, but now that I think of it, you always pause before saying Meera. Why, Bua?"

"Nothing, nothing; why this question suddenly, beta?" Mala replied with a hesitation in her voice.

"Please tell me, Bua."

"There's nothing, as I said! We used to call you by some other name when you were very young. Your… ah, in fact, your father and I used to call you something else."

"Janvi."

"What… huh! How do you… how do you know? Who told you that name?" On the other end of the receiver, Mala shook upon hearing that name after so many years.

"Bua, the fairy keyring that you gave me… where did you buy it from?"

There was a long pause.

"Your mother gave them to me. Beta, come to Mumbai. I can't answer your questions over the phone."

"I will come soon. I have to do a few things before that."

Dear Maa,

17 May 1982

It is Pratap. For months, this hide-and-seek game has been going on. He is making my life miserable. I had not known earlier what he wanted from me, but it is now clear that he wants me to become his slave—he wants me to do whatever he wishes, and give him money from time to time. I am scared, Maa. I don't want to lose my life, my Meera. If Adarsh finds out about my past, he will not forgive me, and I am sure of that. He has that much trust in me. If that is broken, it will finish everything.

I had, earlier, been a fool to have gotten involved with a thug like Pratap. But now—now, my family is everything to me. Meera clings to me all the time. Even in her sleep, she does not leave me. She is equally attached to Adarsh. How do I choose what is best for her and who is the best for her? No, no, I should not be thinking about this at all. Everything will be fine—Pratap will go away from our life. I will not bow down to his demands, and I will definitely not cheat Adarsh. He has met the new Janki—not the reckless, old one!

Your sins have come to bite me now. If anything happens to me and my family, it will also be on you.

I had ignored his threats but then he showed up at Atul's wedding and met everyone in my family. He also spent an entire evening, drinking with Adarsh and his friends. He teased me with things that I don't even remember happening. Maybe, he is making them up, but I want to forget that period of my life. Not sure why life is doing this to me!

I have told everything to Mala. She has understood, maybe not fully, but she said that she will support me, and that I should not surrender to Pratap.

Papa will retire next year. I want him to go into his retirement phase with content and a happy smile.

There has been an awkwardness between Adarsh and me after Atul's wedding. But everyone is busy with the post-wedding celebrations, and maybe, that's why Adarsh hasn't asked me about the details of my friendship with Pratap yet. I don't know for how long I can keep my secrets safe.

I am scared; I am feeling lonely again, and I don't know what to do. I wish Pratap dies somehow.

If I am able to pass this challenge in life, then Meera, Adarsh, and I, will live happily ever after.

Your dear daughter,

Janki

"Clearly, she did not pass that challenge. Maybe this was the reason why your parents broke up."

Meera took a sip of water. "I knew nothing." She paused for the gulp. "I had been just told that she left me and stopped interacting with me. All my later interactions with her showed that she was not interested in me or the family."

"This letter clearly shows otherwise."

"I am not surprised. One only reaps what he sows, isn't it? I just want to know what exactly had happened. I will go to Mumbai, and talk to Mala Bua about it."

Meera
(2015)

Chapter 9

MEERA LOOKED OUT of the window. As a kid, she had thought the world was flat. Looking out of a plane window, she had made her strongest argument, and her biggest supporter had been her Bua. No matter what she said, Mala Bua would always say that her daughter was wonderful and intelligent. Meera recalled when Mala Bua had fought with Kavita Maa. Later, they didn't even see eye to eye. An incident that Meera couldn't forget easily was when Mala Bua ran after Kavita Maa to hit her with a book. This memory brought a smile to her lips. Suddenly, her nostalgic trip was interrupted by the air hostess, who had already called her thrice.

"Ma'am, we are about to land. Please fasten your seatbelt," said the airhostess with a well-rehearsed smile of courtesy. The passenger next to Meera smirked. Meera drifted back into her memories as the plane landed at the Chhatrapati Shivaji Airport in Mumbai.

"Won't you say anything?" Mala said later in the car. Meera was now looking outside the car window and avoiding any kind of conversation.

"How is Rita? Has she joined that company?"

"No. After working so hard and getting those beautiful scores in Grade 12, she had gotten into a good college and got wonderful results there also. Do you know she scored the highest at Mumbai University? And, see what she is doing now!"

Meera knew very well what Rita was doing, but she didn't want her Bua to know that Rita had been taking advice from her all along.

"So, what does she want now?" Meera said in a disinterested tone. She knew exactly what Rita wanted.

"She wants to open a boutique with her friend Kishore."

"Kishore, who?"

"You remember, we used to tease her that he was her boyfriend? That Kishore!"

Meera smiled.

"See, how pretty you look when you smile!"

Meera's smile faded as quickly as it had come. Mala regretted complimenting her. Goodness knew what kind of mood her niece was in!

"Is Mohan Fufaji back from Prague?" Meera changed the subject as the driver pulled the car into the driveway.

"No. He will be back exactly next month and four days from now."

"Wow, you guys still have the spark between yourselves!"

"Don't forget that I am your Bua, not your friend!" Mala chuckled as she opened the door.

Truth be told, Meera had already started regretting coming here. Had she done the right thing? Then, why was everything so awkward? She told Mala, "I am tired, Bua. I'd like to sleep for some time."

"Tired with a two-hour flight?"

"Yes…"

The anger of the past had raised its ugly head inside Meera. She could now feel the anger trying to burst out. Mala sensed it and poked her further so that the volcano would burst.

"Don't be a coward, Meera. It's time that we address the elephant in the room."

Meera turned red on hearing that. She had referred to her mother so casually as a liar and also accused her of being a coward, and all this time, it was her Bua who had been the liar.

"You are calling me a coward. What about all your lies?" Meera snapped.

The sudden outburst took Mala by surprise. "When did I lie?"

"All those gifts that you gave me—they were never from you; you lied!" accused Meera.

"I didn't lie; I always told you that they were from a fairy."

"Hah!"

"Meera, look at me. The truth had always been in front of you, but you always kept your eyes closed. You and your father are similar… Your mother…"

"Bua, don't even take her name! After what she did to me, after all that, you were there...You know what happened to me! She kidnapped me! She wanted to drug me, and still, you had given gifts to me..."

"Meera..."

"And, why now? It took many years to have a child. Sujit had always wanted one, but I was scared that I would become like her—I would have had commitment issues because of her."

"Don't put it on her. You have had these issues because of yourself. If she had been around, she would have made you into a better person."

Meera could not hide her surprise despite her anger. No one in her family had said anything about her mother all her life—all thirty-five years apart from the repeated fact that she had abandoned her. Why? About whom... the details had always been avoided, and now... now, after all these years, her Bua was standing by her mother's side.

"Is this a joke, Bua? Because of her, I still have the mark on my lower back. You know it—you were there at the hospital."

Meera pointed to her lower back, indicating the spot where she had hurt herself while trying to escape from Janki. That was when her mother was trying to drug her.

"I know that very well, Meera. I was there. But I am fed up with pretending that she was some kind of a villain, and you were a victim. The truth is that she had been the victim. Leave it, Meera, go to sleep. You will never understand her!"

There was disappointment in Mala's voice. She did not have the strength to fight for this again after so many years.

"I know. Her mother did not love her, and she had affairs that probably led to her divorce. So, to sum it up, she was a total bitch!" Meera said matter-of-factly.

The words fell on Mala like a slap. She waited for her anger to subside.

Then, she said, "Okay, she may have done some stupid things. But the kind of love she had for you—even I don't love Rita or you that much." After another pause, and with a deep breath, she added, "Let me tell you what had exactly happened.

"I remember... I remember it clearly, still... It was Alok's first birthday when we first went to see your mother, Janki Bhabhi. We had gone together—Mummy, Papa, Dadaji, Arti Didi, and I. I was awestruck when I first saw her. She looked so beautiful in a red sari. I was actually jealous of her fair complexion," Mala said and laughed.

"Is this important?" Meera asked.

"Yes, it is, or else, how would you know that your mother had transformed from a troubled child to a sincere wife, daughter-in-law and a loving mother?" said Mala. "I think it was my jealousy that made her think that I would create problems for her in her *sasural*, and probably I did too, at least initially. But I think that is fine, isn't it?" Mala looked at Meera as if she wanted her approval.

"I wouldn't know," Meera said with a weak smile.

"I think we became friends the day when I went for a movie and Taiji had caught me," Mala reminisced. "Janki Bhabhi said that she had sent me for some work. Otherwise, I would have received a good scolding from Dadaji."

She continued, "What I am trying to tell you is… that your mother came from a very small family. Though she had other relatives, only three of them were together, not in a cordial environment, though. She was very scared and hopeful at the same time, and she learned a lot. The way she cared for Taiji made her everyone's favourite in a couple of months. Even Adarsh Bhaiya was walking tall that his wife was loved by everyone! Do you know that she even fought and convinced Dadaji and Taiji about Kavita? And, look what that Kavita did later on… betrayed Janki Bhabhi!"

"Why? What happened?" asked Meera.

"You only remember that you were kidnapped. I don't know how much you remember of that day, though. It was because of Kavita that they had found your mother and accused her of kidnapping you."

"So, hadn't I not kidnapped? I only remember that I was alone in the park, crying a lot, and then Kavita Maa and you had come."

"Yeah! Because Janki Bhabhi was arrested, and Kavita lodged the complaint. She knew where you both had been. We—your mother, Kavita and I had made that plan, but later Kavita ditched us."

Meera was astonished. "You had planned my kidnap?"

"Oh, don't say it so harshly! It was never meant to be a kidnapping. We had just wanted Bhabhi to spend some time with you alone. But, anyway, don't think anything bad about Kavita. She cared for you as a mother would. Yet, I had been very angry with her, and at some level I still am. We had never got along well after that incident. But it was her love for you—your safety that made her betray Janki Bhabhi. I did understand her, but I can't reverse the wheel now. This regret will remain with me."

Then again, a mischievous glint appeared in Mala's eyes. "You know your mother confided things in me. She had told me about what her mother did to her and also about her boyfriends."

"Boyfriends!" Meera whistled. "Were there many?"

"Why not? Your mother was a gorgeous woman."

"That doesn't mean…"

"Anyway, that's beside the point. She was loyal to the core to your father, her house, and you. But unfortunately, one of the serpents raised its head. You know that that had also been sorted, but by that time, it was too late. The guilt had begun to kill her from within. She thought Adarsh Bhaiya would understand it. I told her not to tell him, but she didn't listen to me."

"How did everyone come to know?" Meera asked.

"She told Adarsh Bhaiya. He couldn't forgive her and then the matter got worse. Everyone tried to explain to Adarsh Bhaiya. At first, even Taiji, who was so fond of Janki Bhabhi, asked Adarsh Bhaiya, instead of Bhabhi, to leave the house. When he agreed, Bhabhi said that she would go, instead. You know she was in contact with almost everyone in the family after she had left? I mean not in the former capacity, but still whatever we could do for her and whatever she could do for us…" Mala explained.

"So, you think she deserved a second chance?"

"Most certainly I do," Mala said, with great firmness in her voice.

"And what about forcing me to have drugs?"

"You have to forgive her for that. She cut her veins to punish herself for that twice. I was there at the hospital when no one had gone to see her. I think that was a major blow, and it went against her terribly."

"I am not convinced, Bua," Meera said. For a moment, her voice had lost its steely edge, but it was back to being cold and ruthless.

Mala waved her hands in despair. "You should have been there and seen that. Live her life, maybe, and only then would you understand."

"I had been in her life, in a way."

"Ah, the letters! She had this habit of writing everything that happened in letters to her mother though I don't know if she ever sent them to her. I think that is one habit she had acquired from your Nani. God will punish your Nani for her sins."

"I think she is still alive."

"I hardly care," Mala said nonchalantly.

"I am reading those letters now."

"What was his name… er… yes, Simon. Did he send them to you?" Mala asked.

Meera was surprised to hear Simon's name from her Bua. "You know him? Of course, my mother…"

"Yes, your mother had told me about him. I was so happy for her. Finally, she seemed to be getting what she deserved." Mala took a deep sigh and said, "Wait, I will show you something." She went inside her room.

The wait was killing Meera now. She had thought that she would get answers, but she now realised that she had probably only wanted her Bua to blame her mother for everything that had happened. Yet, everything that she had said so far was the complete antithesis of her expectations. Meera was now left with more questions, and she only wanted to run away from them—far away from her memories of her mother.

"Look at this!" Mala said as she came out. She was holding an old bottle that appeared to have some mud in it.

"Look at what, mud?" Meera said, squinting at the bottle.

"This is as close as you can get to your mother's ashes—this is the mud from Ground Zero. I had brought it with me when I went to see your mother. I mean when I had gone to New York after that terrible incident."

"Oh, my God" Meera shot up, and then, continued, "You went to New York?"

"Do you want to take it in your hands?" Mala asked.

Meera looked at the bottle for a minute and said, "No."

Mala was disappointed, but she hid her disappointment in her smile and said, "Go. Go to sleep; you must be really tired now. "

Shakuntala

(1976 - 1982)

Chapter 10

MEERA LEFT HER Bua's house the next morning. Rita wanted her to stay for a couple of days, but since Sujit was handling Jia all alone, and she knew what a handful her tiny daughter was, she had to get back.

At one level, Meera wanted to read through her mother's letters first. She wanted to know the reasons for her mother's behaviour and the excuses she had left behind in those letters to justify her acts.

"Could we skip a couple of my grandma's letters and finish Maa's first, instead?" Meera asked Sujit.

She wanted him to say 'no', as on another level, she didn't want to face what her mother had to say. As if almost reading her mind, Sujit replied, "No, I think we should go chronologically. It will be more fun that way."

"Really? All this is stressful to me. How can you find fun in it?" Meera asked.

"I understand. But, you need to relax a bit. These things had happened so many years ago, and for the most part, they will not have an impact on our lives."

Sujit ran a loving hand over her head, and they began reading.

> ***Dear Maa,***
>
> *28 Nov 1976*
>
> *I don't know whether to laugh or cry, or be happy and feel lucky that Shekhar is alive and is now recovering. Or should I be angry at him and hit him for having a keep? And worse—he has a son from this other woman, too.*
>
> *I suspected it for the first time when I saw that woman four times on the day we moved Shekhar from the camp to the main hospital. She was pale and looked as if she would die. She wanted to come near us, but she stood at a distance. I didn't register the*

fact for a week until I constantly began seeing that woman and her son, mostly remaining silent throughout the day, near our room.

I asked Ramesh, our driver, to follow and make inquiries about her. And, look what he found out! I had wanted to run away when I first heard about it. I felt choked—I couldn't breathe, and I don't know for how long I kept walking in the opposite direction. If it were not for Ramesh, I would not have known my way back. He said that his Sir needed me now, more than ever. This was all he said. Maybe he had known it from the start. He must have dropped Shekhar many a time at her place. I asked him—I questioned him as I was angry at him, but he didn't say anything after that.

I saw Janki before she was taken to rehab. She agreed finally, as it had been months since her father had looked at her. I know it was killing her, but she deserved it.

Maa, what do I do? I had kept quiet then, but it is killing me now. Every time I visit him, that woman of his, looks at me. She stares at me, and I think she laughs at me, too. Shekhar looks at me, and I don't know if he still sees me—I don't know if he sees Manav, his son, in Janki, and wishes that they had been here with him.

Disaster and opportunity come without any prior warning. My NGO is sending a team to Diviseema in Andhra Pradesh, where it is feared that more than 25000 people have died. The official figures are way less. I really want to initiate the relief work. We have been discussing about carrying out such projects for a long time—this is the right opportunity for me.

The pain in which I am in right now is more than what the entire population of Andhra Pradesh is feeling! I am scared that if I leave him, he would return to her forever. Should I go, or should I leave?

Your beti,
Shakuntala

"I don't blame him," Meera said disinterestedly.

"What do you mean?" Sujit asked her in surprise.

"It's simple. She had made his life a living hell for so long that he was bound to find solace elsewhere," Meera said.

"I don't know. Hey, this one is rather small!"

Dear Maa,

28 Dec 1976

Maa, my prayers have been fulfilled. Manav died in an accident involving a truck last week. They both deserved it. She survived, but God will see her, too. I just have to pray a little harder. It was an error of judgement on God's part. He should have planned things better.

Shekhar is mine, and I will not let anyone come near him, and I will do what I have to do, to make this happen.

Things are really bad in Diviseema. We have been asked to go further away from the shore, but these authorities do not understand that there might be so many people still stuck there. The unofficial count has gone upto 50000.

I will have to leave soon. Shekhar must be shattered, and he needs me now, more than ever.

Your beti,
Shakuntala

"NO, SHE DIDN'T!" Sujit shouted, making Meera almost jump.

"Why are you shouting?" Meera asked.

"Did she kill your uncle?"

"He was not my uncle!" Meera replied angrily.

"Whatever, OMG! What the hell! I should report this crime!" Sujit said quickly, his words falling over each other.

"Based on what? This letter is 37 years old, and who knows they might have already caught her!"

"Or, maybe she didn't do it at all?" Sujit said, now relaxed enough to weigh other possibilities.

"More likely."

"Let's read further."

Dear Maa,

9 Aug 1977

Shekhar came clean to me. It had all started during the promotion celebrations. We had an amazing celebration last month. Shekhar was looking so handsome—the best he had ever looked! She was also there. You know that I do not question him when he goes out to meet her as I know that both of them have to pass this phase of grief together. You had called me stupid in your last letter, and said that I will lose him. I don't agree with you. I want him to grieve the death of his son and come out of his relationship slowly. I want him to take his time, as it is because of me that he was pushed onto this path. He has had and still has love for me. I can see that. (still, he did what he had done, and in a way that made me love him even more because I realised that I had been so jealous). Had he stopped loving me, he would have left me long back.

And, Maa, don't worry; I know how to win him back if it ever reaches to that point.

Moreover, things at home are settling down now that Janki is well-behaved. She, still, does not have her father's love, but we have started having small conversations every now and then. She is happy about her alliance with Adarsh.

But, I drifted away from the main point. Actually, I wanted to actually prove how wrong you had assessed the situation. Shekhar came clean to me. He told me about her. I haven't seen him this weak in my entire marriage. It was as if he were pleading for something outside his control. I asked him why he was telling me now after seven years of relationship. He told me about Manav and that he and his keep, were not able to move forward in life. He had even suggested to her that she should get married to someone else. He also told her that he couldn't leave me.

I am not angry with him, Maa—not anymore, and I think he knew that I had known it all. I did not show any surprise when he came clean, and he didn't ask why.

At an unspoken level, he knows that I want this to end, and so does he. But he has gone so far that it will take time for him to come back. I am ready to wait—I am ready to do this for our family.

Maa, I also came clean to him about that incident that had happened twenty-one years ago. I told him that when we were in Vindhya Pradesh, which is now Madhya Pradesh (somehow, I still like Vindhya), I had touched his Javan's body, then ran into my room, and nothing had happened between us. He said he had known it since then. The Javan could not keep his mouth shut, and, in guilt, had confessed everything. But Shekhar had trusted me, and I was sure that I would always remain his. I was shocked to see his love for me. If I could give him half of what he has given me, my life will be full.

I do not feel for her, but I do want her to find happiness. A little less than one year ago, I would have killed her. But now, I am more assured of myself and Shekhar. I know he will always be with me.

I hope Adarsh treats Janki in the same way.

Your beti,
Shakuntala

"It's very easy to judge someone based on their actions, but we don't know what it feels like to be in their shoes," Meera said, folding and putting the letter on the pile.

"Agreed."

Dear Maa,

9 Sep 1978

I am writing this letter from Morbi. The situation is maniacal here. I am heading my NGO, Manav Sansthan, this time and working with volunteers to help the people here. I don't think we can return the 35000 lives (official figures are low as usual) and help the remaining with their crops, but we can surely provide food and safety to them so that they can live to die another day. This will also help me in my political ambition.

Shekhar is handling most of Janki's wedding preparations and probably taking help from his keep. He is trying to get her settled, too and in any case, Janki won't miss me at the wedding celebrations, as she is probably hoping that I wouldn't be there, anyway.

We will go to Rajkot from here the day after tomorrow, taking more than 100 people along with us. We will be back once they are settled there and bring in more supplies.

I was able to secure the highest funds ever given to a private organisation to tackle this tragedy. This is really good news for my political career. All the NGOs are raising their eyebrows wondering what the connection is, but they will never know. It's the hard work of our volunteers that has helped us achieve this goal. With 5 crores in funding and 250 volunteers, I can proudly say that I have achieved whatever I could in my role as a social service worker. Now, I have to think bigger and move forward. Shekhar has been advising me to start from the grassroots level to contest MLA elections from a nearby state in four years. If that is the case, then I have to start my work from now onwards so that I can reach each and every voter in the constituency. I have to do really hard work, but I can always use Manav Sansthan's resources, and the Janta will also get benefitted.

You know my devrani's son, Kishore, is also getting married. He is marrying outside our caste. Maaji had been really angry at the start, but the girl is really sweet. She is a better version of Janki.

And finally, I don't know Maa, if Janki is well. There are no complaints from her sasural. No news is good news for me, and if you are that worried, why don't you write a letter to her, yourself?

Your beti,
Shakuntala

"I just looked up for this Manav Sansthan. It seems fishy. There are loads of things they have done right, but there is an equal number of controversies as well. And, guess what? Your Nani is a two-time MP. How could have you not known all this?" Sujit asked, with a grin on his face.

"They had never existed for me, before… before these letters. In fact, they are, still, all fictional characters to me." There was a sense of helplessness in Meera's voice.

"Still, they should have contacted you when you had passed that dependent age. She was definitely alive in 2001, and it has been a long time since then," Sujit said.

"Maybe, they did not want to keep any connection," said Meera.

"Then, why do you bother reading about them? Why do you want to know if they were concerned about you?"

Meera could not deny the reason in his voice, but she said, "I am… we are not reading these letters for them. At least, I am reading them for myself. I know this for sure. All this must be entertaining to you, but I have to find meaning in it. The more I read, the more questions arise in my mind…"she trailed off.

"But I am seeing the difference in you already… before and after reading these letters."

"What are those?" Meera asked.

"I will tell you later."

Dear Maa,

13 Dec 1979

Please forgive me; I was not able to reply earlier. You know that my entire focus is to take Manav Sansthan to a whole new level in Punjab, so that I will be prepared for the state elections in the next three years. A lot of people say that Prakash Singh Badal will not be able to complete five years, and there might be State Elections sooner than that. So, I have to be prepared, and under the guidance of the High Command, we are sure to win them.

Shekhar is aloof from politics and wants to spend his time enjoying his retirement after three years. But, for me, I feel that this is just a start—the start of something amazing to come in the future! I do want to hold a minister's post and—who knows?—I might soon be in Delhi!

But, I must say the situation in Punjab is not what I had thought it to be from outside; I had thought that the public service will bring me a certain social and political level in the state, but I have to do more. The tension within the Sikh community is growing. I was there on the 300th Shaheedi (Martyrdom) Commemoration of Sri Guru Tegh Bahadur Sahib Jee when Sant Jehad said that if it were not for the Sikhs, Indira Gandhi would have been wearing a burkha, and greeting everyone with "Ae-salaam Alaikum". I was shocked to hear this, and so was everyone else. It is now interesting to see what Indiraji's reaction would be.

Shekhar suggests that we move our political base from Punjab to Gujarat, or even Rajasthan. But my hands are already into the mud, and getting out of this means that I will have less than one year to prepare for Rajasthan and Gujarat. At least in Punjab, I have time till' 83. Even if the elections are held earlier, I have established my NGO base here. Lifting and shifting it to a different state, will make me lose my edge. I have invested so much here already, and people in all the high circuits know me.

I have asked Rukmani to handle Manav Sansthan, but she is hesitant to shoulder such a big responsibility. I have shown her all the perks. She can even manage the funds of Shyam Bhaiya and use Manav Sansthan to increase her earnings. She is okay with that but is still not fully on board. I have asked her to give me an answer within three weeks. I really hope that she agrees. If not, then do you think Bhairav, Kanha Mama's son, will be able to do this? He doesn't have to leave his factory. He can put the right people to do both jobs and manage along with me. I want someone from the family as I can't open my trade secrets to the outside world. Could you speak to Mamaji, and let me know?

We celebrated our 35th wedding anniversary on Kishore's wedding day. Our wedding anniversary was not on that day, but it was really good fun. The only one missing was Janki, and we didn't press her to come. In her situation, it's good that she takes rest. Maa, I want a girl for her. I wish she has a girl, and I will give her the love that I couldn't give to Janki.

I have asked you a hundred times now, at least, in seven of my last letters—will you and Papaji come and live with us for a few months? I know that both of you are not keeping well. Awaiting your reply.

Your beti,

Shakuntala

"Sameer did that too," Meera said, folding the letter and putting it on the pile of read letters.

"Did what?" Sujit asked.

"He also founded an NGO a couple of years ago to move funds, and he saved almost fifty lakhs in one year." Sujit punched his fist in the air. "Wow, then we should also do that!"

"I don't think we need it. In any case, we don't have that much money to move about."

"Maybe, your grandmother has left behind a fortune!" Sujit pulled Meera's leg.

"Why do you think she has left anything for me? And, how do you know she is dead? She may be alive in her ashram, and in any case, I do not want any money from that family." There was determination in Meera's voice now.

"Your family, you mean!"

"No! Read on," Meera picked up the next letter and started reading it.

Dear Maa,

19 Aug 1980

I had gone to Delhi last week, and saw Janki really very happy. It seemed like she had got what she wanted from life. She had got the love she deserved—the love that I could never give her. No, I didn't give her anything. You know how her sasural family is. They don't take anything at all, even if we say that it is our custom. They feel a bit awkward now as I go to their house with all the security. But I did give her your great-grandmother's and my great-great-grandmother's ring. She was very happy to receive it and wished you could have also come to meet her. She did spend more time with you and Maaji than with me. She said she would come to meet you in a couple of months. I am sure she has written to you as well.

She wanted to name the girl Janvi, but Kaushalyaji's father's dying wish was to call her Meera. To be honest, Maa, I did not feel anything at all, after seeing the baby. If anything, I felt happy, happy for Janki. I now wish it was a boy so that our family name would have been carried further, but I guess this is what fate had in store for us.

Maa, congratulations to you and Papaji, too, for your great granddaughter! I am sure you must be really happy.

I have been an MLA for a couple of months now, and they have been really eventful. I am surprised that I did not know much of what my role and responsibilities were and what exactly I would be doing as an MLA. Do you remember that I had written that I may get involved in getting the roads constructed for my constituency or help in the allotment of funds to various schemes? The reality is bigger than that. One of the main powers that I can exploit will be the creation of laws related to forests and the protection of wildlife at the State level. Here, I can combine my goals for Manav Sansthan as well, and this will work without any issues as I have found that the administrative leg of the Government is extremely lethargic. It works only when they get a slap on their back, but I don't mind it. I have not come here to change the world but to see myself in an important post in Delhi, and this is just a stepping stone.

With all the security, it is a new world for me. Even Shekhar complains about it. But I feel I am meant to do this; I had been born to do this.

Your beti,
Shakuntala

"Is this the ring?" Sujit pulled out an old ruby ring from the box.

Meera looked childishly at the ring. "Is there any other ring in that box?"

"It does feel good to wear a piece of history. This must go back more than a hundred years."

"Way more than a hundred years, and we don't know how the first one had got it," Meera said proudly.

"There may be some mark on it. We can try and trace its origin, or at least the year. It can be classified as an antique," Sujit said, turning the ring around.

"It shows a lion or a bird—can't make out properly, with initials S. J. Does it mean anything?"

"You look it up on Google while I will read the next letter, or better, let's finish reading the letters, and then you look it up," Meera said and patted the chair beside her.

Dear Maa,

30 Sep 1981

Things are really bad here, Maa. Shekhar is worried about my safety, but I guess it's important to choose the right side. I had never favoured our party's decision to support Bhindranwale in any form earlier, but Indiraji has helped him rise to great heights. Eleven people were killed when he was getting arrested ten days ago—first, Gurbachan Singh and now, Jagat Narain. The movement is picking up to create a Sikh State and it is not going to slow down anytime soon.

I had also warned the party before the July World Sikh Convention at Manji Sahib that they would come up with demands that no one could meet. Now, see the demonstrations in Delhi, and these killings as well. I don't agree with their misplaced arguments, but I am in no position to speak against them on their own home ground.

So many people have died in the last couple of years and for what! No one can see the country split into pieces.

I agree with some of their demands that they had proposed earlier this year. For example, the ban on tobacco. But giving in to most of their demands would be wrong, in my opinion.

To be fair, this has been a long-standing issue for many decades now. But the growth this movement has seen in the recent past, is unimaginable. We, as the party, have a reason to believe that they are getting support from outside India—not just from their community, but beyond that, including from people who want to see Indiraji lose power. All the good work done by our Government in the State is getting ruined by these protests. Even in my constituency, the protests got violent and caused destruction of public property. When we visited the sites, there were stones thrown at us. We apprehended the teenager who was doing it, and to think that he was acting on his own! What kind of poison are they filling into the children's minds?

Even Manav Sansthan has faced a backlash. We wanted to organise a charity event here to raise money for children, mainly orphans. But in the light of this insurgency, the Collector requested me to cancel this event.

I had called Janki and Meera for the event, and they had agreed to come as well. Adarsh was anyway not in the city, so he was counted out. I sometimes wonder, Maa, whether Janki has told everything to Adarsh as I do not feel the warmth in Adarsh's behaviour towards me.

If it were not for Rukmani, I would not have been able to handle both of them. You know, she is quite innovative! I never knew she had in her to manage accounts at this level. She is even thinking of getting support, mainly financial, from NRIs in Africa. There is a huge population of migrants from India in Kenya, Nigeria, Ghana (and they are cash-rich), who want to send money back here to support the causes that they believe in. If Bhindranwale can get it, so can we.

Your beti,
Shakuntala

"It seems like it was anti-Khalistan Movement," Sujit said with a whistle. He was not able to contain his surprise.

"Does it matter?" Meera asked.

"It *does*! I had a friend, Surjeet. Her entire family was killed after Operation Blue Star. I was only eight then, but I had seen her going from living with her entire family to becoming an orphan overnight. I don't know why they left her alive. Her uncle took her. She also doesn't remember much, but these wounds will never heal."

"To be honest, Sujit, I am not very close to this. In fact, I don't have any friends or acquaintances who were affected. What happened was terrible, though. Look at the Babri Masjid occurrence, India-Pakistan Partition, or for that matter, any riot or uprising. All of them have left unimaginable marks on the lives of many."

"I dislike your grandmother."

"I dislike my mother and her family, too. You are free to say as much as you like," Meera countered.

"But, weren't there many people against Khalistan? That's why all this happened, isn't it? Imagine how India would have looked without its crown," Sujit reflected.

Dear Maa,

19 Nov 1982

Maa, I am writing this letter from Delhi now. As expected, Indiraji has rejected their demands. Now see what they have done—hijacked a plane from Bombay to Delhi. What will he achieve by taking the plane to Lahore in Pakistan? Had he thought that he would be welcomed with open arms? Had he thought that history will remember him as a hero? I am glad that he was killed. Foolish man, foolish cause! These militants from Dharam Yudh Morcha have taken this to a new level—a level from which they can't see the sky or the ground beneath. As the Asian Games are coming up, security has been beefed up; and rightly so, no Sikh is allowed in the Delhi region. Indiraji is talking about having more talks with them after the Haryana elections, but as I have said earlier, nothing good will come out of this. I don't know why she is risking her position.

Anyway, I will not drag you into the problems of my daily life. Politics is the most important food I have these days, but because of all these violent and militant activities, my work is going unnoticed in my constituency, which is my bread and butter, and I have to find ways to bring that into the frontline now.

Have you heard from Janki? I asked her to meet me when I was in Delhi, but she never replied to my letter. A mother can only hope that she is fine, but I am really glad that you got to spend time with your great-granddaughter. Whom does she resemble? Does she look like her father, or our Janki?

This year has been the best for me in a very long time. I am at the centre of discussions regarding Punjab and in the close circuits of Indiraji when it comes to manipulation. I know how to use Manav Sansthan for its best. Janki is settled. Meera is two years older; I don't know how fast time flies! Shekhar is also finally free from that woman, who had been my biggest grief. I did not press it—not even once. It was his decision, and I don't think he has made this decision due to my position. I want to think that he has made this decision for us—for our family, the family which he wanted to build and preserve. I think she is going out of India. Shekhar told me that she would never be back, and this has made me the happiest. For me, at least, this is a closed chapter now. I don't wish her well, but I don't wish her bad, either. What more harm I can do to her and myself!

Shekhar is retiring next year from a life lived with the highest dignity. We are planning to take a holiday trip in the early months of the year. I will also have some time in Feb, so I have suggested that we go for a short holiday, away from everyone. Shekhar likes the idea and says he will speak with a travel agent to book the tickets and hotels. I don't want to stay in the Army guesthouses, circuit houses, government dak bungalows, or anywhere that mirrors my past or the present. I want this trip to be free from my political and social life as well as his army life. It will be only us, and we plan to go to a place where no one will know us—where we can be just us again, singing in the rains from heaven.

Your beti,
Shakuntala

"Wow! She was so power-hungry!" exclaimed Sujit.

"Aren't all politicians like that?" Meera asked wryly.

"Yeah, but still when you see them up so close, you realise how they manipulate the situations in their favour." Sujit said and began rocking Jia to sleep.

Meera picked up Jia's bottle of milk. "Is it wrong, though? Don't you want to excel in your field?"

"But lusting for more power is not their job. You see, they should do more humane work," Sujit said.

"Ah, some things will never change! They will remain the same for centuries," Meera said and went out into the kitchen, laughing aloud.

Janki

(1983 - 1988)

Chapter 11

Dear Maa,

5 May 1983

It's her birthday today, but I am not with her. Today is my angel's birthday, but she is not in my arms. I spent two years, seven months, and twenty-three days with my angel, when she had always been in my arms, since she first called me Maa, her first walk, her first smile, long before she started to see the world. Those were the best days of my life.

What have I done to deserve this life? First you did not love me, and now, Meera is taken away from me. Mala was right. I should not have told Adarsh about my past. I still remember the look on his face—the look of betrayal, the look of anger. He had walked away that night only to return after two days. I had to tell everyone that he was out for work. I had thought that he would forgive me when he came back, but he didn't. I couldn't live a lie after Pratap threatened me. I had to tell him lest I was dragged into this kind of situation again, and I might not be able to come out safe every time. I had to come clean in front of him. I loved Adarsh, I still do, and it wasn't fair to him that he lived a lie all his life.

When he did come, he just asked me one thing—why did I lie to him at the Taj? It had been his best memory of our love as well. More than my past relations, he feels that I have betrayed him with that lie. He cannot let go this feeling. I cannot hold back my surprise on seeing how divided the family is. There were those who stood by my side—Maaji and Mala advocated on my behalf. I was surprised to see Kavita's behaviour. She took a neutral stand despite the fact that I had supported her so much during her marriage. No one, in fact, stood against me. They were either neutral or trying to convince Adarsh, but he couldn't get over the whole thing. Maaji even asked him to leave the house and said that she wanted me to stay back for Meera's sake. But how could I let that happen? How could I let Adarsh suffer for my sins? I don't know what will happen to me. I will just have to remember the time with Adarsh as a brief period of happiness amid the rest of my dark life.

I thought though he was angry with me, he would not have any problem with me meeting Meera. But what he has done in the last one or two months is beyond my comprehension. He is altogether a different person. He does not care anymore if I live or die. If he does not want Meera and me to meet, then regardless of who tries to convince him in his family, he will not budge.

Today, on her birthday, he did not let me meet her in the morning when I had gone there. This is not fair, Maa. I am her mother. She is the only thing in my life that I cherish. I cannot live without her. Why can't Adarsh understand this simple thing? Initially, I thought that he is hurt, and he would heal with time. But now, I think that he had always wanted this to happen he always wanted to get separated from me. He had never loved me; else he would not have kept my daughter away from me. He is as selfish as you are.

But I don't care about him, either. I will not give in—I will not give in to my urge for alcohol, or give up on my daughter. I do not care whether anyone is supporting me.

Yes, I will not give up. I will go to his house now and celebrate my angel's birthday. I don't want her to be alone, without her mother, on her birthday. I will take her favourite banana-flavoured cake. She misses me, I know. She wants me to be with her on her birthday. I can't be alone, no! I have to go and meet her... I have to...

Your daughter,

Janki

"Was it fair on Papa's part to do this to your mother?" Sujit asked.

"This is only one side of the coin. I don't know at all if this version is correct. There has to be another explanation for this," Meera said.

"Yeah, it could be. Still, from what you have read, do you think...? Or let me put it this way—if I say I had a past, would you break all relations with me? I know, for sure, I would not do so."

"I wouldn't do it, either, but people were different back then. Society was different," Meera said after a thought.

Sujit shook his head in annoyance. "Really? Was it so different that it allowed a three-year-old to suffer and grow up without her mother, all because of someone's ego?"

"Why are you getting so worked up? I don't remember any of it, anyway."

"Well... all of it had had a huge impact on you and still does. So, don't give me the bullshit that you don't care!" There was an edge of irritation in Sujit's voice now.

Meera flared up too. "You don't have to take out your frustration on me, Sujit. When did I ask you to get involved in my things? These things had never been spoken for my entire life. If it were not for these letters, I wouldn't have known this or discussed it at all."

"You are really impossible! Your decision to not get married—where did that come from?" Sujit asked.

"Oh, so this is why it is coming now?"

"I can't talk to you right now." Sujit got up and walked away in a huff.

"Then leave me alone!" Meera turned her head to the other side.

Dear Maa,

23 Nov 1981

I can say that I had a smile on my face after months. I had met—or, in fact, seen Meera only twice since I left Adarsh's house. Even getting Adarsh beaten up by Pratap's boys didn't help. He hates me even more, now. He said he was the one who hit the goons, but whom to trust? Don't worry. I don't owe Pratap a favour. He has failed miserably in scaring Adarsh. But today was different, and it was all because of Kavita. I had met her in a restaurant last week and pleaded with her to bring Meera along so that I could see her. All I want is to spend some time with her.

Hopefully, after our divorce, she will be with me. She has grown so much in the last couple of months. I was disheartened to know that she has started calling Kavita Maa. I am her mother; she is all mine! I don't want her to call anyone Maa other than me.

But, what I want to tell you, are the best things in the world. I saw her sitting on the chair, trying to see what was on the table. She is like me, inquisitive! She also likes to explore things, and understand them better than anyone else around. I think she will become a journalist and conquer the world with her stories. Kavita was sitting next to her. They were looking in opposite directions when I went there and sat next to Meera. She didn't look at me at first, but when she did, there was this enormous smile on her face—the expression that she had discovered something extraordinary! I can live my next hundred years with that smile, but I don't want to live with that smile—I only want to live with her.

She looked at me and smiled, but within seconds, her expression had changed from smiling to being angry. She grew confused and started to cry and shout that she wanted to go home. I had thought that she would recognise me within a second, but her sadness overshadowed her happiness, and it all faded to confusion. I have always maintained that a child needs her mother. She jumped towards Kavita, and Kavita had to rush along with her, out of the coffee shop into their car.

But I am not sad, Maa. Even if it was just for a couple of seconds, I could see her happy. I was able to see her smiling. I was with her, and she will always remain one of my happy memories.

I am really thankful to Kavita, who went against Adarsh and brought Meera along, to meet me. No one understands me. I had no one to fall back upon. You have never been there for me, and now you are busy with Parliament. But don't worry, I am done complaining to you. I don't even need you, and I don't care whether you are there for me. I will move out of Dadi's house soon. Radhika gives me this look these days; she does not even let me go near Jai. She had even pushed me aside when I tried to get up from the sofa to go and play with him. I had not even had any drink that morning.

God will punish Adarsh. He will suffer in hell for keeping my daughter away from me.

Your daughter,

Janki

"God! Your family is so violent!" Sujit exclaimed.

"Did you forget what happened yesterday?" Meera asked.

"No, I loved the make-out sex."

"I am not talking about that—I am talking about your fight with me!" Meera glared at Sujit.

Sujit started laughing. "I never fought with you. It has always been you… and see, you couldn't control your laughter at the dining table!"

"Anyone would laugh at your grumpy face," Meera grumbled.

"I don't mind being treated like that after every fight. But seriously, your mother sent goons to get Papa's ass kicked?" Sujit said, amazed.

"Super melodrama! But I do agree with her that, at least, he could have let me meet her. After all, she was my mother."

"Hmm, hmm… there is a sudden change in someone's attitude here!" Sujit teased.

"Not sudden," Meera replied.

"Hmm!" was Sujit's only response.

Dear Maa,

3 Jul 1985

I will kill him, Maa, I will kill him. He blames me for Meera's school change. He is so selfish. He doesn't understand what I am going through. Even the court has ordered that I can see Meera once a week, but he is getting standing orders to negate that, too. He does not want me to see my daughter at all.

He does not understand that I can't live without her. I had to take refuge in alcohol, but that day, I didn't have any… okay, I had only had one before meeting Meera. Even she did not realise that! She would not know the smell, anyway. This is all because of that stupid English teacher. Meera had complained that a boy from his class does not let her eat during lunch and misbehaves with her. What did I do? I just went and slapped that son of a bitch. I slapped him so hard that he will remember it his entire life. But what did that English teacher do? He complained that I was under the influence of alcohol, and I had hit a child. He was no child! He was a monster! He was troubling Meera; I will punish anyone and everyone who troubles her.

Adarsh told me that Meera's classmates have stopped talking to her since then. She wants to change her school now. I am telling you, Maa, that he is making a mistake. He should encourage Meera to fight her battles instead of running away from them. He is teaching her a very wrong lesson. He should teach her to fight her way. Life outside is not easy, and it won't be easy for her, either. I hope she never faces what I have faced in my life, but I am sure there will be challenges.

She's five now, and it is very important for her to learn these lessons. Okay, maybe not become as abrasive as I am, but she has to stand up for herself.

I will kill him if he goes ahead with the order. I will surely kill him, even if I have to go to jail; at least, he will also be away from Meera in hell, and then only will he understand how it feels to be kept away from your own daughter.

I have promised him that I will not drink, but he does not listen. He even alleges that I am taking drugs. I promise you, Maa, that I will never do that. I don't want to lose what I have besides Meera—I don't want to lose her completely.

Maa, why don't you help me at least once in your life? Why don't you speak with Papaji and Amma, and ask them to put some sense into that madman?

Your daughter,

Janki

"You know it's easy to get back to drugs if you have done them once?" Sujit said.

"How do you know? Have you tried?" asked Meera.

"No. I treat my body like a temple. But I have seen many players taking drugs to enhance their performance, continue doing so, even when they are not playing."

"But that is not the larger issue, is it?"

"What is it, then?"

"You know a child needs both mom and dad. I actually remember this incident, and I never thought I would say this, but I agree with what Maa says. Papa took me out of that school, and it took me ages to make new friends," said Meera.

"So, you are saying that what your mother did—slapping that kid—was correct?" Sujit asked.

"No. I am saying that Papa should not have taken me out of that school. Eventually, kids do get along, and it was not that I was in some kind of danger," argued Meera.

"I don't know. Sometimes it's better to avoid confrontations," said Sujit and picked up the next letter.

"You are saying this despite being a sportsperson?" teased Meera.

"Precisely, the point!"

Dear Maa,

5 May 1986

Maa, it's not what the police is saying. I never wanted to hurt Meera. It was never my plan to kidnap Meera and run away with her. Where would have I gone? It's all Kavita's fault. Mala was there; you can ask her. It's not my fault, and, in fact, it was Mala's idea so that Meera could celebrate her birthday with me. They had brought her to the park. She looked so pretty and radiant in the blue dress that I had bought for her. She hid behind Kavita when she saw me coming. I don't know what Adarsh and his family had been telling her. I know Kavita did not want to get her in the first place and that Mala had convinced her. But I didn't mind because she takes good care of Meera. But a mother is, after all, a mother, and no one can take my place.

I asked them to take a walk and come back after a couple of hours. They agreed with some hesitation and left Meera with me. Meera knows that I am her mother. I could sense the excitement in her voice when I would ask her something and she thought of an answer, but then there would be a sudden drop in excitement, and she withdrew from me. I had just got a bit irritated as she was not communicating with me. But I hadn't hit her as they told the police.

She started to cry and, unfortunately for me, the local police were nearby. They came and began asking questions. I told them I was her mother. But when they asked Meera, she said "no". That was when I hit her. Seeing her crying, the policemen asked me to stay away from her. How could I have stayed away from her? She fell to the ground when I tried to push them. One of them hit me with his stick. Luckily for me, Kavita and Mala came and stopped them from hitting me more, but before Mala could say anything, Kavita said she was the mother and took Meera away without saying anything to me or anyone else. I could see the surprise in Mala's eyes, but she had to go after them.

The police took me in for kidnapping my own daughter. It had been two days before you got to know and came for my bail. I didn't want you to come, anyway. Mala would have come and enquired about me, my whereabouts and whether I was safe. I think she did not know that the police had taken me. But Kavita—why did she lie? What did she gain out of humiliating me when I hadn't done anything to harm her in my entire life?

I remember the look on your face—the look of disappointment, but trust me, I was not kidnapping her. What would I have achieved by doing that? I didn't want to hurt my angel, and. I would never do that. But she hadn't been listening to me. I had asked her to come with me to have ice-cream, but she started crying. I don't know now when I will see her again. These people would be really strict about where she goes and even Mala will not take any chance.

Can't you use your power to speak with them? What is the use of you being an MP? What good will you do for the country when you cannot do anything for your daughter?

Your daughter

Janki

"I don't remember this incident as it has been written here," Meera said, still frowning at the letter.

Sujit shook his head. "You never told me that anything like this had ever happened."

"What is there to tell? I don't remember it that well. I just remember that she was pulling me towards a place that I didn't want to go to and that she hit me. Not once, but a couple of times," said Meera. The effort of recalling the incident was now visible on her face.

"Evil!" exclaimed Sujit.

"I think she was drunk. Well, I didn't know what 'drunk' meant back then, but she was definitely acting weird… I just remember that I didn't like the whole experience, and it's like that thing in the back of your mind—that sad memory that does not want to go away…" Meera trailed off.

"Maybe she was on drugs," said Sujit.

"I don't trust what she has written in her letter so far. I think she conveniently twisted what had really happened."

"Isn't it obvious? It's her narration!"

"I have to find the truth from Kavita Maa," said Meera. "Now, on to the next letter."

Dear Maa,

7 Nov 1987

Maa, look what Meera has written for me. She is so adorable. No, Adarsh still does not let me see her, but look what she has written.

My dear mummy
World's best mummy
She loves me a lot, and she never scolds me
She buys me toys
I love my Barbie, and I love my mummy
She buys me dresses
In which I look like an angel
I love my mummy

The last couple of months have been really good. Well, it's called relatively, isn't it? Adarsh has been helping me get onto my feet again, I don't know what it is. Is it the love he still has for me, or is it pity, or maybe, he feels that he is responsible for my situation? I don't know what it is, but I don't mind it. I am getting even the little details of Meera's life from him. My princess is seven years old now. Adarsh thinks that I am dangerous for her. How can that be possible? I love her more than my life, and I have stopped drinking. I can't even remember when I had drunk last. Maybe, seven months ago, when Adarsh stormed into that friend's house and forced me to come out with him. I don't know what had gotten into him. Maybe, you or Amma would have asked him to do so, but he still does not trust me. He still thinks that I am dangerous for my own daughter. I don't know the motive behind this sudden change in him, or maybe he has not changed; perhaps this is just a facade.

But whatever it is, he tells me stories of my daughter. She has started making friends now. Adarsh tells me that she can't stop talking about Ritesh whom he calls his son-in-law. He laughed so much when we had gone out for dinner last week. I had promised him that I would think about the business proposal that he had sent last month, but we ended up talking about Meera the entire dinner. I can't get enough of her.

I am also sending you Meera's pictures that Adarsh had given to me.

Your daughter,

Janki

"Ah, that's so sweet!" Sujit said with a smirk on his face.

"Ah, really, that's so sweet!" Meera said, holding the letter close to her.

"OMG! I was kidding. Are you seriously thinking about it?" Sujit tugged and pulled at her hair.

"About what?" Meera said, perplexed.

"About your first love, Ritesh!"

"I don't remember anything like that. Stop pulling my leg!"

"Then?"

"That poem I wrote! It's giving me goose-bumps, see? Just to think that I am reading a poem I had written some twenty-eight years ago! It's like discovering a side of mine that I had never known to have existed," said Meera.

"Sweet! And, it looks like your kidnapper's life is also getting back on track. Do you think that your father still loved her back then?" asked Sujit, now quietening down.

"I don't know. Only he can tell."

"Let's find out." Sujit pulled out the next letter.

Dear Maa,

23 Dec 1988

Maa, the situation here, in the US, is electrifying. There is great excitement for the new President George H. W. Bush. Elections in the US are very different from what they are in India. There is such a frenzy; it looks like they are celebrating some kind of festival. And, why not? Their economy is growing, and there are no clouds of gloom anywhere in this part of the world.

George H. W. Bush had been the Vice-President already, so it was probably an easy win for him. The Americans say that he didn't have a proper opponent. Why don't you come and try your luck here in the US?

Adarsh has been very kind to have brought me here. We are staying in separate rooms on the same floor. I would be lying if I say that getting back together did not cross my mind. I watched him the entire time he slept on the plane. I think he knew that I had been watching him, as a few times when our eyes met, he continued looking at me, and so did I. It was late in the evening when we reached the hotel. Both of us were terribly tired, and he just tucked me into the bed.

Maa, we had a moment as well, and I thought that he would kiss me. But then, I think he regained his senses and went to his room. I can't thank him enough for doing this for me. He came all the way from India to help me set up my business here. He has a big network, and initially, we thought that I would do something in steel, but things are very different here. People have been talking a lot about computers, and Adarsh thinks that this might be the right time to get into this line. There are many sceptics as well—people who think the computer craze will all die down. I don't know, to be honest. We have a meeting with a senior executive from IBM tomorrow. I will write to you again if things materialise here.

The only thing is that I will be more than 7500 miles away from Meera. But Adarsh tells me it will be good for her, as she has started asking questions now, and seeing me off and on, will only disturb her.

I think I do agree with his reasoning. I don't want my daughter to grow up having the same complexes that I have had.

And, more importantly, I am not sure about the USA, either, as it's very far. I told Adarsh that we should find a place nearer to India, like Dubai, or Singapore, or even London may be fine, for that matter. Let's see how things unfold here.

Your daughter,

Janki

"We are sure those things did materialise, didn't they? She did die in the US," Sujit said without realising that he could be causing Meera hurt.

When Meera said nothing, he continued, "Or not. Maybe she just happened to be at the wrong place at the wrong time."

"Less likely," Meera said. "I know she was in the US. That's what was told to me, that she had to go for some work in the US initially. I think I was ten when Papa sat me down one day and told me that my mother might not come home. He told me that she has her own house now in the US," Meera explained to Sujit.

"Did you see her during those times whenever she was in India?" asked her husband.

"I did and that was the worst time of my life," said Meera.

"Oh! How is that?" asked Sujit.

"You will see. But first I have to get some answers from Kavita Maa," Meera said with determination.

Meera
(2015)

Chapter 12

THE NEXT DAY, Meera and Kavita were having tea in the living room at Adarsh's house. Meera, unable to sustain her curiosity any longer, had arranged the meeting with Kavita over the phone.

"I will tell you everything from the beginning," Kavita said, taking a deep breath. She had been trying to avoid the discussion, but Meera was persistent. After much coaxing, Kavita decided to tell Meera her version of the events. She didn't want Meera to interrupt her with questions, though, as this would only confuse things.

Meera sat in front of her, scared but listening intently.

"My marriage had been planned one year before it actually took place. I was new in this house, and it so happened that my path would cross with Janki Bhabhi's, often. She was an outsider, too, like me. Maybe, that's why. You won't believe how big the family was then. There were, at one point, 25 people living under one roof. When I had got married, I think we were about fifteen or sixteen." She paused here, perhaps trying to assess where the story was going and what point she wanted to make.

"Yes," she continued. "I had only my father and a younger brother in my family. Since I met Janki Bhabhi from day one, she had shown such warmth for me that I still cherish those memories."

"I saw her real character and strength when Dharam Nanaji had passed away that year, and Atul's family—now my family—wanted to have a simple wedding with just 50-60 guests. The point was to get married. It was our period of mourning, but they couldn't delay the wedding due to some reasons of their own, which ideally should have been the case. Anyway, my Papa agreed to keep it simple, but I was not happy. You get married only once, and it should have been according to my wishes, shouldn't it? Things went really bad. There was one point when they wanted to cancel the marriage altogether. Papaji had even said in my presence that I was not fit for the family and if I was behaving like that, then what would I do when I actually become a part of their household… And, what did I do?" At this, Kavita again paused and laughed.

"Is it bad that I had that one wish? There was no one standing with me, back then, not even my father. That time, Janki Bhabhi stood with me, asking everyone why they were doing this to me. I still remember the level of voices everyone was speaking, but your mo… Janki Bhabhi raised her voice equally. I think she survived that incident as Adarsh Bhaiya had supported her, else; both of us would have been out of the house then and there, itself."

"Why did you hesitate in referring to her as my mother?" Meera asked Kavita.

"You… you never wanted that reference to happen, do you remember?" Kavita reminded her.

"Yes, then what happened?"

"Well, you know, I am here, sitting in front of you with 35 years of married life due to be completed next year. Ah, you were so beautiful! I think you were 2 or 3 at my wedding," replied Kavita.

"Two."

"Atul and I had moved out of Delhi. His job took him to Bhubaneswar. We were called back when the situation got out of hand and Adarsh Bhaiya had gone really out of his mind for a couple of years. That's when Atul joined the business."

"Why did he do this to himself? Why couldn't he get over the past?"

"See, I have never judged anyone, neither Janki Bhabhi nor Adarsh Bhaiya. Who am I to judge and intervene between them?"

"Well, Maa did speak up for you."

"I am not her. I was not, and neither would I be like her. For what she did for me, I thank her even today. But I didn't agree with her. Actually, I didn't have any opinion. We were all shocked."

"What do you think now?

"I still think what I did was correct, and I have no regrets. It pains me a lot to recall Bhabhi pleading before everyone, just for you. It was so humiliating for her. All these things should have been handled in their bedroom, but they were out in the open, and everyone came to know about them. Ah… it was so sad to see—and now to remember—here in this room—there, in front of that door, Adarsh Bhaiya was standing, crying, hitting himself, and Bhabhi was almost on the ground, tears running down her cheeks, shouting, asking him to stop. She was pleading to everyone to think about you."

"Dadi favoured Maa, correct?"

"No one favoured her. There were those who were looking forward to this moment. I will not get into that, don't even ask me to, but those like me didn't know what to do."

"So ultimately, she had to leave," Meera said.

"In the end, Amma had to make the choice between her son and her daughter-in-law. She left it to Janki. I still believe that Amma could have done more—she could have stopped Bhabhi, but she didn't do enough," Kavita said.

"You said Papa suffered a lot after she left..."

"It was the most difficult period. Those were the darkest years for this family, perhaps. Adarsh Bhaiya had lost it completely. He didn't even come near you for a couple of months. He stopped going to the factory. He had an accident, got mobbed, there was a goon attack... so many things, and he didn't even let us go to the police for these incidents. Whoever did all this kept repeating it. We used to discuss who it could be and listed down all his business associates, but we could never find out."

"Really?" Meera smiled. She didn't want to tell Kavita it was her mother.

"But I must say he loved your mother a lot. He never got married. There were two girls. Twice, he came close to marrying someone after Bhabhi had moved to the USA. To the last one, he had said 'no' on the day of the ring ceremony."

"Oh, I didn't know that!" Meera said.

"Yes, you were kept out of this. I used to take you away from the house, and this was all done to protect you."

Kavita continued, "One thing I didn't like is that Bhabhi did not get any support from her family neither from her mother nor father, even though her mother was an MLA or MP then. I remember that your Nana and Nani came a day after Bhabhi had left this house and had just apologised. It felt as if they had known about her past, and they didn't want to get involved or do anything to save this marriage. I still believe that your Nani could have saved her."

"Yeah, she was a real monster from what I have read so far," agreed Meera.

"Hmm… I will not go that far. She must have had her reasons, but yeah, I agree what she did was wrong. She did support her afterwards, but not as much as she should have."

"Do you remember that she had kidnapped me?" asked Meera.

"Oh, I can never forget that dreadful day. You were six then. How much do you remember?"

"Not much. It's just that I have this very sad feeling about it, somewhere in the back of my mind, and it does not go away. The anger, the disappointment… all I think originated from there."

Kavita sighed and said, "It was your birthday. Mala and I had been planning for you to meet your mother for many days. We had thought of numerous ways to blindfold the rest of the family. Trust me; it was not easy, as everyone knew we still had a connection with Bhabhi.

"On the day when we took you out, we had thought that it would be a two-hour thing, and we would come back before anyone noticed," Kavita continued. "We went to the park and saw Janki Bhabhi. We were also seeing her after a long time. She had lost so much weight that I didn't recognise her at once. Her eyes had popped out, and there were black marks all around her eyes. I thought someone had, actually, hit her."

After scrutinising Meera's expressions carefully, Kavita resumed, "She asked us to leave. I was not willing to do that, but Mala signalled to me. We must have been away for only twenty minutes. I wanted to check in on her, but when we came there, the first thing I saw was that she was hitting you with two or three hard slaps. There were two policemen who were stopping her, hitting her… there was chaos everywhere."

Meera gulped.

"We took you out of there within seconds and rushed out," Kavita said. "We bought you ice-cream on the way and told you not to tell anyone. But the first thing you did was to have started crying as soon as we entered the house. You ran and told everything to Amma and Adarsh Bhaiya…"

"It must have been terrible!" Meera said.

"It was horrible!" Kavita said. "I had never seen Amma so angry. She slapped Mala twice. She couldn't slap me as I was the daughter-in-law, but she didn't leave any stone unturned in lecturing me. She continued with that till she was alive. Even on her deathbed, she told me she could never trust me about you." A tear rolled off Kavita's eyes.

Meera stood up, hugged her, and said, "You are my mother. Whatever I am today is because of you. See, I am not doing that bad!" Meera gave Kavita a kiss on her cheek.

A weak smile broke out on Kavita's face.

"Did you know that she was in jail for two days?" Meera asked when she settled a bit.

"Not right away, but we came to know to know about it after about a week. Our problems felt so petty before that. I just wish the situation was not like that, and she would still have been with us, in the family."

"I can't even imagine that," said Meera truthfully.

"You know what was the breaking point for me?"

"What?"

"When Bhabhi forced you to take drugs. You were just eleven, my child, and see what she did! I went to confront her, but she got violent and I had to run for my life. Like a fool, I took Sameer with me, and he banged into the door in that rush to get badly hurt," said Kavita.

"Oh!"

"I didn't speak to her after that. And, on that fateful day of 9/11, she was killed in the terrorist attack."

"Do you regret anything that you had done?" asked Meera.

"Yes, I do." She paused and said, "It took me so long to forgive her for what she had done to you. I could have spoken to her sooner, or at least, before she left us. I have always considered you before Sameer, and you know that, don't you? Unintentionally, if I have done anything wrong to her, may God and she forgive me… if she is still looking at us."

"Yes, Kavita Maa. I always have and will always consider you before my biological mother."

Kavita hugged Meera and held her tightly as if a weight she had been carrying for many years had lifted off her shoulders.

"Kavita Maa, do you remember my third birthday? Did Maa come to our house to celebrate my birthday? I think that was the first year when she was away from me."

"Yes, she did come, and we did celebrate your birthday. It feels really good now that we did it, but back then, it was another terrible event." When Meera urged her, Kavita continued, "I still remember it clearly. Adarsh Bhaiya had instructed our guard not to let your mother in. Poor fellow! Bhabhi was always nice to servants, but he had to do what Adarsh Bhaiya had asked him to. Bhabhi didn't challenge him. She stood outside the gate and called you. Her cries were so painful that they could have filled anyone's heart with sorrow. Mala and I were in the kitchen. When we first heard her voice, we just ran towards the main gate. But by the time we had reached there, Amma was already outside, pleading with Bhabhi to leave the house. We stood behind her."

"Did I come out? Did Papa come out?"

"Mala ran inside and came out after a couple of minutes to tell us that Adarsh Bhaiya was holding you close and crying his heart out. Still, Bhabhi was adamant about seeing you, and she wouldn't go. By that time, the news had spread that there was some problem in the family. The neighbours came out and cursed us for being evil and not letting a mother see her child. It was a long time before Bhabhi fell silent. Then, she just kept standing there quietly."

"What happened, then?"

"Amma did something which still amazes me. She called for a table to be placed on the road outside the house, and put the cake, that Bhabhi had brought, onto it. We sang the birthday song, looking at the window of your Papa's room and wished you loudly so that you could hear us. She kissed her hands and sent you a birthday wish."

Meera was in tears, and so was Kavita. By the time, she had finished detailing the incident, it was ingrained second by second in Meera's mind.

She felt as if that wish had reached her now, after all these years. She closed her eyes and said—*Thank you, Maa.*

Shakuntala

(1983 - 1988)

Chapter 13

Dear Maa,

12 Dec 1983

Maa, it's dreadful everywhere. Janki is struggling to survive without Meera. I have been asking her several times to come and live with me, but she wants to live her life alone now. If she is this adamant, I am telling you that she will die alone.

Things are not smooth in my constituency here in Punjab. You know very well what has been happening here, at the ground level. Indiraji needs us to manage the state during the President's rule. We have to advise her where the major uprisings are taking place and how to curb them. I had written to you about the Dhilwan incident last month. The militants had killed six innocent people, and the retaliation from the government has been severe. The militants don't report their losses in full. Most of them are dead in the street—unnamed and unclaimed. There are lots more people dying on the other side. They just don't admit that Indiraji is too big a force to handle.

You and Shekhar are alike, in some ways. He also wants me to leave the city and come back to Delhi. 'What am I doing here without a government?' he asks. Both of you fail to understand that this is the best time to come to the High Command's notice. I am here for the long haul and will not get scared by these tiny dog barks.

Don't worry about me being here. I will take care of myself. I was quite worried about your health. It's good now that you are also well. Do you know what people have been saying? Soon, you and I will be able to talk to each other, sitting in different places as if we are next to each other. I know we can do that by telephone, but these new phones are much better. They have already been launched in Bombay last year and will soon reach all parts of the country, and then every home. I will still write to you once in a while, if not regularly. They say that people will also be able to see each other from a distance. I was reading an article in the New York Times, which said some of it has already been achieved, but it will take ages for the technology to come to India.

Maa, having said all this, I am really worried about Janki. She is holding up till now in the hope that Adarsh will take her back. I don't know what is going on in Adarsh's mind. He refused to talk to me. I spoke with Kaushalyaji and Sagarji, who are also helpless, and it's not something I can argue against, either. She probably blames me for what has happened to her, but did I tell her to sleep with all those boys? No, I didn't. I did warn her this would not do her any good. Finally, when she had started seeing things in a positive light, see what happened! Shekhar does not even want to speak to Janki or her parents, but I can't tell this to Janki. If she comes to know that her father has not done anything for her, she will break down. I think, sometimes, lies are better than the cruel truth.

I have to focus now and get my hands on how central politics works. I believe that regional politics is not for me. These people do not want to come out of their bins. The militants are fighting for a lost cause. I am meant to be bigger than this, and all these things, including Janki, are dragging me down.

I may not be able to write to you for a couple of months. But you keep sending me letters, and I will reply to them whenever I can. Give my regards to Papaji.

Your beti,

Shakuntala

"I don't like the way she refers to the Sikh cause and the group as militants," said Sujit.

"Well, weren't they known like this, back then?" asked Meera.

"I don't know."

"Yeah, but I agree with you. It is a black mark on India, which we can't get rid of no matter what we do. Do you know James Markfield, the British journalist whom I met at the conclave last month? We discussed at length about Indian politics, and this episode stood out on its own. They see us in a dark light when it comes to basic human rights."

"Did they have any view on the killings like the bus attack in Dhilwan or other similar attacks?" Sujit asked.

"You shouldn't be surprised if I tell you that many of them, not all, but still a lot, were orchestrated by the Government of India, just to spread confusion. I am not saying this one was, and I don't know, to be honest, but the other side also does things like this," Meera said.

"Yeah, it could be true. Unfortunately, this is politics, and I am getting a feeling that your grandmother was just starting with it."

Dear Maa,

12 Jan 1985

Maa, I could see the pride in both yours and Papaji's eyes during my oath-taking ceremony. It is a feeling that will always live with me—more than the actual ceremony itself. Under the leadership of Rajivji, we will unite again against all these evil eyes from the North and the East. I missed Shekhar at the event. Now that he has taken the reins of Manav Sansthan into his hands, he had to go to Kenya for our ambitious African expansion.

I will now take on larger responsibilities. As you know well, it had not been easy to get here. My seat in Haryana was also not an easy win as I had to battle against all odds to win this position. I hate these newspapers, in particular, that regional one—that guy, a reporter—can't remember his name now—had been after my life. He raked up my past that I was an alcoholic who had spent some time in mental asylums and hospitals, and about Manav Sansthan. Actually, he was not completely wrong. Initially, I had thought he was financed by Gattumji, my opponent, but I later found out that he was working on his own. His objectives were to make Indian politics cleaner, at least in the cities.

It was very embarrassing for the party leaders to respond to allegations against me. At one point, they had even almost decided to take me off the candidate sheet. Then, I met Rajivji's Chief Advisor to explain things to him. He got convinced but asked me to diffuse the situation. Maa, you were wrong about the situation. You had told me that I would not be able to bribe him, but everyone in the world has a price tag; we just have to find out how much it is. I got him an editor's post in a Lucknow-based newspaper. He had been trying for that job for a couple of years, and with the speed and direction he had been taking, he could have never reached Lucknow, though it is only 700km from here. He did continue with his dream to throw me off the radar after moving to Lucknow as well, but a little bit of threat solved it. Ah, everyone loves their children more than they love themselves!

It was very unfortunate for me that Janki was not there. Actually, she is never there—never ever there for me. It was a big moment for me, and she didn't even acknowledge the fact that I had achieved this position in my life. But even if she turns a blind eye towards me, I have one eye on her. I have asked Sudesh, my Security Head, to have someone to keep a track 24x7 of what she does, who she meets. I have also asked them not to allow themselves to be seen, and only take her out of grave danger, which has not happened until now, thankfully. After incidents like throwing stones at Adarsh's residence and getting him beaten up by goons, I have to be careful as she has created more enemies for herself.

She has even started taking drugs now. Drugs with drinking will only take her faster to her sad demise. I no longer see a future for her, and I am tired of running after her. I will just do whatever I can so that she does not kill herself. Rest is up to her destiny, and I can't change that for her.

She is getting worse now that the date for her divorce is nearing. I really feel bad for Shekhar. He is struggling to come out of this. Manav Sansthan is keeping him busy; else, he would have become mad, thinking about his precious daughter.

But I hope now that you and Papaji will come to stay with us for a couple of months, and Janki can also come and stay with us again. See you soon.

Your beti,

Shakuntala

"Your grandmother was pure evil, *yaar*!" exclaimed Sujit with a whistle.

"Well, I don't think so. She did quite a lot of good as well. I think these are just circumstantial things," Meera said.

"Circumstantial, my foot! What about threatening that poor journalist? You are a journalist, too. Don't you feel for him?"

"I don't, for there are ones who give up on their ethics if a bone is thrown at them."

"Would you do that?" Sujit prodded her.

"Do what?" asked Meera.

"I mean… do you have a price-tag, which, if someone gives it to you, will make you back off from the cause?"

"You probably know the answer better than I do. One thing that I learned now, is that I have inherited this adamant nature from my maternal family—this urge to get what I want… Morality is a very relative thing, don't you agree?" said Meera.

"Yeah! I don't mind using performance-enhancing drugs for my players," said Sujit.

"That will get you into trouble."

"I have not done that, and in any case, the level where I work does not need it, anyway. Maybe someday… "

Meera patted Sujit on the head. "Just don't get caught."

Dear Maa,

28 Aug 1985

Maa, the last couple of months have been tough for me, with my responsibilities in office and Janki's troubles, which are growing by the day. And, now this… Shekhar is not allowing me to utilise Manav Sansthan effectively.

He has forged a collaboration with a couple of international NGOs and has moved our organisation towards making it more aligned with their rules and ethics. It is no longer controlled in the way I did… I feel like I am losing my child. It is, in fact, my child, whom I have nurtured for all these years, and now when the time has come to pluck its ripe fruit, Shekhar has become a beacon of moral values.

This has created a rift between Shekhar and me, and I am unsure of what to do next. You had heard the arguments when you were here, but the situation is far worse now.

Apart from funnelling the money through Manav, I needed it to use it to my political advantage, too, but now, they are moving towards more focused goals. Shekhar argued that they should contribute towards one or two areas at the maximum rather than issues concerning the whole world. Though I, at some level, agree with that, I still want to be able to use it for whatever I want to do in my constituency.

It had become embarrassing when the Sarpanch saw us arguing over this matter at a local event. At last, Shekhar had to agree, but I am unsure if I can continue like this. I don't think moving Shekhar out, will do any good as he has taken the NGO to heights that I could not have taken. Maybe, I should also give up easily like Janki, and divorce him.

I really find it hard sometimes to believe that she is my daughter. She is so weak! If something untoward begins to happen, she just goes in the opposite direction instead of facing the problem.

Like, you have always supported and guided me with all my questions during my difficult periods, please guide me this time too. I am unable to focus on larger things due to these issues at home.

Your beti,

Shakuntala

"I have looked up this Manav Sansthan in detail now. It's pretty big in number and in terms of what they do," Sujit said later.

Meera's reply was in one word—"Okay."

"The most interesting thing is that Shakuntala Devi Sexena is the President of the Group, which now spans 12 countries."

"So, my grandmother is still alive," said Meera.

"Perhaps..." replied Sujit.

"I am getting a feeling that I will meet her soon."

"Best of luck with that!"

Dear Maa,

9 Jul 1986

Janki has crossed all limits and, no, I will not listen to your justifications and defences about her. You have always been biased towards her, and you are the frontrunner to save her whenever she does anything wrong. But not this time. I had spoken with the Delhi Police Inspector to neutralise the matter, else; she would have stayed in jail for days. Hitting one's child is barbaric—let alone hitting her in a public place. I am still shocked by the event, and you know how these people are; they got a weak link and are now exploiting it. They say if I can't even control my own child, how will I control my constituency?

I have been telling Shekhar for very long to bring her back home now. At least we can put some control on her wings here, but he won't listen to me. He says she has to find her way out of this on her own. That might well be, but not at the cost of my career. Earlier, people used to whisper, but now they are openly threatening my position in public.

I will not let that happen; I will not let these people take away my sheen. I am tired of saving her from the world now, and that too, without any recognition. She still thinks that I am the villain. She does not see what she has done to me and what she is doing to herself.

Anyway, they are after me for the Kumawat land scheme fraud. I am sure they will not find anything, but both these incidents put me in a difficult position. Also, Bhairav is not able to keep up with the fast pace that Manav Sansthan is spreading. Since Shekhar opted out of the organisation, virtually all the responsibilities have fallen back upon me. He had taken the organisation to its greatest heights in a short period, and now people are finding it difficult to manage. With funds assured from the UN, it's the execution that matters now. And this is where they are struggling.

But they do not understand it. They think we have solutions to all the problems. But don't worry; I will fight this phase as well. It seems Janki and my life are interlinked. Bad things happen to me whenever something bad happens to her. It's odd. Do you remember Dr Shyamlata? She had helped me a lot during my low period, which is fine. In the end, it was her job, but she now wants something in return. She wants to start an orphanage on the lines of Manav Sansthan. She thinks that I would be able to get her land at zero cost. I don't know why these people have unrealistic expectations; I would have still helped her if it were not for these hawks that are after me in the land scheme scam. And, there is also Janki who is sapping all my energy. They react in such an ungrateful manner as if we have not given them their due.

When people reach the top, they forget those who had helped them during their low periods. But they also have to come up with reasonable demands. I can't give them the moon tomorrow if they ask for it.

Please don't judge me. When the dust settles down, I will mend my relations with Dr Shyamlata again—she is not dying tomorrow.

I have sent you some money now, and I will also be there on the day of Papaji's operation.

Your beti,

Shakuntala

"Did you look up this scandal? On Google?" asked Meera.

"I have been trying but could not find even one article. Maybe your grandmother has twisted history in her favour after all." Sujit rolled his eyes.

"Hmm..." was all that Meera said.

Dear Maa,

26 Aug 1987

My first foreign trip to Sri Lanka was as eventful as could be. We were all shocked to see that a Sinhala soldier was attacking Rajivji. There is growing hatred towards Indians in Sri Lanka, and I don't know what they will do next.

Other than that, the trip was good. I did utilise the trip to propagate about the Manav Sansthan. They will be issuing a tender of 500 crores for various projects in Sri Lanka, and Manav Sansthan will get a larger portion of the pie.

As you know, we are here to help humanity, and we will always jump upon such opportunities and take pride in them.

Do you remember the journalist for whom I had got an editor's job in Lucknow? He sees the light properly now. I took his help to reinstate myself after my position was punctured by the land scam. He is now in Team A along with me.

Unless Janki does something really stupid and gives my opponents another chance to stab me, things are looking fine now. Shekhar is trying his hands in the printing business now. He doesn't want to be mainstream and work behind the scenes. I hope that he does better than his other endeavours, though. There is a knot in the thread of our relationship, and we are not on the same page when it comes to morality and ethics, but as they say, at the top you are all alone. I am finding it harder day by day to see Shekhar with me—standing next to me or supporting me, but he is a highly principled man. He is an army soldier at heart, and this spirit will not go away easily. At least now we know where the boundaries are. We don't cross each other.

I feel sometimes that he regrets the decision of not leaving me and going with her when there was time. But then again, I don't know. I can't tell what he is thinking these days, like I used to earlier, and to be honest, I don't find the time. Our delegation will be going to five countries, including Japan, to study their best practices in manufacturing and agriculture. Shekhar and I are in our separate ways now, and I don't know when and where we will meet.

Maa, you have asked me this again and by not replying or mentioning it, I hoped had hinted at what I wanted to say, but you still keep pestering me with that issue. So here is my answer—loud and clear.

No, I will not have anything to do with Adarsh and his family. Meera belongs to that family, too. Even Shekhar is clear that we don't want any more drama. If they don't want us to be part of their family, we also don't want to disturb that equation. Moreover, Janki has just started to learn that I don't like to even discuss it in her presence. I want to avoid anything that might push her into the same state again.

I know it must be really difficult for you. But just forget that there is someone called Meera. I don't want the cycle to start again, and I have to focus on my future. I can see the cabinet berth being much closer than ever.

Your beti,

Shakuntala

"Ouch, that hurts!" said Sujit.

"No, not really. They are all, for the most part, fictional characters to me. I won't be surprised to wake up from this dream just to see this box here, along with all the letters and people—the stories in it, all vanishing," said Meera.

"Are you again shutting out one side of your life?" asked Sujit in mock surprise.

"No, it's like a can of worms. Now that it has been opened, they will all come out—bad, ugly and disgusting," Meera made a face.

"Ah, you just killed my appetite!" Sujit made a gagging sound.

Dear Maa,

5 Jan 1988

Have you heard of the phrase—playing with fire? This is what is happening with me. The fire is a wonderful thing—I have realised this now. You are attracted to it, but then the more you go into it, the more you are turned into fumes.

Manav Sansthan has achieved great heights, and it's all because of Shekhar's vision. Though he is not actively involved in the day-to-day executive decisions, he is always there for me as a mentor. Due to our earlier campaigns, we have generated enough name among the charity, and it is widely recognised, but I have to take it further to make it a truly global conglomerate. I have to think big; this is where the Ramesh Group and Co have come into the picture. Their twelve-thousand-crore empire needs a reputable firm for their corporate social responsibility activities. After several meetings, I have come to know that if we help each other, we will also be able to help society profoundly and effectively.

Maa, I don't mind bending the rules for social benefit. I have to secure our future, and after us, all of it will go to Janki. She is also off to a great start now. I still don't know what she will choose in the end, but I did speak to her about handling our US leg of operations so that I, along with Bhairav, can manage the rest of the world.

Now after the Ramesh and Co interactions, we are starting an office in Switzerland as well. Analysts say it cannot get better than this, and what safer place can there be, to secure the organisation's future?

Some people have alleged that I had favoured them, got them tenders in coal and petroleum and moved crores of funds overseas. They name Mauritius; they are fools. They don't understand that I need to help the socially-backward so that they can rise to better social levels. For that, I need Manav Sansthan to function properly, and we also need funds.

But you can understand it now that it's like playing with fire. I can get my hands burnt or even myself if I am not careful. Even the people I deal with, have no ethics, and all they can think of and want is, money. They don't understand that we have to show that we care and that we have a responsibility towards society.

If I wish for big things for myself and my family, I will have to take this plunge.

Your beti,

Shakuntala

"Manav Sansthan has done actually a lot of good work in the recent years," Sujit said.

"I am just curious to know what plunge she took. It can't be as simple as that—moving funds to Swiss banks and allocating of coal and other natural resources in her favour," Meera said. She was now sorting the letters and also keeping an eye on Jia, playing with her toys on a mat beside her chair.

"Do you think this shit goes deeper?" Sujit asked.

"I do, yeah…" Meera replied.

Janki

(1989 - 1994)

Chapter 14

Dear Maa,

23rd Oct 1989

We have survived an earthquake. We were at Candlestick Park wherein Oakland Athletics and San Francisco Giants were meeting each other after a gap of 32 years. It was a grand event. I suggested to Adarsh that we reach the stadium early to avoid the crowd. I think it happened a little after five when the stadium had been almost half-full. The stadium was amazing, though. There was a recent structure constructed on the upper deck. I thought that it might fall on all of us. The entire stadium was vibrating as the earthquake wave passed through it, and the light poles were shaking precariously. A few minutes later, a police car entered the ground to inform us that the game had been postponed. To be honest, it was, at one point, more exciting than scary. You should have seen Adarsh's face. He was badly shaken up, and he kept taking Meera's name. Later, he told me that she only has one parent and asked me what would have happened if she had lost him as well

This is his second trip to the US in a year. At one level, I don't think he needed to come here anyway, but I am glad that he did. He was accompanied by Mr Prakesh from Jaipur, who will be our export provider of Khadi from India. I will manage the exclusive outlet here in California and also the distribution to various other stores in the state.

I did manage to convince him to stay with me. Mr Prakesh is also staying with us. But I don't mind it as long as I am with Adarsh. I am sure there is something still lurking in his heart for me, and I have to find these answers. He did not say anything; he did not even give me a hint or lead to proceed, but it's just what I feel, so I am putting it down.

Meera is nine-and-a-half now; it has been three years since I saw her last. But I don't feel that she is away from me. I call Adarsh and ask him about her almost every week, and he tells me all the stories of how happy she was when she had got selected for a school play, her jealousy about her former best friend Garima, and all that. These days, she is obsessed with drawing. Adarsh told me that she draws well. He had even brought a couple of her drawings for me. They are really good, and I am sending you one of them, along with this letter.

Mala had told me a couple of weeks ago that Meera feels bad when she sees her friends with their mothers. Mala thinks this was the reason of her fight with Garima, but when I asked Adarsh about it, he said that it was not true and that she is happy with Kavita. I am sure that Kavita must be taking good care of her, but ultimately, a child needs her mother. I told Adarsh that his ego is spoiling an innocent heart.

I am sending you a camera and a slide projector. You don't get these things in India, and I have no plans to come here, either—I don't want to do that anytime soon. If I come, I will be drawn towards Meera, which will not be good for either of us.

Your dear daughter,

Janki

"Oh, so these drawing are yours! I did say they were yours, didn't I?" Sujit said with a grin on his face. He picked up the drawings that were lying under the letters in the box.

"I don't remember about them," Meera said with a plain look on her face.

"You do. Why are you lying to me?" Sujit teased.

Meera pulled a face. "All right, I remember about them. I also remember the fight with Garima who was my best friend. I used to tell her everything, but she was jealous of me and used to taunt me about Maa in our fights, which incidentally increased after that quarrel."

"Why, what happened?" Sujit said, tickling Jia's tummy and making her laugh.

"Nothing but a simple kids' fight. But they all knew that I had a weak spot, and they exploited this even when I had reached college." Meera ran a hand over Jia's hair.

"Were you affected?" asked Sujit.

"Of course, yes! This is why I don't like my childhood very much. I do not have many happy memories of that period, and it was much later that I learned to separate from them." Meera picked up the next letter.

"But that made you a cold bitch," her husband said.

"Maybe. But that worked out for me. And for us."

The two of them looked at Jia with smiles on their faces.

Dear Maa,

28 Dec 1989

Some unfortunate incident has taken place. I have just returned from a coffee date with a guy called Simon. It all started a week ago when I was invited to a party by an influential distributor here. I didn't want to go, but I had to because he is the one who can generate interest for Khadi in the US. He introduced me to his family, including his younger brother, and everyone there. When we had settled, his younger brother, Simon came with drinks and we started chatting. I don't remember when the discussion reached his bedroom. But by the time I got back to my senses, we had already been kissing, and some of our clothes were off.

I didn't want to do this. Things are so wonderful with Adarsh, and I want to go to Meera as soon as possible. Adarsh hasn't said anything this time as well, but he looked as if he was more determined to stay here a little longer.

I should not have done what I did, and I am feeling guilty. It's not that Adarsh is my husband, but still, I have hope. I kept dreaming about Meera calling to tell me that I was wrong, and I couldn't sleep that night. When I went to work next day, Simon was there. He followed me the whole day, trying to persuade me, apologising to me, and doing all sorts of things that would normally make someone throw herself into his arms, but I tried to stay away from him as much as possible.

I had to go to this coffee date with him to stop him from following me. I don't know why and how I could do this. What will Meera think about me?

Your dear daughter,

Janki

"Before you say anything, Sujit, I am warning you…" Meera said as soon as she had finished the letter.

Sujit was waiting for her to finish, to start with his comments.

"What did I say?"

Meera could almost hear him laughing within. "You have to promise me that you will not comment on my mother's or, for that matter, anyone's personal life, else I will not let you read these letters," she snapped.

"Done! I was just going to discuss that earthquake. That was a pretty amazing thing to experience," Sujit said, his tongue firmly in his cheek.

"I know what amazing things you wanted to discuss." Meera pulled out her tongue at him.

Dear Maa,

19 Jun 1990

I am glad that I could come to India for Nani's last rites. She loved me a lot, and had been always there for me, even when you were not there. She was so kind and loving, and look what she has left for me—this necklace! I have carefully put it into this box I bought yesterday from a pawn shop. You know, when I lived with her, she used to wear this! I used to ask her to give it to me, to which, I still remember, she used to say, 'All my love is for you.' I used to tell her, 'I don't want your love; I want the necklace.' But now I understand she meant that I would have it, and her love will always be with me in this form. I feel as if she is watching and blessing me from up there. I will give this to Meera when she is old enough to understand the importance of this love that has cascaded to her through generations. I hope to have an amicable relationship with her in future, and you would also agree that we—you and I, are now at our best place in our entire life—our relationship has never been this good!

I had shown this necklace to Simon who suggested that we sell it at an antique market. I had an argument with him over that. Later, he made funny faces that made me smile. He is so adorable!

I got a chance to see Meera as well, on her 10th birthday. She was looking like an angel—my angel! I entered Adarsh's house after all these years. One thing that I have understood is that he does not want us to be together again. He even approves of my relationship with Simon, and I did need his approval. I had told him so many times that there is no relationship between Simon and me, but he suspects that I have it.

Along with the other things that Nani has left for me, I found this box of old letters, which you and Nani had written to each other. While Nani's letters are very short and to the point, I am getting quite a bit of insight into your early life from your letters. It is interesting to read that you and Papa were practically kids when you had got married. How great it sounds to grow up with your husband and then be like his friend! Do you know that Adarsh's Kuldeep Kaka's son Lakshman was also into street fighting? He was a bit off track, just like Papa. I can't believe that Papa had ever been like this as I have always seen him so disciplined and focused like a proper army man. Nani has organised these letters into ten-year bundles, and I have read through the first bundle. It has been like a fairy tale so far! I will write to you once I have read further.

Please take care of Nanaji. He must be feeling really lonely. I can understand how he must be feeling without a partner, but I am glad that he will now come and stay with you.

Your dear daughter,

Janki

Later, at the dining table, Sujit admired the necklace for several minutes. Even while putting morsels of food into his mouth, he could not let go of the ancient ornament. "This necklace is really exquisite," he mumbled. "Hey, tell me one thing…"

"Go on; I know what you will ask," Meera said.

"Then, why don't you ask and answer it?" countered Sujit.

"You wanted to ask me what I intend to do with the things in this box," Meera said.

"Yes."

"I don't know yet whether I want to keep them."

"If you want to sell them, I am fine with it. It might actually fetch a good amount," teased Sujit.

"You are a dog."

"I know."

Dear Maa,

20 Aug 1990

What the hell have you done? What does your letter dated 19th Nov 1956 mean? Does it mean that you had sex outside your marriage? How could you? Papa has done so much for you. He took so much upon himself when you were miserable and alcoholic, and you did this to him! I had, at least, thought that even though you didn't love me, you had still worked hard to keep our family together and that you loved Papa. But you are a born politician, and you deserve to be what you are right now—a corrupt leader who only fills her own pocket in the name of charity. I know what you are up to in your Manav Sansthan.

Go to hell! I don't care if you loot innocent people. But you have stabbed Papa in the back, and I will not forget that.

My hands are trembling as I write this letter. Am I what you have told me? Am I Papa's daughter at all, or am I a product of your lust?

Janki

"Wow, I didn't know it would come and bite her like this. What if her father is some Javan and not your actual grandfather?" The two of them looked at each other after putting the letter down.

"Hold on to your horses. We know that this is not the case. She had confessed it later on to her husband, and I think the issue was sorted." Meera gave his hair a little tweak.

"Oh yeah, you are right! I had forgotten about that," Sujit rubbed his head.

"I think this is the initial shock of knowing something like this. And it will die down."

"Or get worse. I don't see your grandmother being the consoling type. She would have left your mother high and dry to think whatever she wanted to and not given any justification," Sujit said shrewdly.

"We'll have to see how everything shapes up."

Dear Maa,

10 Oct 1990

WHY DIDN'T YOU REPLY TO ME? Tell me who my father is, tell me if I belong to this family.

Don't even try to talk to me on the phone. I will not hear your terrible voice. Just reply with the details of my birthfather. I don't want to do anything with you anymore.

Janki

"You were right. This short yet powerful letter clearly tells us that my grandmother had given no explanation to her daughter," Meera rubbed her forehead.

"But why didn't she? They were so much happier right now. This small confusion could have led to a lot more issues." Sujit shook his head and put the letter aside.

"I don't think it was a small confusion as it cast aspersions on her existence. Anyone would panic if he had reason to suspect his paternity. Anyway, you can ask my grandmother when we meet her. You mentioned that she is still alive." Meera stood up and picked Jia up to put her to bed.

"Yeah, but she could be on a ventilator for all we know. Her sins must have accumulated at some point." Sujit carried his plate to the kitchen.

"We will find out," Meera replied.

Dear Maa,

6 May 1991

You are as evil as it can get and because of you, my angel, Meera will never look at my face again.

I had come to India to get answers, but you refused to meet me. I have warned you repeatedly, and I will tell Papa everything this time. You have to tell me what you have done, and who my father is. I will not leave India even if I have to stay back here for months.

I had promised myself that I would not write you another letter for my entire life. But I am writing it here. You must be laughing at me, thinking that I have gone crazy with all the drinking and marijuana and that I will kill myself and all your problems will be solved.

Meera had come to see me on her birthday yesterday. Adarsh had sent me her pictures earlier. But when I saw her—her beautiful innocent face as she entered the house after five years, I couldn't recognise her. I had been talking to Adarsh about her at least once a week, but I couldn't recognise her. It could have been because of the alcohol. She felt bad; I got to know it at once as after all, I am her mother, and I had got worried that she would leave me just as everyone else. I wanted her to stay with me, and this was when everything went wrong. I had thought that she would stay with me if she became like me. So, I had forced her to take marijuana.

What I had been thinking! I could see the look—scared and disgusted with hatred all over again, but I wanted her to be with me—to always stay with me, and I thought this was the only way out. Why didn't you just tell me who my father is? I would have never come to India, and this would never have happened. Simon keeps my drinking in check. He is also not there to support me. What will Meera think about me?

Adarsh and I had planned that Meera could spend some time with me in the US after a couple of years. But now that dream has been destroyed, and it is all because of you. How can I be sane when I now know that my entire life is a lie? Maybe, this is why you could never love me?

But whatever the case is, you have taken away my hope to live—you have taken away my angel from my life. God will never forgive you, and you will die alone and miserable.

Janki

"How do you remember this?" Sujit asked Meera.

"Kavita Maa had told me she was back to India for a couple of months and that she would really like to see me. As it was my birthday in a couple of weeks, I could even ask her for a present of my choice. I was eleven then, and more than meeting her, I was drawn to the idea of getting the present I wanted. So, I got all dressed up. Kavita Maa said that she would wait outside in the car. I think my mother was staying with her friend or someone else. When I went inside, it was dark. There were guys and girls all over each other—it was a bit awkward. Then she came out. To be fair to her, I didn't recognise her at first. Because of this, everyone had started laughing and I felt so embarrassed that I wanted to run away."

Meera paused at this point, but Sujit said, "Go on, Meera…"

With quivering lips, she continued, "She grabbed hold of me and started shouting. She was drunk and high, just as she has written. Everyone was screaming and it had got really chaotic until Kavita Maa came and pulled me out of her hands. I got a couple of scratches on my hands and legs, but she refused to let me go. Sameer was also hurt in the scuffle."

"Then what happened?"

"I never saw her again in my life. She is right; she had lost me that day," Meera said bitterly.

"It was a terrible incident, but it doesn't sound like something which could not have been mended."

"I was in child therapy for one year. Not because of only this, but in general," Meera grimaced.

"Yeah, I know. You had told me," Sujit said sympathetically.

"I still have social and emotional issues, and this is the reason I had to struggle hard to be a journalist. I wanted to overcome my fears," Meera said in a rush.

"You are doing well."

"Not well enough," Meera said, rubbing her forehead.

"Don't be hard on yourself." Sujit drew her close.

Meera closed her eyes. "But I do wish we had sorted out all this."

"Now that you have said it loud, we can deal with the problem," Sujit consoled her.

"This is not the first time I have thought about it, though," Meera said.

Dear Maa,

16 Jun 1991

I am leaving this letter with Adarsh. I have asked him to hand it over to you in-person. He will not judge you by your past. After reading the letter from 1957, he said that it does not say that you had had sex with that Javan, but I wanted to hear this from you.

Simon is here to take me back and I will go with him to never come back. Hopefully, this was our last meeting. May you rot in hell!

Janki

"Were your mother and Simon a couple? There is no mention of this in any of these recent letters," Sujit asked.

"Not sure. They could have been so, as he was the one who had sent these letters and this box," Meera replied wryly.

"But in that letter, he had said they were close friends. He did not mention himself as her husband."

"We'll have to read further to find out." Meera picked up the next letter.

Dear Maa,

5 May 1992

The more I think about you, the more I hate you. At times, I think this anger will consume me. Meera has had twelve sessions till now, one each month. And, each time she goes to the session, it kills me to think that this has happened because of me, but there is nothing I can do about it. Well, I can—I can do her good by staying away from her.

Simon insists that I continue writing letters to you. Do you know that I can even imagine killing you? But one thing that I acknowledge is the fact that I was high that day. It is my fault as well as yours, what has happened to Meera. She will never forgive me, and because you made me go through all this, I will never forgive you, either.

Out of habit, if you must know, I am not sending you these letters, so you won't read them, but anyway, here is the latest news—this is what has happened in my miserable life. There is hope in the form of Simon. He had proposed to me, but I declined. He understands that I may never be ready for a commitment again, but he is still ready to support me.

I have opened three more stores in the neighbouring states of California: one in Phoenix, Arizona, another in Carson City, Nevada, and the third one in Salem, Oregon. I keep myself busy so that I do not have to think about you or my angel.

I just hope that wherever she is and whoever she is with, she is happy and has a full life, unlike mine.

Don't worry; I am not dying tonight. Adarsh said that he would start the process of my reconciliation with Meera again in a couple of years because Meera doesn't want to hear anything about me now, and even Adarsh's parents won't agree to it.

I think now that I have realised my mistakes, I am able to breathe a little freely.

Janki

"It must feel terrible to go through these things as a child. It actually disturbs your entire outlook, doesn't it?" Sujit said.

"It does, but the love that I got from my entire family, and mind you, it's quite a big one, has helped me a lot. And now, after reading all this, I am realising that they—I mean everyone in my family—have never actually said anything against Maa—not even once in all these years," Meera said. "Even when I used to throw tantrums and call her names, they would never say anything at all."

"Why do you think they didn't?" Sujit asked.

"Maybe, at some level, everyone believed that things would go back to normal some day?"

"They never went back to normal, did they?" asked Sujit, putting the letter away.

"No, they didn't," Meera said.

Dear Maa,

15 Aug 1993

Happy Independence Day! Have I got independence from you? Maybe, not. But we are connected by birth, so that is a bit difficult. Am I still angry? To be honest, I do not have any feelings for you—none at all; or whatever they are, they are not of anger. But that does not mean I have forgiven you or that I have stopped looking for answers.

Meera, my daughter, is thirteen now. I remember when I was thirteen, you had sent me away to Dadi's house. Life is so funny! When I was younger, all I wanted was, to somehow stay with you. I used to cry through the entire night. Initially, Nani and then Dadi, or Rukmani Chachi, used to calm me down. Now that I am a woman, all I want is to be with my daughter. Life has given me neither a mother's love nor a daughter's affection.

I think, if I were to put it in perspective, I do not have time at all to think about you. With three stores and two more in the pipeline, Simon and I do not have time to live in the past. And, for me, my future, my Meera is more important than anything that had happened in the past.

Simon is another person who embarrasses me every time—at least once every few months, in front of our entire staff. He does it deliberately when we have our get-together, and all the reps are in California. He thinks this will put pressure on me, and I would say 'yes' to his marriage proposal. This time, I had to say 'yes' as it had been getting too much. Everyone was relieved that finally, something concrete had happened.

But when everyone had settled down and Simon was in his senses, I told him what we have now is fantastic, and I don't want to ruin it. I told him that I don't want to get into a relationship. I think he has accepted that and respects it. Anyone seeing us through their Indian specs will call us a married couple, anyway.

Adarsh had been shying away from telling me this. I had to get this out from Mala. My little angel has a boyfriend; his name is Samar.

I am so excited for her. I teased Adarsh that he has got a son-in-law now. This boy, Samar, makes it a point to visit their house once a week and meet everyone. Adarsh has sent me his photo. I hope Meera would marry him. He is quite good-looking, too; they will have beautiful kids.

I know I am going way ahead of the league, but it feels so good to know that your daughter is now old enough and that young boys are chasing her. Don't worry; she is not like me. I think that the boy is after her—not the other way round. Kavita, Mala and Adarsh have paid so much attention to her and inculcated such good values into her! Adarsh keeps on telling me that she is too good to be true. Perhaps, she thinks that she has to compensate for my actions, so she has matured ahead of her age.

She will never be like you or I—she will be the best that our family would have seen for generations.

Janki

"Your list is growing. First, that guy and now this one! How many have you kept in the closet?" Sujit looked up with a mock frown.

"Samar Rajput… I had almost forgotten him. I will look him up on Facebook and send him a friend request," Meera stood up, laughing.

"Hey, hello…" started Sujit.

"Don't be jealous; I love you, too. But not more than him," teased Meera and ran out of the room, wagging her thumb at Sujit.

Dear Maa,

29 Nov 1994

I had to fly back to California within three days of reaching there. A fire had broken out in one of our stores, and Simon needed me to be there. Papa is feeling better now, anyway. I should thank you for agreeing to stay away from the house for those three days when I had come to see him as I did not want to see you.

I did see Meera from a distance. She has grown into a beautiful girl; no wonder so many boys are after her!

Papa was happy to see me. We talked a lot. Actually, I did all the talking, and he listened to me. I told him all about Meera—I told him about Simon. He liked Simon—I showed him Simon's pictures.

One thing he told me was that everyone has skeletons in their closet, and at times, they tumble out. He told me about his keep and his son Manav who had died in an accident. I was not angry with him. How could I be given his current condition? He was expecting that I would walk away from him. It was part of his guilt that had kept him away from me; maybe that is why he told me everything. I couldn't be angry with him. He told me that you have known this for many years now. How did you manage to forgive him? In my case, I was not even married to Adarsh when I had my liaisons, and he still couldn't get over my past. But we have moved on, now. What about you? I did not know that you had been carrying so much weight on your shoulders. You have even named your NGO Manav Sansthan after his son.

I will still not send you this letter. I would probably never get an answer to my questions, but there is an ounce of respect that has been generated towards you in my heart. Maybe, one day, when we see eye to eye, I might ask you these questions in person.

Till then, take care of Papa.

Janki

"It is hard to do that, isn't it?" Sujit asked.

"Well, she was a bitch. She forgot everything that she did—the alcohol and everything!" Meera said with great irritation.

"Still…" Sujit remarked calmly.

"Don't worry. We are not sailing in the same boat as theirs."

"I hope not," Sujit said. Meera glared at him, but he was saved by the ringing of his phone.

"What do you mean by that?" snapped Meera.

"Nothing, read on…" said her husband and answered the phone.

"No, not now. I have to fly to Delhi," said Meera. "I am going for this party meeting coverage with a senior editor. I will speak to Papa, too. He will have to give answers to all my questions now."

"God save him!" Sujit pulled a face once he was done with his call.

Meera looked at him and folded the letter in her hands.

Meera
(2015)

Chapter 15

"SO, WHAT DID you find in those mysterious letters from your mother?" Adarsh asked, looking intently at Meera.

"Everything…" Meera said.

"Is that all you have got to say? Are you not angry at what I did to your mother?" Adarsh asked. He knew that he had to poke her hard for the volcano to erupt. Meera had been quiet since she came from Mumbai, and Adarsh knew that sooner or later, she would erupt and had been preparing himself for what she would say.

"I have spent half my life angry with one parent, and I will not spend the second half angry with the other," Meera said, kneeling by his chair.

"You are not angry, then? Don't you have any questions for me?" Adarsh asked in surprise.

"No, Papa. Trust me; I don't have questions for you. You did what you would have thought was right for yourself and me. Who am I to judge you?"

"I had imagined the conversation was going to be a lot different when you called and told me about the letters…" Adarsh said making a wry face.

Meera put her hand over her father's. "Did you think that I would come to fight with you? It's hard to fight for someone whom you have hated all your life, and this change in my emotions is not enough for a fight."

"Till where have you read so far?" her father asked. There was some relief on his face now.

"Till 1994 when Maa had to come to India as Nanaji fell ill."

"Ah, I can't forget that incident! I was the one who had gone to your grandmother and told her Janki wanted to see her father. She understood what I had meant without me putting anything into words. Her very next sentence was that she had some work in Mumbai and would have to leave the same day your mother arrived," Adarsh said.

Meera was perplexed. "Why did you help her when it had been clear that you did not want to have anything to do with her?"

Adarsh looked at her. "I had thought that you wouldn't have any questions for me?"

"Maybe, one or two," Meera said, sitting on the chair next to him.

"Fair enough; ask me what you want to know." And as if he was preparing for a battle, Adarsh slumped into his chair and closed his eyes.

"Like I had said earlier, why did you help her after you had left her to suffer in the first place? Why didn't you ever discuss all this? Why did you not tell me, ask me, or force me to open the box when she had died in 2001?" Tears were rolling down her cheeks as she tried to bombard her father with all the questions that she had held back for days.

"Hold on… one by one, Meera," Adarsh held up his hands to make her stop.

"Then, tell me one thing—how could you have been so selfish to put your ego before your daughter's happiness?" Meera accused with tears still rolling down her cheeks.

"I don't know where to start from…" Adarsh looked at her. The volcano within Meera had now indeed erupted as he had known it would, but he was finding it difficult to gather words.

"Start from wherever you like, but I want answers to all my questions."

Adarsh took a deep breath and said in a low voice, "Meera, you have to understand that your mother was an amazing woman—there is no doubt about it. Before meeting her, I had had two relationships which ended because the girls were seeing other guys too, besides me. So, once your mother had told me about her past, I could not live with that, and she had understood that it was more of my issue than hers."

He paused for a low cough and then continued, "You may call me selfish, but I loved your mother from the day I had seen her, and, at some level, I still do. That's why I never got married again. People told me that I could not be both mother and father, which might be true, but what guarantee was there that any new mother would have taken good care of you? Well, to be honest, I just couldn't get over the fact she had hidden all this from me, and all these were excuses that I made on the way. I know they seem paltry, but…"

It was clear that Adarsh was now making an effort to speak. His eyes narrowed and his words were coming slowly. "You know, I could never love her as the same earlier after we had got separated. There were numerous incidents that had brought us close—close enough for us to think of getting back together, but I think, by that time, the idea of us being together had been lost. Your mother said the final 'No'. I had had let her go once, and, by the time, I had got back to my senses, she was completely gone."

"Why? What happened?" Meera asked.

"It happened much later after your grandfather had died. I will leave that to your mother to tell you," Adarsh continued with his part of the story. "You asked me why I had helped her. To be honest, I don't know. Sorry, you must have been expecting a great tragic love story, but it was nothing of that sort. I guess that I had become used to her. 95% of the time, we used to talk about you. This gave me the strength to be the parent that you deserved. She would call me from the US at nights, and we used to talk for hours. It used to get awkward, at times, but I guess we didn't try to work out another option."

He paused for a moment as if to recollect a memory, and then said, "You know, she used to tell me what fun she had been having with Simon. I think there had been another guy, too, for a very brief period until Simon scared him away. He had to spend three nights in jail for that."

"Had they been together?" Meera asked.

"Yes and no. They were never engaged, I think, never married, either. But he was the only one for Janki, and Janki was the only one he had wanted for a friend. I used to tell them that they had become like an old couple who did not need anyone except each other in their lives."

"Why had she made him wait?" Meera asked.

"The only thing that she had ever wanted was you, and she hoped that one day you would turn up at her doorstep. She wanted to be there for you—that's all," Adarsh said.

"And I never went to her."

"You did actually, several times, but something terrible would happen every time. Because of that, you had drifted further away from her."

"Yes. I can recall having gone to her, for more than a couple of times," Meera said.

"You know what she used to say towards… towards her end?" Adarsh swallowed.

"What?" Meera prompted.

"She had said that whatever happened to her, was a sort of punishment for whatever she had done to her mother in her adolescence."

"Did you ever have any relationship after… like Maa had with Simon?" Meera asked hesitantly.

"I had you, and directly or indirectly, I had been still in a relationship with Janki. In fact, I want you to believe that she had been in a relationship with me."

"I wish that you guys could have got back together."

"I had wished it, too, but I guess that we had been so filled with the past baggage that we made mistakes for which we had to pay dearly later."

"Why didn't you try once I had become a little older?" asked Meera.

"We wanted to, but you had gone into a shell and had to be put in therapy. I had tried speaking to you several times, but all I got was a closed door.

"Kavita and Mala also tried, but we had hit a stone wall, and we realised that the risk would be greater than the reward," Adarsh said wearily.

"And, why hadn't you told me all this since 2001? In fact, you had never told me about Simon and my invitation to New York."

"We had spoken on the latter if you can remember, and for the first part of the question, I didn't know where to start from, and I also didn't know that you would get these letters to tell you the whole story from their point of view. I had just sort of let it go, and I am sorry for that."

"Did you read these letters?" asked Meera.

"No. Never! Not now, and neither, then. This was one of the things your mother hadn't shared with me," replied Adarsh.

"You should read those letters," said his daughter.

"I will do it now, probably. Are you done reading them?" asked Adarsh.

"Yeah, mostly. I am just left with Nani's letters from 1989 to 1994 and a couple of miscellaneous ones from 1995. That's it, and then I will be done with them," Meera said.

"What about after that year? They should have continued till 2001..." surmised Adarsh.

"Maybe, they had stopped writing and started using phones..." said Meera.

"I doubt it. Maybe, your Nani will be having some..." Adarsh said and called for tea.

"Did you go to see her?" inquired Meera.

"No, not recently. She had moved to her Sansthan in 2006-2007 when met her last, and there has been no reason for me to see her since then," Adarsh said.

"Has she ever wanted to see me?" asked Meera.

"She had wanted to, at least until we had last met. But I had told her, there was no point in complicating her life further. I have also not met her since then. But I know that she is still alive as I am her second next of kin after her nephew," Adarsh said.

"What is that one thing you would have done if you could turn back time?" Meera picked up a cup of tea and handed it to her father.

"I would never marry Janki! Do you have any more questions for me?" Adarsh took the tea from Meera.

"No, just tell me more about her. What had she been like?" Meera said, taking a sip of tea.

Adarsh shook his head. "This is a trap—this is the most difficult question."

"Take your time. I will set dinner. You can tell me over a dessert" Meera stood up and picked up her phone to call Sujit.

Shakuntala

(1989 - 1994)

Chapter 16

Dear Maa,

12 Jun 1989

Janki is doing well in the US. I had met Adarsh a couple of months ago, and he mentioned that she is more interested in some import-export business than in technology. I have suggested to him to deal in khadi as there could be a huge demand for Indian garments in the West in future. I have also introduced him to Mr Prakesh; we had worked together in 1977 in Andhra Pradesh, and benefited from the engagement in supplying clothes to the affected areas. I have asked Adarsh not to tell Janki that I have been helping her as I know she would not like it. It's better that she feels that it is Adarsh who has been doing so. Politics is a funny business. Do you know Mr Sinha? Yes, the opposition leader who had been the first to start with the mudslinging by writing a newspaper article about Manav Sansthan, and me. But when I offered him partnership in my deal with Ramesh and Co, he promptly agreed on the condition that the mudslinging would continue in public, but what we did behind closed doors was up to us.

Actually, he is a fool because he does not understand the larger picture. He is happy, making around 30-40% profit in land deals. What he does not understand is that the land will give us a lot more profit when we build our factory upon it. And, you know… I do everything for a social cause. With the government subsidy on land and basic amenities, Manav Sansthan would make huge money, of course, for social causes.

But there are those who do not understand my vision for Manav Sansthan. To be honest, I don't blame them as their land has been taken away from them. There would always be some people who are fool enough to go against me. One such thing had happened last week, but I have now ensured that it would not happen again.

I am sure that you must have read about it in the newspaper as it had created quite a scene. I had been invited to this school's golden jubilee function. During the distribution of the sports awards, and trust me, there were quite a few, I had to maintain a fake smile time while handing out the children their awards. Once everything was over, they asked me to go and give a motivational speech to the leaders of the units who had participated in the march past.

It happened when I was about to complete my speech, I hadn't known, at first, what struck me, but one of the students threw cow dung at me. Thankfully, nothing hit my face, but my saree was completely soiled. No, I hadn't done anything then, but I did ask the boy why he had done that, to which he said that I had taken his land and home. Goodness knows who puts this poison in the minds of these young children!

It did not take me long to find out who his father was, and I made this boy see reason when my men broke his father's leg. He has to learn a lesson, and he would have known it by now that he is working for Manav Sansthan as a cleaner. I have also ensured that he does not go to any school. Don't worry; they will not go anywhere outside and speak against me. I have also ensured this.

It has to be understood that these things indicate that I am not in control of my constituency, which is something I can never let happen, with so much being at stake.

I know what you would say, but we have to do things like this to maintain our position. We can't let the image slip; else, everything would be finished.

I have booked your tickets for a trip to Europe, and as I had informed you in my last letter, we might meet in Switzerland.

Your beti,

Shakuntala

Meera had returned just a couple of hours ago. The first thing that she did upon her return was to bring Sujit up to date about her discussion with her father. And, as soon as that was out of the way, the two started going through the letters.

"I should get these letters published in my newspaper—they will be a huge scoop," Meera said.

"No one will care now about a politician who had done something in the Stone Age. But wait, let me show you something. If I am not wrong…" Sujit went out of the room, preoccupied with his own thoughts.

"Where are you? What are you doing in the attic?" Meera called out to him.

"Just a minute!" Sujit shouted back.

Sujit came back, holding an old-looking trophy and asked, "Do you know what this is?"

"Your ancient award. You have so many of them in that trunk, upstairs," Meera said with a hint of pride.

"Yes and no. Now listen, this is very special. Read what it says," Sujit told Meera.

"Awarded by MP Shakuntala Devi Saxena on 26th of May 1989," he read it out.

"OMG!" Meera jumped up.

"Yeah, and you know, I remember that incident about the cow dung thrown at… your grandmother. Three or four of us had planned it together, but at the last minute, we had chickened out, and Shyam was the only one who could gather the courage to do so. And so, now you know what had actually happened…" Sujit said.

"So, did he study any further?"

"For at least a couple of months, he did not. Then, our principal went and brought him back. The principal retired sometime later, but he had done this one last good thing for Shyam. And hey, do you know one funny thing? Shyam had joined an NGO some years ago, and if I am not mistaken, it was Manav Sansthan. Let me call him and ask."

Sujit called Shyam to confirm what he had read and found out that he was indeed working at Manav Sansthan.

"Is he seeking revenge or something? Should we warn your grandmother?" Sujit said apprehensively after the phone call.

"Later. Let's first finish this pile." Meera pulled Sujit down beside her.

"Yeah, but isn't it amazing that your grandmother had given me an award?" Sujit said, still thinking about the incident.

"It is," Meera said.

"You know… these awards that I got in the 8th and 9th standards, had inspired me to become what I am today. And now having known the other side of the story, I am a bit shocked that these politicians inspire and praise you on your face, but all they want is, to just get over with it!" Sujit said pensively.

"I am not defending her, but isn't that the case everywhere?" asked Meera.

"Can be. But when you are young, all you know is that you have received an award from someone important," said Sujit.

"Maybe, we can question her about this when we meet her," suggested Meera.

"When you meet her! I have absolutely no intention of meeting her."

Dear Maa,

4 Nov 1991

I am all alone. I don't trust anyone to confide my thoughts in. Shekhar is there, but he does not want to get involved in anything related to Manav Sansthan. I have realised it now that you are gone—How lucky I had been to have had you as a mother! I can confidently say that I had not been the best of daughters for you. At times, I felt you loved Janki more than I.

For me, you haven't gone. For me, you are still here, guiding me at each step. I will continue to write letters to you each year, at least once, even though I know that no one would read them. I hadn't got to know until very late that you had left all my letters to Janki. I am sure that you must have thought that if she reads these letters, she would understand my perspective. But your approach was completely wrong. I have written to you my innermost secrets—those things that no one knows about and no one should. The letters that you had given to her, had my incident with the Javan, which both Shekhar and I had been done with. And now, that has come back to haunt me among so many other things. Maa, it's not your fault—it's mine. Now I can't even reason this with you. I don't know what you have had in mind, but after losing you, I also did not think about these incidents and had given the letters to her as per your wish. I hope she does read the rest of the letters to know that nothing had happened that night. But by the tone of her letters, it looks like she will never read any of them again.

She is asking for answers—she is asking me to prove my innocence and my loyalty towards my husband. I will not do that. Anyway, she has not given me any peace since she has been born. Why bother trying for it, now? I am fed up with her. It's good that she is no longer in India.

I have a bigger fish to fry, than to deal with the tantrums she gets into once every five years. There is something seriously wrong with her. I have discussed this with Shekhar, too and he thinks that time will heal everything and that I do not have to justify myself to her.

Things haven't been good since you left me. You had guided me—steered me away from all my problems, and now I have no one to look up to. Do you know… I had to call the same journalist from Lucknow to save me this time by burying the recent issue. I had been relying far too much on him, and he has also started showing signs that he has some authority over me. He is wrong and will be corrected, but I have to keep quiet for now.

It's simple, Maa; there are many people who need help from Manav Sansthan, and if we have taken government grants to construct centres across India, why is this a problem for these people? It's not that I would eat up the money. They can see the buildings and daily operations very well which cost money. There was also this local municipal commissioner who did not understand this. Now, what is my fault if he is dead in an accident? They are linking everything with me, and this has created tensions with our partner Ramesh and Co, too. They don't want to be dragged into this mess, as they have threatened to withdraw support if it continues. Their hypocrisy is now apparent. When they needed land for the factories, I had got it for them then at a decade-old rate, and now when I am having issues, they are running away.

Maa, rest in peace. I know that you are looking after me from up there, and your prayers are with me. This, too, shall pass.

I miss you, Maa, I miss you a lot. Papaji has become very weak since you have gone as he is not keeping well. I am just worried what I will do when both of you would be gone.

Your beti,

Shakuntala

"But what is wrong in clarifying a simple thing?" Meera asked in frustration.

"I think it is ego," said Sujit.

"It is more than ego. Did you read she has written that Janki had been a problem since the start and that she didn't owe her any explanation and all that? I think she had reached that stage in life where she did not even care about her," Meera said in a serious tone.

"Isn't it because she had been actually causing trouble for you, them, and, in fact, for everyone around?" Sujit asked.

"But isn't everyone who had been around to be blamed for that?" Meera said pensively.

"I don't know. After a certain age and time, it's all your decision. No one can preach to you for your entire life. You have to take responsibility for your actions," Sujit reflected.

"I don't know where you are taking this discussion to. I am just saying that people should communicate with each other to resolve minor issues; else, it does not take much time for them to become major ones," Meera remarked.

"Agreed."

Dear Maa,

4 Dec 1991

Maa, this year has been worse than the last. You had left me last year and see what's happening to your daughter! Look at Janki... look at her forcing her own daughter to have drugs! That is a horrendous act, and she should be sent to jail. If it were not for Adarsh, I might have done so. I don't know why I am cursed with a daughter like her. On the one hand, she has been doing well. Her relationship with that American is going on steady, and her business is also doing well. I get all the news from Prakesh who had been to the US thrice in the last couple of years. And, on the other hand, she has done this. I don't know what to do. She is still after me to give her answers. We don't speak at all now, but I know why she is after me, and she will not get it from me.

Papaji's health has started improving, but he is worried about me. He misses you a lot, Maa. I miss you, too, and wish you had been here with me in this difficult period.

It has been difficult for Manav Sansthan as well. The High Court has ordered a state-level inquiry into the assets and operations of the organisation. They will not find anything; I am sure of this. This is merely an inconvenience to me rather than any trouble. These newspapers are hilarious. They are saying that it is the end of an era—an era of corruption and that people of India will give me justice now. They also say that it is the end for me, and I will rot in jail once the inquiry has submitted the reports and the judgement arrives.

What they don't know is that I am so deep that they cannot, for that matter, touch a single strand of my hair, let alone finish me. Let them pray, Maa, because they will not have anywhere to hide once I strike back.

The only issue I have is that they have frozen the assets of Manav Sansthan and because of this, all my units, where we have people to take care of, are suffering. In the interim, there are many beneficiaries who have been supporting us with running day-to-day operations. All future projects have been put on hold, and all this is costing me crores. They had even taken Bhairav into custody, but we had seen this coming early on, and were prepared.

Maa, I need your guidance, like always; I need your help to come out of this situation. Even Shekhar has not been supportive. I don't have anyone to discuss this with.

Your beti,

Shakuntala

"Don't worry. I had read about it when I first looked up the NGO," Sujit said in a matter-of-fact manner.

"I am not worried at all. This does not have any impact on me," Meera said.

"But, you must be curious to know if your dearest Nani had gone to jail."

"Well, did she?"

"No. Her organisation was cleared of all charges. There are people who are still trying to find needles in the haystack, but it's stale food now," said Sujit.

"Good to know." Meera let out a sigh of relief.

"That means that all the funds are still there in the safe havens of the Swiss banks."

"Maybe," said Meera.

"When I had married you, I didn't know that you were so rich," Sujit teased.

"Your love makes me rich," said Meera, putting her head on to his shoulder.

Dear Maa,

24 Dec 1992

Another year has gone by without you. Another year of struggle has ended, and now I feel that things are looking up. The past two years had been really bad—much worse than Janki's teenage years, when she had slept with every boy in the city, or when I had been in and out of hospitals, getting treated for various mental issues. They had written me off at one time, and I had been at a worse place than those years when I had lost my two babies.

You are not with me. Janki still hasn't been talking to me; she is already dead for me. Manav Sansthan has also almost faced a shutdown. My political role was saved as I had not been involved directly in its operations, at least, on paper. There had been huge pressure from the High Command that I resign on moral grounds.

All because you had not been there to protect or guide me as you had always done when you were alive.

I had met your great granddaughter, our lovely Meera yesterday. I had asked Adarsh to bring her along to the Manav Sansthan Reignite Ceremony, which he did. I immediately recognised her. She looks just like Janki; she has her smile and eyes. For a second, I had felt that Janki was looking at me with a sense of betrayal in her eyes and anger lurking behind that gorgeous smile. But I was pulled out of my illusion only when she said 'Namaste, Aunty'. My own granddaughter was not acknowledging me! I looked at Adarsh, and he signalled to me to let the moment pass. I confronted him later, and he promised that he would talk to Meera about him, me, and our family.

She must have felt awkward as my eyes were following her the entire night—the entire time she had been in the hall. Her way of talking, walking—her gestures… everything reminded me of Janki. I wish she had been there with me. Surprising, isn't it?

With your blessings, the clouds of despair have begun to scatter, and a new beginning awaits. I will have to shine brighter now. But before I can do that, I need to ensure that all those serpents who had shown their fangs meet their proper fate.

Your beti,

Shakuntala

"I don't remember this encounter at all," Meera said.

"Well, you didn't know who it had been. For you, it was just another unimportant event where Papa had dragged you," Sujit said reasonably.

"True," Meera acknowledged. "But it's curious to know how often our paths have crossed without us knowing about it, including yours as well."

"True," said Sujit.

Dear Maa,

27 Dec 1993

I had almost missed writing to you this year, but I promise that I will make a greater effort next year.

Janki is still not speaking to me nor have I made any attempt to contact her. But she is doing really great in the USA, creating an empire of her own.

Several things have happened this year, but the best for me has been the earthquake in Maharashtra. Our base camp was in Osmanabad—the area that had been the worst affected by the earthquake. My heart goes out to the 10000-12000 victims of the natural disaster, and we did our best to support the affected. But this had also been an opportunity to put Manav Sansthan back on track, restore its sheen and give a fitting reply to those who had maligned its image and purpose. All this has been possible due to our work in Osmanabad, for which the efforts were undertaken by me, Ramesh and Co, and our supporters in the West. All the discordant voices have been silenced now.

The links which I have made, sometimes, scare me. I have not even discussed them with Shekhar as he won't be able to handle them due to his ill-health. Papaji and I are worried about him, but he worries about Janki and misses her a lot. They do speak to each other, but not as often as earlier, and the strain in their relationship is still apparent.

Your beti,

Shakuntala

"Evil! Pure evil! Thank God that she is not a part of our lives," Sujit whistled.

"Well, it's just perspective, isn't it?" asked Meera.

"Yeah, you will find those who support her actions. But, in general, I feel that we have had a much simpler life without her being around," said Sujit.

"I don't know about that. I am really curious to know how Manav Sansthan and Maa's Khadi business in the US function now."

"Simon can tell you about the latter. Give him a call," Sujit said reasonably.

"No, not now. I need to finish the remaining letters and then speak to my grandmother, if at all, after all these years, she is still willing to speak to me about it."

Dear Maa,

12 Dec 1994

Shekhar is so ill that I am scared that he would leave me as you did. His health has completely deteriorated.

Janki had come to see him on the condition that I would not be there. Adarsh had come to tell me this—he did not actually say it, but I had understood and since the Winter Session of Parliament was about to start, and I had some pending work in my constituency as well, I left them alone.

I have also consolidated the operations of his printing press with Manav Sansthan. He might not like it but I don't have any other option or time to manage it alone.

It all seems so unreal, so unnecessary! Why do I have this anger for my daughter when she is the only one I am left with? Where will I take all this wealth that has been sitting as the mountains? I will not take anything with me—not a single paisa, and whom it should all go to, doesn't even want to see my face even when her father is on his deathbed. Whom do I leave it all to?

I can leave everything to Meera, but that would mean Janki will not get anything. What, if in the future, she would come back and manage Manav Sansthan with Bhairav and his family?

Sometimes, I feel that I should leave everything, and just sit and watch Janki managing things, advising her if she needs and watch Meera growing up. All I have done in my life seems meaningless now as I don't have anyone to share it with.

I will try to reconcile with Janki and even convince Adarsh and Janki to get back together for the sake of Meera. I know that it is probably too late, and I should have attempted this long ago, but I had been stuck in a world which, in the end, has given me only loneliness.

I now know what you had meant; why you had always tried to make me see reason and why you had always tried to make me aware of my greed.

But I think now it's too late for me.

Your beti,

Shakuṇtala

"Retribution time!" Meera said with sarcasm dripping into her voice.

"For all we know, it could have been just another ploy—another phase and then back to square one," said Sujit, looking at her.

"Yeah, we don't know that yet."

"When will you contact her?"

"I am thinking of contacting her now, or should I just read the remaining letters from 1995 as those are the last ones that we have?" asked Meera.

"Yeah. Might as well complete them and see if there are any more shockers," remarked Sujit.

Janki
(1995)

Chapter 17

Dear Maa,

23 Feb 1995

A lot has happened on this trip, and I am grateful to you for calling me. I know that it had been short, but at least I got to spend time with Papa, and I am grateful to you for this. I am grateful to you for other reasons as well. You have unknowingly given hope to Papa, and now he can leave us in peace. Yes, I want him to go to the other side as I can't see him suffer now that he is on ventilator. There is little hope, and I don't want him to suffer. I had met Papa when he was still in his senses. He was happy to see me by his side; in fact, he was happy to see all of us by his side. After all these years, I didn't mind sharing space with you, and I think you also didn't mind it. Sickness and birth bring families together, don't they?

His one wish, which is difficult for me fulfil, is to get back with Adarsh. I knew what he had meant when he had held our hands. I could sense that his weak hand was trying to take my hand towards his other hand, in which he was holding Adarsh's hand. He might have sensed the resistance in my hand, though and dropped the idea, but things are different now.

Adarsh had come to the room to drop me off the first night when I was staying at the hotel, I couldn't say 'no' to you when you had asked me to stay with you and Papa from the next day onwards. It had actually given me an opportunity to stay with Papa and… and with you a little longer.

It so happened that when Adarsh came to drop me, I asked him to stay for a little longer. I was confused as I had been evaluating what Papa wanted to happen, and I guess Adarsh also wanted to. One thing led to another, and there we were, close to each other after two decades. It felt, good, it felt complete—I have never felt the same with Simon.

I did not know what to do next. Adarsh did not speak with me for the entire day. He was supposed to come home as we had planned earlier, but he came in very late and had gone away immediately. He also shied away from making eye contact. I will not be surprised if he comes and tells me that he regrets what had happened.

You might call me selfish, but I also think that it should not have happened. However good I may feel, it still does not mean that I can bring this to a logical conclusion.

Simon has been waiting for me in the US, and I know he is better for me in every way. We have a good partnership, and I cannot leave all that, can I?

The moment I think that my life has been going steady, something happens. Whoever is writing my fate, does not like me, for sure.

Your daughter,

Janki.

"So, this is what Papa had wanted my mother to tell me," Meera said with irritation.

"Well, for one thing, we know that they did not get back together. Otherwise, we wouldn't be sitting here, reading these letters," Sujit said.

"Yeah, but it does not make sense. If she had been with Simon, why did she still spend the night, or maybe nights with Papa in India?" Meera said, agitated.

"How do you know that Maa and Simon had been like together… together?" asked Sujit.

"It doesn't make sense. I think this was very careless of them."

Sujit tried to calm her down. "Why are you getting worked up?"

"I feel that there had been too much action in their life. Why couldn't they just get on with their separate lives and stay where they had been?" Meera shook her head in annoyance.

"You have to ask your mother… oh, sorry… maybe, you can visit Simon and ask him about his relationship with your mother?" Sujit suggested.

"Are you mad? I will not go all the way to the US to just ask that!" exclaimed Meera.

"I think you should, and you will go. He is a very important piece of this puzzle."

Meera contemplated. "You think so?"

"Yes," said Sujit firmly.

Dear Maa,

5 Apr 1995

I had to tell him. I couldn't just hide it from him as, after all, it's his child as well. Don't think it otherwise, as I am certain that this child is Adarsh's. I was in India when it had happened just before Papa expired, and Simon had been, anyway, into a different relationship for the last couple of months. That's how I know.

I was also not surprised by Adarsh's reaction. He didn't have anything to say. After all the time we had spent together, he didn't have anything to say! But I am not angry with him; I also don't want this child as I had not been a good mother in the past, and I can never be one in the future. Whatever I say or do, history will always remember me as a bad mother, and my own child will always remember me in the same way. Adarsh says this child does not have a future as far as his or her parents are concerned, so why do we need to complicate another life even before it is born? I do agree with him.

I also did not know what Simon had planned for me. For the nth time, he proposed to me and for the nth time I had said no, but yes, I did tell him about this incident—I mean I could not have hidden such an important thing from him. To my surprise, he is willing to give his name to the child, but it is not fair on him, either. I know how much he loves kids, and I am sure he will love this child as well, but at the end of the day, it will not be his, and moreover, I have not yet decided if I want to live with him.

Simon has been the one thing in my life which is not jinxed with my bad luck, and I don't want to spoil what we have by getting married.

Adarsh had told me that we can get back together, but I had to come back to India. I don't mind coming back to India, and now that I am on speaking terms with you, I have more than one reason to come back with the primary one being Meera.

But do you think that I should take the plunge? What good will come out of this self-pity that Adarsh has for me? What if he cannot live with my relationship with Simon tomorrow? What will happen to this new life then, and what will happen to Meera? She will be the first one to get disturbed by this sudden and unexpected change.

I now know what I have to do, and I pray to God that he gives me strength.

Your daughter,

Janki

"I WANT TO BURN THESE LETTERS!" Meera jumped and screamed.

It was a sudden shock to Sujit who had been engrossed in the letter. "Hey, calm down! What happened?"

"WHAT HAPPENED, YOU ASK? I SHOULD NEVER HAVE READ THESE FILTHY LETTERS." Meera didn't even know that tears were running down her cheeks—tears of anger.

"HEY, calm down! Jia will wake up." Sujit caught hold of her shoulders and shook her.

"I should not have read these letters!" Meera said with tears in her eyes and collapsed into the sofa.

Sujit rushed to her and asked, "Why are you so angry?"

"How could they do it? The two of them had done so much wrong as far as I was concerned, and in their lust, they wanted to get another child into this world so that they could torture him or her as well." Meera was openly sobbing now.

"For all you know—you might be having a brother or sister somewhere," reflected Sujit.

"No. I don't think so. Papa couldn't have kept this from me," Meera said, quietening down a bit. "I am just disgusted with these guys."

"I think you are overreacting."

"Overreacting, you said? You don't know what it means to live a life like this—constant fear, the constant building of hope, and then the crashing down again like a house of cards. You don't know anything." Meera buried her face into her hands.

Sujit put his arm around Meera and drew her close. "Probably not, but at least, this incident did not have an impact on you then, and it should not have it now, either. That is what I am saying."

"It is! All of this is having an impact on me. Do I regret my decision to open these letters?" Meera put her head on his shoulders.

"No, I don't. The way I see this is—these things are coming before you, but you are fighting and winning against demons that you have had stored in this head of yours for all these years," Sujit said, running a hand over her hair.

"I just want to get over with this." Meera, now calmer, picked up the next letter.

Dear Maa,

5 May 1995

Today is Meera's birthday, and as every year, she is far away from me. As the years pass, she will just remember me as a mother whom she had never wanted because she regards Kavita as her mother, anyway.

And, I have killed any hope now that her parents would get back together. With the abortion, Adarsh and I have closed all openings for reconciliation, and I don't think we will get close again, ever—not even if we would be the last people on this planet.

Simon has been very supportive of me throughout the phase. I might well say 'yes' to him in a couple of years if I find enough courage to be in a committed relationship with him. But, for now, I need some time to just heal myself.

After Nani, Papa, and now my own child, whom I have not allowed to come into this world... What had been his fault? Only, that he had me as his mother.

But all of us—Simon, Adarsh and I—believe that it would not have been fair for him or her to live a life like Meera's. I have already troubled my angel, and I could have made the same mistake again.

Simon said that he is ready to adopt kids if I don't want my own. But it is not fair on him, if he parents my child or an orphan, for he can't compromise his life because of me, and I won't let that happen, either. I think I should start looking around for a suitable partner for him, who will give him the love he deserves.

Lastly, Maa, I do not feel sorry, and I have no regrets. I know my decision concerning my abortion was the correct one.

Your daughter,

Janki

"What do you want to do now?" Sujit asked, putting the letter down.

"What can I do now?" Meera countered.

"Do you want to read them? Only two are left, or pack everything and dump them into the attic, or burn them?"

"I don't think the letters can give me anymore answers. The only two people who can, are my father and my grandmother," reflected Meera.

"Why don't you finish these two as well and then take all the questions at once to them?" Sujit suggested.

Shakuntala
(1995)

Chapter 18

Dear Maa,

30 Mar 1995

Shekhar has left me, too. Well, it is better for him since he had been suffering a lot since last year. But it was not his age to go. He was a soldier. How could he have been so weak and leave me like this?

Now, I don't know anyone to go to and no one whom I can trust. You know how people in politics are. I have told the party High Command that I won't be contesting the next General Elections and asked them to relieve me from all the party duties as well. In my last years, I will now focus only on running Manav Sansthan, not the way I wanted it to run, but the way Shekhar wanted it to. This is the only way I would be able to pay tribute to him. This is the only way I could look him into his eyes when we meet on the other side.

For whom will I do this? Janki has created her own world; she doesn't want my money, and I can't give Meera mine. Adarsh had come and helped me with Shekhar's last rites, but why will he come back now? There is nothing for him here.

One thing that Shekhar had done before he passed away was to get Janki to forgive us. We had failed her as parents… I, and only I, have failed her. It was Shekhar who kept the family together. He made my daughter talk to me and stay with me for some time, and I am happy to tell you that she was happy when she was leaving for the US. She must have thought that she would be alone in life. She has not regarded me as her mother for a long time now, and I know she must have thought that after her father, there would be no one whom she could call family. But she had been happy when she was going back. She was happy that she still has family in Adarsh and me. Hopefully, one day, Meera will also realise that her mother is not the bad person she thinks now.

But, Maa, I will be lying if I say that I am not concerned about Janki. She had got close to Adarsh when she came this time. I just hope that they handle the situation carefully with Meera if at all they want to come back together. For Meera, her mother is actually far away, but if she comes back into her life, I don't know if they will be able to handle it. History is repeating itself. I am concerned that the same thing that happened between Janki and I, will happen between Janki and Meera, too. I just don't want Janki to make the same mistakes I had done...

I just wish the best for my daughter.

Your beti,

Shakuntala

"What would you have done, Meera? Would you have accepted your mother?" Sujit asked Meera, looking at her with narrowed eyes.

"I don't know. Probably I would have. I have always longed for her, even when I hated… and still do, at some level. Even though I had hated her, I wanted to be with her. It's a feeling I can't explain." Meera shook her head.

"I can understand… So, are you ready to end this journey with the last letter?" Sujit asked.

"How do you know that there are no more letters?" asked Meera.

"You can check the box."

"No… I mean how do you know that when I go to see my grandmother, she won't hand me letters from 1995 to 2001? She had died in 2001. There must have been some communication between them," Meera said.

"Yeah, but by then, the phone had been starting to gain ground," said Sujit.

"I think this had been a family ritual thing rather than a communication tool," Meera reflected.

"Hmm… we have to wait and see," said Sujit.

Dear Maa,

7 Sep 1995

I might go to the US next year for a couple of months after my retirement from politics. I just want to spend some time with Janki and live with her. I also want to know how it feels to live with your daughter, especially when you and your daughter are not after each other's throats. No, Maa, you can see me from up there. I will not do anything now to spoil the equilibrium between your granddaughter and I and the state where we are into.

I have also created a trust into which I have moved the assets that I can show and made Janki and Meera its nominees. Adarsh had shown some resistance earlier, and I had to reason with him, but he ultimately agreed. Meera is not 18 yet; he signed the documents as the guardian, but he would need to get Meera's signature when she turns 18 and submit it to the trust if he wants the money, and why wouldn't he? All these years of hard work that I have done along with Manav Sansthan and the money that I earned—where will all of that go? It will go to Janki, and after that, to Meera, unless Janki decides to have a family of her own with Simon. In that case, they can make arrangements according to the guidelines that I have set. But I have made sure that neither Meera nor Janki will have to suffer because of the money. You know… there is a common saying: Maa, they have so much money that seven generations can sit at home, and there will still be some left for the coming ones to spend. Irrespective of what Adarsh says now, I know he will get those signatures when Meera turns 18, and I will make sure that Janki gets her share while I am still alive. I am going to the US to convince her to come back and handle Manav Sansthan. I don't have the energy now to carry on in this way, at least.

But Maa, there is also another popular saying that goes thus —Once you are into politics, it doesn't leave you. That's so true! The more I try to keep myself away from the dirt, the more it comes back and shows up its ugly face. I know that I had promised that after Shekhar was gone, I would only focus on social issues instead of anything for myself, but I have to put these problems to rest once for all. I had tried to reason it out with him and I tried to threaten his family, and I even took away all that he had had and left him nowhere to go. Still, he is back again.

I have to now lay him to rest, give him the peace that he had been looking for. I know everyone can be bought except this guy. He has to have something else. I have seen different layers of dirt, and I have always done what was required, and now, Maa, this is required.

Maybe, this is the last thing I will do.

Shakuntala

"And here we go. Your grandmother has made us accomplices in murder," Sujit remarked wryly.

"We don't know yet what has happened as this doesn't say anything clearly. Of course, it is not admissible in any Court of Law," said Meera.

"I know, but there has to be something in the closet," said Sujit.

"Let's find out. I will try and call her tomorrow." Meera gave a big yawn and stretched her arms.

Meera

(2015)

Chapter 19

MEERA HAD LOOKED at her phone for the hundredth time that morning. Her phone stared back at her with its blank face. It didn't help her to gather the courage to dial the number. At times, she did try to press the green button, and could even hear the ring a few times, but she would disconnect the phone immediately.

It had been evening when Sujit came back from work. He sat across Meera, putting the phone on loudspeaker. Meera prayed that the Manav Sansthan office was closed, or her grandmother was out of city for months, or something like that, or dead.

"Hello," said a strong female voice on the other side.

Meera's heart sank. Could it be her? But no, it couldn't! She would not pick up the phone at the reception.

"Hello, is this Manav Sansthan?" Sujit asked.

"Yes, that's where you have dialled, sir. What can I do for you?" asked the voice politely on the other end.

"Can we speak to Shakuntala Devi Sexena?" he inquired.

"You can, but you have to take an appointment and give a reason for the meeting. She is very selective in meeting people. May I ask your name and the purpose of your visit?"

"My name is Sujit. I am her granddaughter, Meera's husband," Sujit replied.

There was a long pause.

"Hello," Sujit said again, moving his mouth closer to the phone.

"I have been with Madam for twenty-five years now. Why have you decided to call now?" the receptionist asked in a surprised tone.

Tears rolled down Meera's cheek. She wanted to say a lot of things, but only air came out.

"Can we meet her?" Sujit asked, his voice getting more muffled for the second, seeing Meera in this state.

"I will call her now and then call you back on your number," she said and disconnected the phone before Sujit could say, "Thank you".

Meera and Sujit had been at the phone and would jump at each notification from news and social media apps, but the phone did not ring for another hour. When it did, it was Adarsh on the line.

"Hello, Papa," Meera said, trying to hold back her urge to cry again. She didn't know why she was getting so emotional now considering she had been nowhere close to this state while reading the letters.

"Meera beta, are you okay? You sound as if you have cried a lot." There was worry in Adarsh's voice.

"No, Papa, I am fine. How are you?" Meera asked.

"Beta, your Nani had called me just now. Have you wanted to see her?" he asked.

Meera looked at Sujit. They both wondered why she had called Adarsh instead of them.

"Yes, I have read all the letters. I think now it is time to face the devil herself," said Meera sarcastically.

"Don't say that. She is worried that you will vent your anger on her and she doesn't feel that she can take it anymore," Adarsh said.

"Chill, Papa! That was just an idiom. I have no plans to vent my anger on anyone. Please call and tell her that I just want to meet her. I have a few questions for her—that's all."

"Are you sure about this? Will now be fine?"

"Why not? Yes, I am sure!"

"Okay then, goodbye."

"Bye."

The next time when the phone rang, it was an unknown number. Meera knew this was it. She was opening a door in her life, and she would not be able to close it again.

"Hello" Meera said in a shaky voice.

"Hello…" It was a long hello on the other side, and it was her. It was a sweet but firm voice, and this way of saying "hello" could only be her style. It suited her, Meera thought.

"Meera, here."

"I know," Shakuntala said. "Are you okay? How are dear Jia and your useless husband?"

With the phone still on the loudspeaker, Meera and Sujit looked at each other, stunned. She might have known about Jia from Papa, but why did she call Sujit useless?

"Sorry… did I hear you clearly? Did you just call my husband useless?" Meera said, with a rising edge in her voice.

"Ah, don't worry. I call all husbands useless, who listen to everything their wives say. I am just joking; can't this old woman joke? I know he takes good care of you," Shakuntala said.

She probably knows more about Sujit and I than we had realised, Meera thought.

"Are you still there? What happened? You have called me for the first time. Why had it taken you so long?" Shakuntala asked.

Meera drew a breath and said, "I have read yours and Maa's letters and just wanted to meet you as it seems the next logical thing to do. I have a few questions for you, if you could…"

"Oh, those letters," Shakuntala cut in. "Where did you get them, and how much have you read so far?"

"I had got them in 2001 when Maa's things were sent back from the US. But I opened the box recently, and I have read all of them."

"Then, we certainly need to talk. You can come anytime you like."

"I will come next week on Tuesday," said Meera.

"Okay, beta. See you, then."

"Bye."

"Bye, beta," Shakuntala said and put the phone down.

As soon as Meera disconnected the phone, she hugged Sujit.

"Why did you say next week? You could have gone tomorrow as well. It's only a few minutes drive from here," said Sujit.

"I just need some more time," Meera said.

"You are so near… and…"

"...and yet so far," Meera completed the sentence.

Meera looked outside the window as the world was going on with its daily chores. Though the drive was not more than 45 minutes from her house to the centre, she didn't want to drive nor wanted Sujit to accompany her on this first visit.

She imagined an old woman holding a tiny hand, helping her and teaching her granddaughter how to cross the road. She couldn't understand why she was getting a feeling now that she had missed out on that. She has had her Dadi's love, then, why was she feeling this big gap in her life now?

She walked past the main door of the building and was greeted by an elderly receptionist. I might have spoken to her, Meera thought.

"How can I help you today, Meera?" the receptionist asked in a motherly tone.

"You know my name. I mean, you know who I am?" Meera said.

"Well, the staff here is pretty old, and we are like a family. Madam's family is our family. We have all seen your pictures and have celebrated your birthdays with Madam; we even had a big party last year when Jia was born. She is so adorable," the lady replied.

Meera didn't know what to say. Even if she tried, she knew nothing would come out.

Sarita, the receptionist, sensed this and came out from behind her desk to hug her, saying, "Don't worry! We are happy to see you finally, and I am sure Madam will be, too."

Meera nodded a 'yes' as Sarita showed her the way.

Meera glanced at her as she entered a big oak door into her chambers. *She has got some style,* Meera thought. *After all, some of the money from her Swiss account has to show up somewhere.*

And then, the moment had arrived. Shakuntala was in the room, standing right before Meera.

She looks like an older version of my mother, Meera thought.

Shakuntala came closer and put her hands on Meera's head. She ran them to her cheeks and gave her a kiss.

"You look so much like Janki, just a bit prettier than her!" she said and smiled.

"I was thinking the same for you, Maa looked like you!" Meera smiled.

"Come, come, beta! Sit, sit with me. Let me see you. These old eyes want to see you as much as they can. I am not sure when I will see you again."

"What do I call you?" Meera asked.

Shakuntala was surprised at the question, but she held her composure and said, "You can call me anything you wish to. I am your Nani. I used to call my Nani 'Amma'; you can call me that, or simply Nani, or Naniji will do. But if you are not comfortable with that, you can call me Aunty. My family here calls me Madam. You can call me that, or if you want something funny, then you can call me Netaji, as I was referred to when I was in active politics. What do you want to call me?"

"Papa used to call his Nani 'Ammaye'. Can I call you the same?" asked Meera.

"Yes, you can!" came the reply.

"So, you said you have read all the letters. You must have known everything I had told my Maa and what Janki told me, too. Those letters have created enough problems in our family, but they have also bound us together again. How many of them have you read?" asked the old lady.

"I have read all of them, I mean all those that I had. But… I have tried not to judge anyone of you. If at all, the letters have had a positive impact on me, I have been able to let go of some of my anger towards Maa," said Meera.

"Your mother hadn't reacted in this way. She had been angrier than ever after reading those letters," said Shakuntala. Then she made a sudden request, "May I have them back if you don't mind? After all these years of having lived alone, I will get to live with Shekhar, Janki and my mother, through those letters."

"Yes, of course! I will bring them when I come the next time," said Meera.

"I am glad that there will be the next time."

"I was, at first, fascinated by the letters. They took me to the era when they had been written. It felt as if I was there, smelling the air. But, as the years progressed, the letters unveiled the family secrets, layer by layer. That was when it got difficult, and then…" Meera trailed off.

"I can understand," Shakuntala said. "I remember my mother suggesting to me to write letters about whatever happened with me in my *sasural.* Things were very different, then. Girls used to get married very young. I am sure you know this. Living under a new roof was as difficult as you can imagine, and it was even more so, for a child. When I had got married, things were very difficult for me. Shekhar was a different person altogether. So, she asked me to write those letters and give vent to my feelings. Truly, I would feel less agitated after writing them. Janki had also learnt this from me when she saw me writing those letters."

"But there were good things as well like you continued with your studies post-marriage. In those times, getting a daughter-in-law educated must have been a big thing," said Meera.

"Yes, it was. Life is deep. Each and every moment we live, is like a layer that keeps getting pushed down as the next comes over it. It is not possible to conjure all of it in any written form—Life is too complex for that. Those letters were just a glimpse of our lives, not all of it, though. To answer your question, 'yes', there were good things as well. In fact, good things surpassed the bad ones, and that's why I became what I am," said Shakuntala.

"How does it feel to get married to a complete stranger? Our generation can't even imagine that happening," said Meera.

"We never thought that there could have been another option. That was the culture then, and we accepted it. You never know what will happen in the next eighty years; how society will be, but this is what makes our Indian culture unique. We blindly trust our parents that whatever they do, will be right for us. But that may also go wrong, and I am a living example of that."

"What happened to Maa was unfortunate. I realised it only when I become a mother that no child should go through this," said Meera.

"You must have seen me in a very bad light, isn't it? You must have thought of me as a villain as I didn't give any justification to Shekhar or Janki or anyone else before. But I will give it to you." Shakuntala relaxed in her chair as she embarked on her nostalgic journey. "I was born in a large family. I saw it getting broken, too, and though my father did not say anything, I could see in his eyes how much he had been broken. Being a girl, I was not able to lift his spirits much. He needed a boy—a son. He used to work till very late. He wouldn't have to if he had had a son. Now, things are different, not completely, though, but they are. I have seen my mother sitting alone without hope. She did not have anyone whom she could call family, as I had always been away from her. A son and his family would always have stayed with her. So, when I had Janki, I thought that Shekhar and I, will have the same future, and this feeling grew stronger day-by-day and second-by-second. But with justification, Meera, I will also say that I made mistakes. I spoiled things with Janki; I spoiled things with Shekhar. It is very difficult to admit that you have done something wrong, but here I do admit that after they have left me alone. I can say that it were my parenting mistakes that led Janki to make those choices."

"Then, why did you keep on continuing them? You could have given this a pause and…" Meera stopped in the middle of her sentence.

"If it were that easy! We did try to have another child—a son. But twice they were taken away from me. Perhaps my sin of neglecting Janki came to the fore. With the second one, we had been so close. If it were not for Janki, he would have been alive. She had been getting cranky and fell down. I had to hold her for a couple of minutes till Shekhar could come; otherwise I would have lost both of them. I saved Janki. And God punished me with a stillborn in return."

"Both of you had reasons to hate each other, but how do you see that hatred now? Do you think it was justified?" asked Meera.

"I have no regrets if that is what you are asking. Being in politics, I have learned that there is nothing black and white in this world; everything is in shades of grey. I have learned this the hard way, though some people get it easily."

"What is that?"

"You must have read about Disha and her son Manav?" said Shakuntala.

"Yes, I have read about Manav, but you have never mentioned her name in the letters," Meera said.

"Maybe. Her name was Disha, and she came into Shekhar's life when I had been at my lowest. Shekhar never stopped loving me, but that shrewd and cunning woman made him weak—she made him feel that he needed her. My only regret is that I did not pull Shekhar out soon enough."

"I think what you did was unusual, but it was the right thing to do," said Meera.

"Do you think so? If it happens with you, what will you do?" Shakuntala said interestedly.

"I will, probably, kill the other woman."

There was a pause, and then both laughed.

Meera continued with her questions. "You said that you have no regrets apart from the one you mentioned. But what about the cruel things you did as a politician—your views on Khalistan and what eventually happened to Maa?"

"See, you have to understand that politics is a different ballgame altogether. As I said earlier about the world being grey, the rules in politics are different. There are even more shades of the same colour. Regarding Khalistan, it is interesting that you asked; I had been on the wrong side then. Our country was polarised—there were those who had been wrong then, and as I said, I was one of them. My God knows that we—Manav Sansthan—have done a lot to compensate for that. But after all these years, I do not feel that I have done anything to deserve the kind of behaviour I received from Janki. Every parent makes mistakes. Your father must have made quite a few, too. But that does not mean that you set out to fight the world."

"What do you think of that hatred now? Would you have done anything differently?"

"I don't really know. Had I done things differently, I would not have reached where I am today. Maybe, I would have been happy and content with what I had, but would never have been able to build this empire," said Shakuntala.

"But, at what cost?"

"At the cost of self. Everyone is responsible for his own destiny and his choices. Tell me, Meera, do you believe in a past life? I have been doing lot of reading on it lately and exploring the world beyond ours—the one from where we come into this world. When we come, we choose the path we want. This path can be easy or difficult, but it will lead to only one place; whatever we face on the path is our choice. Anyway, leave all this. We can go on and on about these things. Tell me more about Jia."

"She was the one who opened the door for me," Meera said with a smile. "I got the letters, the box, and among other things, your mother's necklace, but I never had courage to open it. I had almost forgotten about it, but when I lifted her in my arms, the first thought that came into my mind was that I missed my mother, not with anger or frustration, but with just a plea. Jia is now a toddler, and she does everything a toddler would do. She crashes into things, explores them and puts everything into her mouth. I can never stop loving her. I can't even get enough of her."

"She is very lucky to have you as her mother. Let me show you some pictures of Janki." Saying this, Shakuntala pulled out a couple of albums and started showing her pictures of that part of the family which she had never known.

"This is when we had been to Amritsar before all of that happened. It is such a lovely place! Your Nanaji had bought a house in Chandigarh on the same trip. He wanted to settle down there, but that never happened. Now that house is being used by Manav Sansthan for its operations in the State. And look at this one… Janki looks so pretty with Simon; they were good together. Simon helped Janki grow as a person. And, this one is my favourite—tell me who she is holding in her arms?"

"Me," said Meera.

"That's what I tell everyone, but no, she is your sister Seema. The picture is so natural; it looks like it's her baby. I don't have a good picture of you and Janki, so I use this to show anyone as your picture."

"I think Papa has a couple of good pictures. I can get you one," Meera said.

"Ah, your Papa! He does check on me every once in a while. I tell him not to, but I think he considers it as his duty. He is a good man with a bad rationale, but the arrangement works for me. I get updated on what is happening in your life. This is the only source for us to know about you," smiled Shakuntala.

"Tell me more about Papa and Maa. How were they like when they had first met before all the problems started?"

"I saw your father working like a normal employee in your grandfather's firm. His dedication drew me towards him, and I felt he would be able to tame Janki. Yes, I used the word 'tame' as that had been the time when Janki was completely out of hand. I saw values in him, and he had completely surprised her during their courtship period. Their love for epic, the romantic, and the adventurous was similar. They had met so many times before marriage at all odd locations, hidden so much from the world, that I wouldn't have been surprised if they had come up with the news that they were already having you. Thankfully nothing of that sort happened; else, your Nanaji would have shot Adarsh dead. He was completely opposite when he was around Janki, and she, too, was a completely new person for me. They were good for each other, but I guess some things are not meant to be. Our lives would have been so different if we had taken another route," Shakuntala philosophised.

"What would you consider the most memorable time of your life?" asked Meera.

"I think this time when you are with me, will be the most memorable time for me for many years. Before that, the time I had spent with Janki in the US when we built our relationship from scratch and had been in a very happy place before that fateful day. We even planned her return to India. Trust me. I lobbied a lot for a likely meeting with you when she was here, the time spent with Shekhar—each and every bit of it. But most of it is a haze now. That is why I asked if you could give me those letters. I can relive my life—the fears, the celebrations, the anticipation, the wrongs, the rights—all of it. I can live it again one more time."

"Yes, I will bring those letters," Meera said.

"Since we are having a heart-to-heart, I have one more confession to make," Shakuntala said sheepishly.

"Go on."

"You know I have always kept an eye on you. Adarsh or my men have been around you all the time, ensuring that that they were out of sight, though. But they had always been with you, ready to protect you from any danger. A couple of years ago, when your car had broken down in Leh, the mechanic—who appeared out of nowhere—was my man. Also, when you were persistent in going to Kargil for coverage, they might have agreed to take you as an intern, but I had called them to change their decision," Shakuntala said.

"WHAT? That is so unfair! That would have been a golden opportunity for me. No one from our college was selected by that news channel. And, did you help me with the selection as well?" Meera said.

"No, I have never favoured you. I might have stopped you from going one step up the ladder a couple of times, but what you are is all because of your hard work," Shakuntala said.

"This is an intrusion into my privacy and the choices I have made for myself. You should not have done this. I am not comfortable sitting here anymore as I am not sure what else you might have doctored in my life," Meera said, irritated.

"There are a few things," Shakuntala said. "Yes, I will not lie, but trust me, it was all for your good."

"That is for me to decide, and definitely not for you," Meera said, still irritated.

"I am sorry, and trust me, I never say these three words to anyone," said Shakuntala.

"I am lucky, then!" Meera said on a calmer note.

"Yes, you are."

"I am sorry," Meera apologised. "I should not have behaved this way, but please promise me that you will not dictate my life from now onwards. I will come to seek your opinion, and you can advise me then."

"Happy with that!" Shakuntala said with relief.

"One thing I must say—what with your spying activities and the letters, we know more about each other than we would have otherwise," Meera acknowledged. "I know most of your inner secrets, and I assume you may be knowing mine."

"More than you know!" Shakuntala said with a smile.

Meera did not like the sound of the sentence, but she said, "Ammaye, let me tell you one incident which will surely put a smile onto your face."

"Go on then…"

"You remember, ah… do you remember the year when you had gone to some school's Sports Day celebrations and someone threw cow dung at you?" asked Meera.

"Yes, I do remember that. I can never forget it even if I want to."

"Sujit had got a trophy that day!" said Meera.

"Oh, that's wonderful!" exclaimed Shakuntala.

"But I felt really bad about what you did to that poor boy and his father."

"Ah, don't worry about him! You know the boy, Shyam whom you are talking about, handles almost all the Manav Sansthan operations like we do in school. He is my right hand. He realised what he did was wrong once he had worked here for a couple of months, and whenever he could, he came back and worked his way up. He is extremely hard-working, and his pain of a father is still alive," Shakuntala recounted.

"That's interesting! He is Sujit's friend, but never talks about you. He must be knowing about me," said Meera.

"Yes, he does, and I have asked him to keep quiet. But it's funny to see how life gets to you in a full circle."

Meera shook her head.

"Okay, Meera, now that you are here, I want to talk to you regarding something really important. I had asked your father to get your signatures on a few documents related to Manav Sansthan when you turned 18, and he has done that."

"He did that?" Meera asked, surprised.

"Yes, he did that. Neither of you has ever taken an active part in any of my affairs, and it was his request that we keep it that way. But now, I want you to think it over, and let me know what you want to do. I can ask someone to send some papers to your home for you to read."

"I don't know what to say," Meera said.

"Don't say anything now, and even if you don't want to come here, you can always come to see your grandmother, can't you?" Shakuntala reasoned.

Meera didn't say anything.

"When you come here next time, I will take you to meet Rukmani, your other Nani and her family. They will also be eager to meet you," Shakuntala said.

"I don't know what I could say to them," Meera shook her head.

"You don't have to say anything special. Just meet them. They are also your family," Shakuntala said, putting a hand over Meera's. "I have one more thing for you. I have your mother's remaining letters. Simon, I think sent them to me accidently. You can read about a happier period of your mother's life if you want to," she continued.

"Thank you!"

"No, no, don't thank me! I should thank you as you have come a long way, even if it is just a few kilometres." Shakuntala smiled and ran a hand over Meera's head.

"How was it?" Sujit asked once she was back.

Meera told him everything, including the details of the office, attitude of the staff and anything and everything that she could remember. He was as surprised as Meera had been on some of the disclosures.

"Should we do our homework?" he asked when Meera had finally finished.

"Homework?"

"Yeah, these new letters, happier letters as she says," Sujit replied while Meera lay Jia down on the bed to sleep.

"Let's get on with these, then," Meera agreed.

Shakuntala & Janki

(1996 - 2001)

Chapter 20

Dear Maa,

30 Mar 1996

Hope you are doing well! It has been one year since Papa left us, but as you had said the other day on the phone that the last thing he did before he went was to bring us together. I am also happy to say that it has been one year since we have been on the same page, and I, kind of, like this space. It is filled with positivity where I, at least, do not have any baggage.

Simon and I would love to have you here in the US. We have just moved into a new apartment near the store since it helps us in the commute. The flat is a bit expensive, but we will manage, and thanks for extending the offer to pay for us. But Simon and I think that it will not be necessary, and importantly, we will get our final settlement from two distributors in about six months. Then we might buy this apartment as I do not like the idea of renting the place, but we can manage it for a couple of months.

I had also gone to Vaduz as per your instructions. They allowed only me to see the details; Simon had to wait outside in the lobby for almost the entire day, and I felt really bad for him, but I must say that I was amazed to see what and how much could have been kept there. I was also amazed to see that you had managed to do this right under Papa's nose! Please don't get me wrong; I am not accusing you of anything. These were your choices and I remain true to what I have said earlier that I will not judge you again, and I will not ask you any questions that you might not want to answer.

But my position is still the same. I—in fact, we—do not want your money. I am not saying this out of disrespect, but rather out of self-respect. By God's grace, we have built quite an establishment here. We had actually been thinking of doing some consolidation as we want to spend time with each other. The work has now become like a rat race.

Maa, you had mentioned that once you retire from active politics, you would want to go to Amarnath next year. I would suggest that you come here and stay with us for a while. Lord Shiva can wait another couple of years. I don't think he is in any hurry to call you to him!

Meera will clear her 12th exams by next year, and I think we should do something for her. I had called Adarsh, and he asked me to come up with some ideas. I have been thinking that Adarsh and Meera can also come to the US with you, not together, of course, but won't it be fun if we are all in the same country, at least? We can also go to the places they would want to visit. At least, I will be able to see her, though, from a distance.

Finally, I know it has taken a very long time, but I am glad we are together again. Love you.

Your daughter,

Janki

"You know… I told you that I had gone to Disneyland after my 12th exam; that was where it had all begun. She had not yet been my life, but I feel that she was so much involved, and it seems they were all in a happy place, except for me," Meera said.

"Did you enjoy it?" asked Sujit.

"What, being left out?" Meera glared at him.

"No, silly… Disneyland."

"I want to say that I had become too old for that, but I did enjoy it," Meera said with a smile.

"Then why complain? The proper question is—did you see your mother and grandmother during this trip?" Sujit prodded her.

"No, not really."

"How boring!"

Dear Janki,

13 Nov 1996

Time flies. Good or bad, it doesn't matter what it was! I miss him more than anything else. The purpose of my life is lost and dead with him. Yes, I am happy that he has done something that neither of us had been able to do for decades. I will cherish our relationship as long as I live.

Congratulations on moving in with Simon. You deserve every bit of happiness that God can give you. I will always be there for both of you if you want me to do anything. I know you are more than capable of handling yourselves, but what are parents for? All that I have is you which is why I had asked you to go to Vaduz so that you can see for yourself what all you have. I know that as you have accepted me, you will accept the wealth also someday. Pass on my apologies to Simon for having to wait. I know the general process, clearance and stuff, takes a lot of time there; that is why the place is what it is.

Your Papa was an honest man. He was an army man. He never truly understood the operations of Manav Sansthan and my politics. But, when we met, I had told you that there is no right or wrong in politics; it is all relative. Manav Sansthan has done what no other organisation could in such a short period. It isn't that it has got all these international awards for nothing. The organisation gives back to society more than it earns. I will not take offence to what you have said, as I am trying to follow his path now. It is tough; trust me as I have to let go of so many options, but then there is no reason for me now to take any risks.

Also, I have quit active politics. See what had happened this year, though. I did warn the High Command not to take the BJP lightly. Without political support, my hands are, anyway, a bit tight; as you know, in politics, everyone salutes the rising sun, and no one wants to be associated with anyone walking in the opposite direction. But don't worry; I have enough resources here to make things work out for me.

I am very glad that you told me against going to Amarnath this year. What a terrible thing to have happened! Almost 200 people got stranded and were frozen to death. Had it not been for you, I might have been one of them. But life or death, I will go to Amarnath one day. Shekhar had always wanted to go; I consider this his last wish.

I had spoken to Adarsh as soon as I got the letter and, who knows, maybe, we can do a family reconciliation in the US. We can all sit down and explain how things got out of hand with Meera. I am sure that she will think differently, given that she is away from the familiar environment... She is a smart kid. I am in touch with her principal who praises her every time, not because he is speaking to me, but because Meera is genuinely a bright student. With a little support from her parents and grandparents, she will rise to heights that we would have never seen.

Janki, my dear, we had been waiting for each other. I am glad that we have found each other. I love you, too.

Yours,

Maa

"When I had asked her last week if she has ever favoured or helped me in anyway, she lied to me, and said 'never' and that what I am today is because of my hard work."

"What do you expect from a politician?" Sujit asked reasonably. "What about the billions in the Swiss bank?

"We don't know if they are still there, and, more importantly, we don't need that money. If my mother has not taken it, we cannot take it, either," replied Meera.

"I don't mind a bit of cash to sleep on," Sujit said dreamily.

"No way! And I also know you are kidding," Meera said, giving Sujit a stern look.

"Do you?"

Dear Maa,

24 Jan 1997

They say that December has been the wettest month ever recorded and it has not rained like cats and dogs, but like wolves and tigers (this is a self-coined term). Some areas have seen floods worse than those of 1974, according to newspapers.

This rain has spoilt not only our New Year plans but also the ones we had for the next couple of months. And all of this has happened before the final delivery payment. Due to this, we might have to push the decision of buying of this flat ahead by a couple of months. We might even have to move out as the landlord is in a hurry to sell the flat.

Maa, please don't offer any money. We will manage on our own. I am sharing my problems with you, but it's not because I expect you to send me a cheque.

But one thing good to look forward to is Meera's visit to the US in April; I have already started counting backwards.

Can't you bring your plans forward and come here a bit early? You can stay with us and help us clear this mess. We have been planning this trip for so long, almost two years.

Did you get a chance to speak to the Vice-chancellor of Denanath College for Meera? It is very important for her to get through the best college.

Please reply with the date of your travel.

Janki

"You studied at this college, correct?" asked Sujit.

"I did, yes. But this was not the only college I applied to. I mean I needed above 90% to get into this college, and I did get 90% to the dot, so they had kept me on the waiting list. Everyone, including all my friends, said that no one ever reaches the waiting list because seats are filled much before that. I had also applied to the second-best college and, in fact, was on the waiting list there, as well."

"Then?" he prompted.

"Then I got a call and a letter informing me that my seat had been confirmed and that I had to go there and complete my paperwork," Meera replied.

"What about the second-best college?" Sujit asked again.

"They did not send any reply, and I was so happy! I thought I had been very lucky," Meera sounded a little upset.

"Well, in a way, you are," Sujit said reasonably.

"Not, it had been like this. It feels as if I am on borrowed luck," said Meera.

"Everyone does it."

"I am upset not because I had gotten into the college this way. I am just upset because I had been kept in the dark, and not told about it."

"Fair enough!"

Dear Janki,

4 Mar 1997

Janki, my dear daughter, the US will have to wait a little longer for me. As you know, I had already booked the tickets, got the visa, did all the shopping you had asked me to. It was all sitting in the suitcase before me. But with a heavy heart, I have to say that I will not be able to come. Bhairav has had a heart attack, and I have to be here to guide the team on the day-to-day operations. His son is there, and there is one more guy who had left us a couple of years back but has joined us again. Please forgive me; I will make a plan to come as soon as things settle down a bit over here.

I will not offer you any money if you don't like it. But my prayers and wishes are with you, and I know you will emerge a winner as always.

I had been looking forward to this trip more than you could have imagined. It would have given us all a chance, as a family, to see if we could solve the last of these roadblocks.

Yes, I did speak to the Vice-chancellor of Denanath College for Meera. She said that Meera needs to get above 90% if she wants to get into the college. I have also told Adarsh to pay more attention to her now, so that my task will become easier later. Adarsh also wants her to get into this college, and I am sure he will try his best to make her achieve this.

Again, I can't tell you how bad I am feeling. After all these preparations, I have had to cancel my plan. But Meera is coming, and you will hopefully get a chance to spend time with her and resolve your issues. Adarsh had told me that she is not that excited to come to the US; she wants to go to Australia.

Yours,
Maa

"Hey, they are talking about April, but you told me that you had gone to Disneyland around October-November," Sujit pointed out.

"November. Perhaps, they had been planning and it didn't work out. There are a lot of things that even I am not sure of whether they are to be believed," Meera replied.

"Let's find out, then," Sujit stretched.

Dear Maa,

23 Nov 1997

We had delayed Meera's trip just for you, but you still couldn't make it. I know, and I understand the reason, but it would have been really good if you had been here. Maybe, you could have handled things differently.

I would call this trip a success despite what had happened in the last week. I am glad that Meera came to the 25th anniversary of the park. It was spectacular to see Candy Castle, and I looked at the expression of awe on Meera's face. But, to be honest, I did feel that she has become a bit old for all this now. We should have planned this earlier. For the most part of the trip, it was fine, and I don't think she had seen me, but when she did, she created a scene and broke a vase. Poor Adarsh had to pay $1500 for it. The worst part is that she did not come out of her room for two days, and Adarsh had to cancel all their plans and take her directly to New York. From there, they left for India in a week. I am sure, by now, Adarsh must have told you what had happened there.

It seems that I will never be able to overcome her hatred. I wish she would just listen to me.

Leave it! I can't change my destiny, but I remain hopeful that she will forgive me and come to me someday. I hope it won't be too late, then. For now, I am just glad that she will go back to her college. The college atmosphere is really helping her to grow as a person. Adarsh told me that she now has more friends than ever, is quite popular as well. I have asked Adarsh to be cautious as she is very vulnerable now, but he assured me that she has been getting all the love and care required at home. So, whatever path she chooses in life, she will not make the mistakes I had made.

You had to cancel your tickets twice, but I hope you will come next year. Hope to see you soon; Simon and I are also planning to come to India sometime next year, and we might travel back with you.

Your dear daughter,

Janki

"What happened?" Sujit said, intrigued.

Meera made a face. "I don't want to talk about it."

"Why what is there to not talk about? Why are you avoiding the subject?" Sujit gave her hair a tweak.

"I had been just thinking about something else. Okay… first thing, she had been wrong then, I did like the Disney experience. It was one of the most memorable experiences I have ever had, and I had seen her on the second day but avoided her. Even Papa knew that I had come to know about it, but he also kept quiet," said Meera.

"Then, why was there a sudden explosion in the last week?"

"I was sick and tired of keeping quiet when I had known what they were up to, I would see them talk every now and then, and when I would come, they would just move apart. So, I lost control, called her names, and Papa slapped me. Then, I broke the vase and ran to my room." Meera stated everything in a matter of fact way.

"Quite a scene from a 17-year-old," Sujit whistled.

"Yeah, but our New York leg had been even worse. I had promised myself that I would never go to New York again," Meera recollected.

"What had happened there?"

"Save it for some other time."

Dear Janki,

14 Dec 1997

Don't lose hope. You have always been able to steer away from dark clouds, and these will also go away soon. I have full trust in Adarsh; one day, Meera will understand.

Yes, unfortunately, I had to cancel my trip again due to my dream project which is getting halted now after Mother Teresa's death. It's a national tragedy. The whole country is in a state of grief and my project has also got halted. It was a very prestigious project for Manav Sansthan, but we have to do planning again after a couple of months, so I have to be here. Hopefully, I will be there next year.

Yes, Adarsh told me what had happened in Florida as well as in New York. She is getting out of hand, and I have asked Adarsh to keep some control over her. Even if she has had problems, that was no way to behave. Also, after Ramprasadji, there is no elder in their house who will use his stick to pull the children back on track so that they do not go astray.

But let me tell you one good thing. You had seen the Queen in Dubai all those years ago, and I saw her here in India. She was asking about you.

Jokes apart, do take care of yourself and write to me soon.

Yours,

Maa

"Who is she to teach me anything when she, too, has done all that?" Meera asked irritated.

"Correct! Two wrongs do not make a right," corrected Sujit.

"You are saying that I was being unreasonable." Meera glared at him.

"When did I say that?" asked Sujit.

"Just now."

Dear Maa,

26 Feb 1998

Maa, it has been three years since Papa left us. I may think about him a bit less, but whenever I do, the pain tears me apart inside, even though I had not been that close to him towards his end.

He has always inspired me in so many ways. I wish he could have met Simon. We have been going steady, and hopefully when he proposes to me the next time, I will say 'yes'. I know this will be the right thing to do after all this time.

Life is extremely fragile, and after his accident last month, I am scared and anxious like I had been when I left Adarsh. I don't want anything to happen to him.

I might finally need some help from you now. No, it's not for Simon; he is covered by insurance, but for setting up a manufacturing unit here in the US. There are huge benefits of doing it in taxation and stuff like that, and Simon knows it better. But for that, we need some investment, and we do not want to take any loan. Anyway, this house loan is eating up most of our monthly budget.

I will call you and let you know the details.

I have sent some money to Adarsh for Meera's first car, a Maruti 800; I hope Meera will be surprised and happy to see the car.

Your dear daughter,
Janki

"I can't believe that my first car was bought by her," Meera looked up.

"Is that a problem?" Sujit asked her.

"Not now, but it would have been a huge problem if I had known this, then," she admitted.

"What would you have done? Burn down the car?" asked Sujit.

"Yes, perhaps. I love that car and I still have it. Though I don't drive it anymore, it has been my first love," said Meera with a smile on her face.

"Ouch! That hurts!" Sujit made a face.

"Don't get too worked up. You are not my first even among all humans," Meera teased.

"I will die with that pain."

"Then go and jump out of the window now."

"You are evil like your mo…" Sujit broke off.

"Mother." Meera finished.

"I didn't mean that." Sujit was sure that Meera would blow up now.

"Don't worry; I don't mind." Meera smiled.

Dear Janki,

16 Oct 1998

No one can understand what a woman goes through if her partner is not with her. It would have been easier if your father was alive, and I had gone as he would have survived, somehow. But what keeps me going each day is our dream to take Manav Sansthan to heights by the principles which he had laid out.

I was also very disturbed to hear about Simon's accident, and I wish him well. And also, that you two both stay happily.

Whatever I have, is yours, and I don't have the energy as earlier. I have been telling you for a long time now that you and Simon can come here and take over the reins of Manav Sansthan. But, in the meanwhile, I will be happy to support you as much as you want.

I had attended Alok's wedding. The weddings of the next generation have started in Adarsh's family. After Mala's wedding, this is the first occasion where I saw all of them, including Meera. She did not come near me, nor did I call for her. I have told Adarsh to let her come on her own if she wants to come and meet me, then well and good. Anyway, I would just bless the couple for whom I had gone there. To be honest, I don't know why they were in such a hurry. I think the girl is pregnant, but I might be wrong.

Meera was looking so pretty and well-behaved, and I saw a proud mother in Kavita. There are so many boys after her, she said, but I think she is already taken. I could see the way she was looking at one of them. I told this to Adarsh, but he did not agree with me, but I am telling you; these eyes have seen enough of the world.

Anyway, I am happy for her. She is a responsible girl. You take care of yourself and Simon.

Yours,

Maa

"Hello, who was this mystery man about whom I don't know?" Sujit asked.

"Nothing, just a casual fling!" Meera said, trying to avoid the subject.

"Was it? How come you have had a casual fling if you could come to your brother's wedding and mingled with the family? Many of them would have realised that there had been something going on between you both," Sujit said.

"Let them think what they had wanted to. There was nothing, at least not with him!" Meera replied.

"What does that mean? How many more were there?"

"You are my first if you know what I mean…" Meera batted her eyelids.

"I don't trust you, now," Sujit said and winked.

"Let me get that trust back, then," Meera said, and winked back.

Dear Maa,

3 Jun 1999

Maa, I am glad you had been here when it all happened. Simon has sent you his love. I didn't know what Simon had in store for us when we had gone to Las Vegas. I thought he might be trying to impress you with all those fancy cars and casinos so that you get an idea of our lives here, and be assured that your daughter is happy with the man she has been living with.

I was surprised when he had popped the question, though. There was such a crowd on the streets that I couldn't understand what was happening. I was actually expecting many people to stop in their shoes to enjoy the show, but no one did. I still laugh at Simon for this. Perhaps, the streets of Las Vegas have seen so many proposals that they are now clichéd. But, for me, it was an event that I can never forget, and I will cherish this memory forever. The ring is beautiful; I can't believe that he has chosen it. It's not him, but it's definitely me.

I had to say 'yes', Maa. I had to say 'yes', and I could see the satisfaction in your eyes as we hugged and cried again on the street. I asked Simon why he had chosen that setup. He could have proposed at any nice hotel when we had been there. He said he had wanted it to be raw. I don't know what that means, but whatever it is, I am in a happy state of mind right now.

I spoke to Adarsh, and he is also happy for me. Simon and Adarsh actually get along well with each other. Simon insists that we should speak to Meera now. It has been long overdue, he says. One day she will get married and have children of her own. I want to be part of her life, and Simon knows how important this is for me.

I don't know if I would have any say in her marriage. I mean that she might select someone I don't know, or else, Adarsh will let me know if he finds any suitable match for her. I might have just found one for her.

His name, I think, is Sujit. We had met him at the Indian community meet. He happened to be in the US for a sports meet. By God, Maa, that kid is excellent. He is focused, determined, and knows how to achieve what he wants. It is no small feat to beat athletes in their own country, especially when you know that their build and training are much better than ours. If not him, Meera should find someone like him. I know Meera is too young for this discussion, and I will not talk about this to Adarsh as he will get upset with me, but I will keep him in mind while we decide to look for boys for her, and hopefully, he will be single till that time. He had blushed and said 'yes' when I asked him if he had a girlfriend. He saw the expression on my face and was clueless as to why I was speaking about girlfriends. I hope he did not get the wrong message that I was hitting on him.

Anyway, Maa, life has never been better, and we will talk more about it over the phone when I come to India next year.

Your dear daughter,

Janki

"She had got engaged?"

"Was that you who had met her?"

Sujit and Meera spoke at once. Sujit had gotten the letters photocopied so that they could read them together.

"You reply first!"

They said that together, and then burst out laughing.

"I don't remember much except just that a hot aunty was hitting on me. I never knew that she had been your, or for that matter, that she was looking for a groom for her daughter." Sujit was still surprised.

"It is so fascinating that she had met you and approved of you! It was even before we had met. It's like the universe had listened to her wishes." Meera had tears in her eyes and her throat choked.

"She had a strong connection with the universe, then," Sujit looked heavenwards.

"Do you remember anything else? Do you remember Simon?" Meera asked.

"Sorry, I don't. I don't even remember her face but just a feeling that she was a hot woman."

"Stop saying this, now!"

"Yeah, correct, it is not appropriate," Sujit said wryly.

Dear Janki,

9 Nov 1999

I can tell you now, and I hope Simon won't mind it. I knew that he would propose to you. But you are right. He took no help, at least from me, in the selection of the ring. That had all been his decision. Perhaps, he could get the perfect ring for you because he knows you so well.

I am happy for both of you.

Adarsh puts up a brave face in front of you, but it does affect him, and you can see that he had not been in any relationship since you left him. But you don't get worried about him. He has plenty on hand with Meera, and yes, maybe next year when you will be here, we can try and patch you and Meera up. I hope no one would have to die to mend your relationship with Meera as your Papa died for us.

No way! I will not let that happen. These sportsmen are too obsessive about everything, so I don't agree with him—whatever his name is. I will seek a scientist for her as I have always been fascinated with their work.

And, you know that you should come for good, or at least move to the East Coast. The West Coast is too dangerous, what if another earthquake occurs in the Mojave Desert in your state? I don't know how you had been living there. Every two years, something or the other happens.

I had an argument with Adarsh yesterday. Actually, I had been a fool to have told him that I had called up the new channel which wants to take the brightest students of the Denanath College to the Kargil medical base camps, and they have selected our Meera. They said that it would be an embarrassment to the news channel if they withdrew it now. I said I don't care, but my daughter will not go to zones where there were bullets and bombs everywhere. Adarsh told me that she was very disappointed. But he does not understand that it is not safe. Even if he says that the medical base camps are safe and the duration is only two days for the interns, a lot could happen in two days. I hadn't told you this earlier as you would have disagreed with me. Adarsh says that it was the opportunity of a lifetime. I told him that if there will be no life left, what can one do with mere opportunity? Don't you think I am right?

I can't wait till next year for you to come here. I pray that these next few months pass as quickly as possible.

Yours,

Maa

"She did tell me this, and I had felt really bad then. I had thought I might have gotten over with it, but no, I am still feeling bad," Meera said, looking at Sujit.

"This is not fair!" agreed Sujit.

"Thank you! After reading these letters, it looks like my life had been in the hands of these two women whom I hadn't wanted to meet at all. How could have Papa allowed this?" Meera sounded exasperated now.

"You can ask him tomorrow," said Sujit.

Meera couldn't sleep that night; the feeling of living a life like a puppet was too overwhelming. She kept looking at Jia and promised herself she would never let that happen with her; she would not let history repeat itself.

"Hello, Papa!" Meera called Adarsh the first thing in the morning.

"Hello, beta, what happened? So early, everything okay?" Adarsh asked her.

"No, everything is not okay."

Adarsh understood. "Anything to do with your visit to your Nani?"

"Yes."

"What happened? Tell me…"

"All of you had scripted my life, right from college! Who I meet, where I go, what do I do for work… it was all scripted by people whom I had hated for almost my entire life," Meera burst out.

"No, Meera, it was nothing like that. When things had got somewhat settled, I just included them in my conversations about you. Yes, there had been a few instances where they went overboard, but I did warn them, especially your Nani, to stay out of your way. In some cases, I had also been one of the culprits. But it has ended well, hasn't it? Are you not happy with your life?" Adarsh tried to reason with her.

"Not anymore."

"Meera, listen to me… Though you had not been in contact with your mother, she always loved you. Bad decisions or bad fate have led us to where we are today. I want you to stand in their shoes for a bit and then think about it. If you still feel that you had been at the receiving end of injustice, then we can discuss all those incidents—one by one. You can vent out your frustration on me," Adarsh pacified her.

"No, I don't want to talk about it. I just wanted to let you know that I am extremely hurt, and whatever I do next, I will always doubt whether it is my decision," Meera said and hung up the phone before Adarsh could say anything.

Dear Maa,

23 Feb 2000

I hate New York, but Simon loves the city. He says that we will get old and die in this city. But I can die anywhere in the world except here. I mean, I do like some bits of it, like Central Park. It's amazing to see so many people coming there every day and getting involved in various activities. You can see a sea of colours in the midst of green and blue, with concrete on the outskirts of the park. But, apart from that, the only thing I like is the Statue of Liberty. When you go near it, it actually grows on you. It's so magnificent and elegant, that it has to be a Wonder of the World. I will look it up on the Internet to find more information about it.

We had to postpone our trip to India for two reasons—The first being the Kandahar hijack. The Government is on high alert here as well and has issued travel caution to South Asia. The second reason behind it, is our plan to move to New York. It had been going on in Simon's mind for quite some time. He did try his hands on financial services back home as well, but it hadn't worked out. The market is not mature there, he says. It will be a bit difficult to coordinate the business from here in New York, but I have to do it for Simon. He has done a lot for me. In a way, he has sacrificed his dreams for me, and now when he wants to do something he has set his heart to, I should support it.

Why do you keep on asking about our marriage? Perhaps when we come to India and my differences with Meera are resolved, then I might think about it. I want Meera to be with me on my special occasion, and we think that getting married is just a formality and a waste of money. We are at a stage where we have been sharing our toothbrushes. What will marriage change for us?

Is it true that Meera is seeing someone? Adarsh is still upset with you for having blocked Meera's trip last year, and he does not easily share things with me anymore. I guess he has been doing this with you as well. Don't worry, I am still speaking with him, but is it true? Adarsh says that Meera did not tell him, but he got to know from someone anyway that she had been seeing someone. He also said that he likes the boy. He is a national sports star; I hope he is the same boy whom I had met in the US. I can't remember his name now… Sumit… Sujeev… something like that, and Adarsh says that they might get married, too. I am really happy for her.

Your dear daughter,

Janki

"These parents are really bad. They know everything, and we think that we have fooled them. Do you remember that we had promised to not let our relationship be known to even our friends? Then, how on earth did your father get to know all this… did you tell him?" Sujit asked in surprise.

"No way! I don't know either how he came to know about it. I think since every parent has been through that age, he has an idea of what we would do. I am feeling bad that I had spoken rudely to Papa this morning. I should have waited for this letter. He did speak up for me."

"Yes, and I am now hurt about Maa not remembering my name." Sujit pulled a mock face.

"Aww! But she did like you!" Meera smiled.

Sujit was about to say something when Meera's phone rang. She picked it up after three rings.

"Hello, beta!"

"Hello, Ammaye, how are you?" Meera said, looking at Sujit with raised eyebrows.

"I am alive again now that I have you," Shakuntala said.

Meera had thought that she would argue with her Nani as well, but she didn't feel angry any longer after what she said and in the way she did.

"May I ask you something?" Shakuntala continued while Meera did not say anything.

"Yes, please go on. You don't have to ask my permission," said Meera.

"Will you meet your maternal family—your brother and sisters and your other Nana and Nani?"

"Um…" Meera was quiet.

"No problem if you don't want to meet now. You may take your time," Shakuntala assured her.

"I don't know anything about them," countered Meera.

"You will get to when you meet them, and they will be very happy to see you."

"Perhaps in a couple of weeks. This is too overwhelming for me, and I just need a bit of time to absorb things," Meera answered slowly.

"Yes, yes, take your time. We have waited for so long, and a couple of weeks more will not make a difference. But I do hope that your answer will be 'yes'."

"I will let you know."

"Bye, beta."

"Bye!" Meera put the phone down.

Dear Janki,

29 Jun 2000

I don't know why you don't like New York. I loved the city when I had gone there with a delegation. Actually, we had gone to Washington, but a couple of us really wanted to see New York, so we extended our trip by two days and stayed there. We had to write an explanation letter as to why we had extended our stay, but it was nothing that we could not manage. We were there for only one day and a half, and we did that walking tour. I don't remember now what it is called, but they took us to Little Italy, Soho and other surrounding areas. We ate a really good pizza as well.

I will speak to Simon but do wish him luck from my side, anyway. I am waiting for you guys to get married. Getting married is not about how many things you share, how many feelings you share. I am old school, so I have full trust in this institution, and I would want you to take the plunge as soon as possible. You should come to India soon so that we can also speak to Meera. She has grown into a rational young woman, and I am sure she will understand you.

Also, I have no idea that Meera is seeing someone. Adarsh does not talk much about her nowadays, and you know why. Is it my fault that I love my granddaughter so much that I don't want to see her in danger? Anyway, he will come around one day, and with the outbreak of fire in the mill, I do not have the energy to run behind him. The fire has consumed your father's dream. This media is spreading the news that I started the fire deliberately to get the insurance money to fund my dream project with the Missionaries of Charity. But you tell me—will someone kill his one child so that the other one can live? I can't do that, and these fools don't know that I don't need money. I have enough stacked like mountains. If God wants social work to get done with my hands, he will show me which path I need to take.

I will meet Adarsh and learn what has been going on there. I don't want Meera to end up with someone who does not deserve her.

Yours,
Maa

"You know—I have just one question for her…" Meera said, folding her copy of the letter.

"What?" Sujit raised an eyebrow.

"If I didn't go and meet her, why didn't she come and meet me after Maa had died? It's been 15 years since then, and a lot could have happened in those years. She could have at least made one attempt. When you look at the letters, they talk about me in each and every one of them. They were following, dictating my life, but not once did she come in front of me and listen to what I had to say."

"Would you have listened to her?" Sujit questioned.

"Maybe or maybe not, but that's not the point, is it?" Meera closed her eyes and shook her head.

"You will have to ask her that question. You might as well ask Papa. It seems that towards the end, the relationship between Ammaye and Papa was not cordial. It had started turning sour, and you can see that," Sujit reflected.

"I don't know."

Dear Maa,

23 Jul 2001

Simon has set up his office in the Twin Towers. It's a small space—probably the smallest it can get here. We have asked the agent to keep looking for an alternative. He said he will find a suitable place in the next couple of weeks. If not, then we will move our base out of this building. The view is amazing. At this height, you can see miles around. It's amazing, but I still stick to my opinion that I do not like this city. New York is not for me.

Anyway, I have to sit in this office, while Simon travels across the country. His travelling has increased quite a bit in the last couple of months, and at times, he is out for weeks at a stretch.

It's been two years since we had met last, and even though, we call each other and also write these customary letters once in a while, I would still love to sit and talk my heart out to you. Do you know what Meera did to me? I can't speak about it over the phone; it's too painful. Even when I write, it's not that easy.

Adarsh had been lobbying for me for a while now, and she knew that I would call her, but when I did, she disregarded me, and started screaming on the phone. I know that she hates me, but I had expected something better from her.

I had called her, and said, 'Hello, beta.' Without even letting me finish the sentence, she pounced on me, and asked, 'Who are you?' I know she knew who I was, but still her tone! I told her, 'I am Janki, your mother.' She raised her voice and said, 'I don't have a mother named Janki. Her name is Kavita.' She told me that I had dialled the wrong number. I said, 'I am sorry; I know what you feel about me.' But as soon as I had said this, she started shouting. I kept hearing her angry voice; at least I could hear her voice. She called me names—liar, kidnapper, drug-addict, and what, not. I can't even write about a few of the things that she had shouted. In a way, she is right. I am all that, but I am more than that, and this is what I want her to understand. Before I could say anything else, she hung up. Just before disconnecting the phone, she had said that I was the devil in a woman's disguise and that I should stay away from her and she wished that I had already been dead.

Maa, I am not hurt or angry with her. I can understand her anger as I have also gone through this and kept this hatred for you for so long in my heart. I can understand her completely, and when she comes out of her anger, I know she will be happier than ever.

There is one more thing that I need to tell you. I don't know it yet, but probably know in a couple of weeks, but we have started to plan for a child. Simon loves children, and I will be really happy to see him with his own kids. I have also promised myself that I will not repeat the mistakes that I had made with Meera.

Your dear daughter,

Janki

"Do you remember this conversation differently?" Sujit inquired after they had put their letters down.

"No. I had been pretty rude to her, and I felt so good for a couple of weeks since that, but I had also secretly wished that she called again and pleaded before me. A child, I had always wanted to be with her. No matter what you think about your parents, they are always important to you," said Meera.

"Well, she didn't have much time left, did she? Not even two months were left after that call," recollected Sujit.

"Yes."

"Do you regret venting out your frustration?" he asked.

"If you were to put it in that perspective… no, not at that time, but things had been very different then," replied Meera.

"What about your letter? You said that you had started it. You could have vent out your frustration through it," suggested Sujit.

"Read it, yourself."

Maa,

29 Nov 2015

I don't know what's happening to me. My hands are trembling, and tears are rolling down my cheeks. I have just written 'Maa'. I have realised today how powerful this word is. It connects me to you. I have called you many names in the past, but not 'Maa'. Now that I am calling you 'Maa', I can't realise how hard it could have been.

I have hated you all my life. A large part of me still hates you, but my hate can't be bigger than my relationship with you by birth. Jia has helped me realise this, and I will not make the mistakes that you had made with me.

"That's it," Meera said quietly. "This is after 100 iterations. I want to write everything that I had felt or faced—how my friends used to tease me, how I used to wake up at nights, screaming her name, how Papa sacrificed his entire life for me, but nothing was coming out."

"Relax, it will," said Sujit. "Why don't you pick up these letters from the beginning, or begin them where you want to start the story from? Just answer her. Laugh with her, cry with her, tell her how you had felt about the incidents that happened with her and also write if you had faced similar situations or better or even worse ones. You can connect with her this way."

"I don't know if I will ever be able to tell her everything," Meera said, with doubt in her voice.

"Start from somewhere and see how it goes. Should we open the final letter?" asked Sujit. "Why has this letter been left unopened?"

"Perhaps, Maa never got a chance to read this letter as it might have arrived after the incident," Meera answered.

Dear Janki,

31 Aug 2001

I am really happy for you. You should start a family soon, and my wishes are with you that you will get the happiness you deserve.

I have asked Simon to consider opening one office in Delhi as well so that both of you can come to India more often. Yes, it's been long, and I am eagerly waiting for your visit in December. I am glad that I had sent the tickets, otherwise, your trip would have been postponed again.

Don't worry about Meera. You and I would have done the same thing had we been in her place. She is a very sensible young lady, and I am sure she will turn around.

My health is not good these days. The doctor has asked me to relax a bit. Shyam is handling the core operations of the organisation, and I have moved into a mentoring role. I don't know how long I would stay quiet as it's not in my nature. But, let's see. Till then, I have lots of time on hand to buy paintings and increase my collection of art. I will show you my collection when you are in India in December.

Take care. I don't know why I have been worrying so much about you these days when everything is going well, by the grace of the Lord. God bless!

Yours,

Maa

"The letter which Maa never got to open," Meera said sadly.

She paused for a thought and then said, "Lots of things could have happened. I would have reconciled with her in December or have had a teenage brother or sister now. Maybe, they would have settled down in India and we would have met them regularly. Maybe we would have again fought on something trivial; life could have taken so many different routes had that attack not happened. It has changed the course of my life… and for so many others."

"For better or for worse."

"For better or for worse."

Meera
(2015)

Chapter 21

"HELLO, PAPA," SAID Meera, with hesitation in her voice. She did not know how her father would react to the idea that she was going to propose.

"Hello, beta, how are you? Are you through with all the letters?" asked Adarsh.

"Yes."

"So, what do you think?"

"What does that mean?"

"I mean—do you feel more burdened or more relaxed?"

"I have few questions for you and Ammaye, but those do not need urgent discussion. They can wait," Then after taking a deep breath, she said, "I want to discuss something with you."

"Yes, go ahead."

"I want to go to New York. It has been long overdue."

There was silence on the phone and Meera could hear the sound of her breath coming back to her.

"You didn't like the idea..." she said.

"No, I liked it. It just struck me that I should have given you these letters and asked you to read them long before. I think we have wasted a decade and a half. You are right. It has been long overdue," Adarsh replied.

"I am glad that you liked the idea."

"What will you do there?"

"I will meet her; I will feel her, and I will go where she had last been and pay my tribute to her," Meera said quietly.

"Do you want me to come along with you?"

"No. I will have to do this on my own. Even Sujit is not coming along with me, and there are many people who can handle Jia for five days, but there… there she is, alone, and I have to free her; I have to free myself," Meera replied, with a crack in her voice.

Sujit looked at the letter from over Meera's head, it read:

When I was in the eighth standard…

"What are you doing, reading my letter? Go away!" Meera hid what she had been writing.

"I have no interest in reading your letters. I have just come back from the travel agent's office, and here are your tickets booked for three weeks from now." He glanced again at the written sheets and said, "You are doing quite well than when you had started it. What? Has it already been twenty pages?"

"I am trying to remember incidents and feelings and putting them into words. It's not an easy task."

"I can't say that. I have never written a letter in my entire life—not even a school leave application!" Sujit laughed.

"Is that supposed to be funny?" Meera scoffed. "Please go. I have to write; I don't know if I will be able to finish it."

"What's the hurry? You can write during the flight, or even when you have reached there. You can show me later what you have written."

"No. I will not let you read my letter."

"That's mean! I read all these letters about your entire family history—wicked history, and you will not let me read your letter! I would want to see what you have written."

"No way."

"Then, have your dinner alone. I was about to get dinner for you." Sujit huffed away.

"Fine."

"Fine."

Meera walked into the main hall where she saw a crowd of people looking at her. She could sense mixed vibes from them. A few of them had tears in their eyes, a few were wondering why they were there, and a few kept their expressions locked away. Meera tried to commit to memory their names and faces as Shakuntala introduced her to each member of her extended family.

Meera came to know that Choti Maa—that was what Janki used to call her Rukmani Chachi—she insisted that Meera also call her Choti Maa instead of Choti Nani. She said that she was feeling as if Janki was here and calling her Choti Maa again after so many years. She lived in Cape Town, along with her husband Shyam, their son Kishore, his wife Radhika, and their elder son, Janak and his family. Kishore Mama had started a jewellery export/import business because he didn't want to continue with his grandfather's law firm. Along with his son Janak and wife Radhika, he also handled the African operations of Manav Sansthan. Shekhar had given him this responsibility and he continued to honour it. They had a four-year-old daughter Kuljeet, who was immediately fascinated by Jia and wanted her all to herself. Their younger son Jai, who was married to Kavya, and had twins Anubhav and Anurodh, was still trying to find his feet. He worked with Manav Sansthan on and off.

"I am glad to know that I have another big family," said Meera. "My family—I mean, my father's side of the family is also very large, and most of us still live together."

"Shakuntala Bhabhi has always looked after us and kept us together through thick and thin. She is the eldest in the family now, and we all do what she tells us to," Choti Maa said with love in her eyes.

"I just wish that Janki and Adarsh along with Meera, Sujit and our precious princess would always be with us," Shakuntala said with tears in her eyes.

"We are here now, Ammaye," Meera said, holding her hand.

"Meera, I might have seen your shows on the news channel, but I had never known that you are our sister!" Jai said when things settled down, and Meera had spent some time with everyone.

Meera smiled; she didn't know what to say.

"May I ask you something?" he asked.

"Sure!"

"Why did you decide to show up suddenly? Why after all these years?"

Meera wanted to reply to him and tell her the story of how she had got the letters and found out about everything and everyone, but she didn't like the tone of Jai's question.

"I didn't understand your question," she said.

"Let me put it in simple English, then. If you are thinking that you will take control of Manav Sansthan and the money, you are mistaken. We have spent our blood and life in maintaining the organisation as well, and I will not let any outsider come and take away what belongs to me," Jai said in a belligerent tone.

Meera laughed aloud, enough for her family to look in their direction.

"Now that you have challenged me, my newly-found brother, I will make sure that you get what you deserve," she replied with a chuckle.

"Ammaye, can I ask you something?" Meera said while they were returning from the Choti Maa's house. It had been a full day, and Meera could see the tiredness on Shakuntala's face, but decided to ask about it anyway.

"I have been waiting for it since the beginning," Shakuntala said.

Meera was surprised. "Do you know what I want to say?"

"I can guess, yes, but go ahead. Ask me what you want to."

"I have two questions, actually. First, why didn't you come and meet me after Maa had passed away? You could have easily come over and talked to me. I don't think I'd have had any problems with you. The place where we are now—we could have been here much earlier."

"I did try many times. I even had many arguments with Adarsh before and after Janki had left us, but he wanted everything related to Janki and me, to be kept away from you," Shakuntala said.

"I don't understand why so."

"I do. You had had a very fragile childhood, just like Janki, and I now understand that Adarsh didn't want the same fate for you. I used to get very angry with him earlier, but after all these years and these incidents, Janki led me to believe that he had been right. He was just scared for you, and I have to say that I completely agree with him now. What was your second question?"

"Why did Maa have such a bad life? Even when things did go in her favour, why did she meet with the worst thing ever?"

"It's the bad karma of parents for which the child has to suffer. I have always believed that Janki had had a tough life because of me—the choices I made, and the things I did. My only prayer for Jia is that she gets a stable house around her and that she grows into a confident woman," Shakuntala said. "Has my reply helped?"

"A little, I guess. The more I think of it, the more questions I seem to have," Meera said.

"Time heals all wounds. It has done for me; it will do for you, too."

"Hello, Simon!" Meera finally found the courage to call the international number that she should have dialled fifteen years ago.

"Hello, who is this?" She heard Simon's chirpy voice filled with energy and life.

"My name is Meera. I am Janki's daughter," Meera said in a single breath.

"Sorry, who? The line's not clear. Did you say Janki?"

"Yes. Janki's daughter, Meera."

"Holy shit! Have you got my letter, then?" Simon asked and laughed.

"I did, yes… long story."

"Ah, my child, we have waited for you for so long! I even contacted Adarsh a number of times. He always said that you were not ready. I had been wondering whether you'd ever call!" Simon said, and then asked, "When did you read my letter? When I had sent it!"

"No, now…" Meera said, a bit sheepish now.

"Oh, I see! Anyway, chuck all that! How's your life, dear? Your mother, the love of my life, would talk about you all the time! I know probably more about you and your childhood than you!" Simon said cheerily.

"I am sure. I am glad that Maa was with you, and she had been happy," said Meera.

"We were happy. You haven't a clue how happy she'd have been to hear you calling her mom. She'd have just… given up everything and come running to you," reflected Simon.

"I know that, now."

"You are a bit late, kiddo, aren't you?" There was a break in his voice now.

"Yes, I am, and I know I will never be able to make up for the lost time, but I want to see her, I want to feel her and that's why I have plans to come to New York in the next week. I will be staying at…"

Simon cut in. "You will be staying with us! My wife and two little devils will love to meet you. I have told them all about you."

"I'd love to meet your family, too."

"Tell me when, and I'll come and pick you up from the airport!"

All the letters flashed through Meera's mind as she took the taxi to the airport. All the images seemed so real! She had relived the life of her grandmother, from being present at the first Independence Parade to the rusty and difficult army life, from being an alcoholic to getting completely involved in social activities, leaving the dark side of politics, to the love which she had shown when they met—all seemed to come back to her as on a projector film.

"Meera, your mother ran away!"

"Meera, your father used to beat your mother. She was rude like you, and hence she had run away."

"Meera, you poor soul! Don't worry! God will listen to your prayers, and you will get a mother soon."

"What happened, beta? What happened? Everything is all right; everything is all right. I will always be with you."

She come out of her thoughts, and her terrible memories as the cab took the final turn towards the airport terminal.

It had been a long journey and Meera was finding it difficult to sleep. She was coming in and out of her thoughts, and all of them were troubling her.

"Why did you lie about your mother, Meera?"

"Yes, Meera, why did you lie about her? If she is alive and your parents have separated, not a big deal! I have seen many children with separated parents."

"This is not done, Meera! We had trusted you. We thought that you were our friend, but we got to know about it from someone else."

Meera gripped her seat handle as the plane landed at JFK.

Meera walked slowly; she didn't want to come out of the terminal. She was afraid, scared.

"Meera, I had asked you not to discuss my issue with anyone, but you spilt it to everyone around."

"You don't know how difficult it is to live with a mother like this, and now I have to leave this office as I can't stand people laughing behind my back."

"I shouldn't have trusted you. How would you know it? You don't have a mother."

Meera saw a board with her name on it, and behind it was a man with a white beard and a white hat. He looked as if he was on a picnic. Meera walked towards him. Sitting in the car beside him, Meera looked out of the window. They didn't have much to talk about. Simon attempted some small talk. He talked about Janki and how much Meera had meant to her, but she had already known that now.

"Can you take me to Ground Zero?" she asked.

"Now? Do you want to go now? You can rest a bit, and I can take you there tomorrow. What do you say? Everyone will be excited to see you," said Simon.

"Maa has waited fifteen years for me. I don't want to offend you, but I just want to go, and see where it has all ended," said Meera.

"I'd say from where it all started. Let me take you there."

Meera walked to the main gate slowly, imagining the horrors of that day—what her mother would have thought then. Would she have cried and called out her name? With each step towards the memorial, her heart was beating faster. Would she have thought of that? Suppose, she was with Meera in India living her life with Papa… She stopped to look around. The place seemed so busy, yet so empty. A thousand feelings… yet a chilling silence covered her.

"Should we go inside?" Simon said quietly from behind her.

Meera was blocking the way, but no one asked her to move away as she was crying without knowing it. This is an emotional place, and people respect that.

She looked at the large area where the buildings were as they walked into the campus.

"This is where the relatives and friends leave messages for their loved ones. Do you want to leave any message for your mother?" Simon asked quietly.

Meera held the bar and closed her eyes. She must have been standing like this for a couple of minutes or a couple of hours; she had no idea. Simon stood across her. He did not want to disturb their meeting after so long. Meera wept her heart out as she spoke to her mother after so many years. She asked for forgiveness for speaking rudely to her. She asked for forgiveness for throwing a tantrum at Disneyland. She forgave her for not being there for her when she had needed her the most. She had no idea of the time. Simon let her be.

She looked around. A lot later, when she was calmer, she saw that there had been other people who were getting as emotional as she was. An old man, a young boy, a middle-aged woman—What were their stories? How did they start? What were their relatives and friends doing in the building on that fateful day that had ended or started a new story?

Meera took out a large envelope and looked at it for minutes. All her fears, her questions, their answers… all that she had wanted to say to her mother, all that she wanted to hear from her were, inside it.

She placed the letters in the sea of flowers and other messages that others had left for their relatives.

Epilogue

IT TOOK MEERA a long time to walk into the main office of Manav Sansthan. As she walked in, she remembered how her life had changed after she read the letters from her mother. She remembered clearly the discussion that she had with Shakuntala when she came back from New York.

"I want you to take the reins of Manav Sansthan. I know this was not the life you wanted for yourself and Sujit, but you have to understand that I don't have anyone else to go to. What will happen to my dream, your Nanaji's dream, after me?"

"I don't know if I will be able to handle the responsibility and there are others in the family who may not like it."

"There will be challenges, but I am sure everything will fall into place."

Things had changed a lot, she was much more assured of herself, and she found that there was so much more to discover in her relationship with Sujit. Sujit had always liked her feisty and now that she was a lot calmer, it had given new meaning to her relationship.

She greeted Sarita, who was very happy to see her. They had been waiting for the day to come when Meera would enter Manav Sansthan and accept it whole-heartedly.

She remembered her father saying, "Meera, there will always be a lot of options in front of you. What you choose makes you who you are."

"I don't know if my choices are correct," Meera had asked.

"Whatever happens, I will always be with you like I have always been with you till now."

Meera wanted to take the stairs. She was not in a hurry. She wanted to take her time; it was a big decision for her. As she took the steps, she remembered how Simon had consoled her in New York, where she had almost fainted. He wanted her to join the import/export business that he and her mother had started. Simon left everything after 2001 to only focus on keeping Janki's business alive and by doing that, keeping her memories alive.

"I want you to take over the company for me. It is my life, but I will not mind Janki's daughter having and running it. She would be happier if you do it. I know that."

"It is not fair to her memory that you have kept buried for so long to hand it over to someone who does not deserve it fully. I am happy to get involved in things, but it is your family, your baby too, and I don't want to tear that apart."

She remembered how Simon had hugged her. He had had tears in his eyes and it was like he had been meeting a long-lost daughter.

Finally, she thought of Jia, who would have a choice. She remembered her discussion and the final decision of her grandmother, and the papers she signed the previous week, which prompted her to finalise the decision and come to Manav Sansthan.

"If you don't take control of Manav Sansthan, I will transfer all my money, here and abroad to Jia, and move all the money to a trust so that when she becomes 18, she will get all that I want you to have"

"But will she understand what you, Maa, and I have gone through? Will she understand the gravity of everything, the emotions?" Meera had asked.

"I am sure she will and you will be there for her to support her, and to explain what had happened to make sure that she learns from it and does not drift away."

As Meera opened the door of Shakuntala's office, she saw her lying down on her couch, blood oozing out of her back where she had been stabbed. Meera shouted:

"AMMAYE!"

… the saga continues …

As Shakuntala fights for her life, Meera embarks on a journey into the depths of history to uncover long-buried secrets.

As the weight of the empire bears down upon her, strains in her relationships with Sujith and Jia start to appear. Meera must confront her past to secure her future, and the fate of generations hangs in the balance.

Will she succumb to the curse that haunts her lineage, or will she muster the strength to shatter the cycle forever?

Vishwakarma Publications

presents

Weight of the Empire

Book 2 in the Letters to my mother Series

Coming

Dec 2024

Acknowledgements

A HUGE SHOUT out and big Thank You to readers of my first draft, my mother Alka Pareek and my aunt Anjali Purohit.

Thanks to my friend and author Saurabh Nirmal, who provided valuable insights to help my characters navigate their momentous journeys.

I can't say enough thanks to an author and friend Neil D'Silva, who edited the book in the first round to make it readable for Agents, Publishers and Editors. I have immense gratitude for you, Neil, and I hope to continue to collaborate with you in future.

I thank my agent The Book Bakers, for helping the book find a publisher.

Thank you, Rhea Chandrachud, my editor, who helped bring the book into its current shape.

Thank you, Vishal Soni and Nupur at Vishwakarma Publishers, for bringing this book to you.

Thank you, Geetika Saini, for ironing out the rough edges in the follow-up editing.

Last but not the least, heartful thanks to my wife Neeru Pareek, who tried her best to read a few pages, even though she does not enjoy reading, and my daughter Miraya Pareek because I just love her so much that even if she doesn't know that I have written a book (yet), I still have loads of gratitude towards her and credit her to have made this happen in her own innocent ways.

Thank you,

Vikkas Arun Pareek

Also by Author

Voices of the Silent Creek

The Adventures of Blue Flamingo - Book Series

